ABOU ___ ___U I HOR

Daniel Grant is a writer and television news producer in London. He lives in Godalming in Surrey with his wife Alison and their black Labrador, Diggi.

Three Way is his second novel.

Also by Daniel Grant:

SEX LESSONS

CONNECT WITH DANIEL:
Blog: http://danjgrant.blogspot.co.uk/
Twitter: dangrantwriter
Facebook: facebook.com/danieljgrant
Website: www.danielgrantonline.com

THREE WAY

DANIEL GRANT

© Copyright 2013 Daniel Grant

Published by Chapter 13 Publishing

Cover by John Chandler at Chandler Book Design

ISBN: 978-0-9926232-0-3

First Edition

A CIP catalogue record for this title is available from the British Library.

For Feeney

BEFORE

'Do you want to see my tits?'

'What?'

'You heard me.'

'Ash, what the fuck?'

'I'm just saying- '

'I know what you're saying.'

'So?'

'What about Gabriel?'

'He's seen them.'

'Ashley.'

'It's a simple question, Ollie. Yes or no?'

Yes or no. Yes, life goes one way, no, life goes another. I'm not sure key life moments should necessarily hang around questions like, 'do you want to see my tits?' But there we are, Ashley and I have always been...complicated.

YEARS LATER...

ONE - THE END

I glance at the three piles of clothes sitting on my bed.

Pile One: Underwear
Pile Two: Tops, dresses, skirts
Pile Three: Jackets and coats

In the corner, a stack of shoe boxes. My eyes hone in on a pair of Birkenstocks, scuffed and dirtied with sand. Svetla walks in, her eyes deliberately not catching mine. She bends down and picks up her iPhone charger.

'Okay, think that's everything,' she says. I glance at the piles of clothes, then back to her. Her shoulder-length blonde Scandinavian hair is tied back roughly. She wears lose tracky bottoms and a baggy T-shirt. Honestly, she's looked better. Her eyes are tired from crying. My fault. Hours of pleading, arguing, shouting and now this. Quiet observing. Acutely aware neither of us can change what's been said and done.

'What about these?' I say, indicating the piles of clothes.

'Charity,' she replies.

'You want me to take these to the charity shop?' I ask, frowning.

'No, Ollie, I'll do it. Just leave them somewhere and I'll do it when I have time,' she replies in a cold voice. I nod slowly. She picks up her bulky pink rucksack and throws it over her shoulder.

'Let me help you-' I say, stepping forward.

'NO. No, thank you,' she replies, correcting her tone. She walks out into the hallway. I follow her to the front door, a zombie. I put on a pair of old slippers and we walk out to her car. She goes around to the boot and throws the rucksack on top of the rest of her things, pushing it down hard. I go to help her, she shoves me away. I hold my hands up and step back. I watch her struggle to close the boot but eventually she succeeds and slams it shut. She turns to face me but doesn't make eye contact.

'Okay, so...bye,' she says.

'Svetla-'

'No. We've said everything we need to say. Let's say goodbye like adults,' she replies, holding out her hand. Two and a half years we've been together and she wants to shake my hand. I look at her palm then up to her eyes. She blinks fast then turns away. There are so many things I want to say. So many apologies for all the stupid things I've said and done. Sorry for being me. She opens the car door.

'Hey,' I say, walking round to her. She turns to face me, tears in her eyes. When I see them my heart melts. What the hell are we doing? 'You sure there's nothing more we can do?'

'We've done everything. You're miserable with me. I'm miserable with you. We gave it a good shot and it didn't work. Time for something else,' she says, staring straight into my eyes.

'Okay well, I just...' my voice crumbles, '...I just wanted to say that I...really loved you and although I didn't show it very often...I hope you're happy somewhere else.' Do I mean any of the words I'm saying or are they just some ploy to persuade her I am a genuinely nice guy? A tear rolls down her cheek. I move to hug her, she lets me but I feel her tense up. No warmth. No affection. Hugging a statue. I release her. She looks down and turns as the tear drops from her face to the ground. She quickly wipes her cheek and sniffs, getting into her car and closing the door. I stand back, my hands finding their way into my pockets. She starts the engine and pulls away. I stand, rooted, imprinting every part of this into my psyche. She indicates left at the road and slowly pulls away. I hear the car disappear into the distance and then...nothing except the sound of birds singing. The end.

I turn and walk back inside my flat. My mind is still processing what's just happened. The girl I love has just left me. The girl I thought I was going to marry no longer lives with me. I walk into my bedroom and sit down on the bed. A tear runs down my face, I blink it away. I take a cardigan from the pile and smell her smell, closing my eyes. What have I done?

TWO – SIX MONTHS LATER...

I wake with a start and check the clock. 05:45 AM. Damn. I'm up half an hour early. How did that happen? I yank the duvet off and tip toe to the bathroom looking like I'm doing some sort of weird pigeon walk. I get to the toilet, urgently needing to go. It's always tricky at this time of the morning. I have to do some serious trajectory calculations and just like some of the world's best scientists, every so often, I'm out. I won't go into details, suffice to say I think we all know what I'm on about. Yeah, alright Ollie, get on with it. Right.

This is me. I live in this two bedroom shithole slap bang in the middle of the crap part of Clapham, South London. And before you ask, yes there is a good part. I saved up for literally years to afford this place, not bad for a twenty-six year old. There's a constant drawl of traffic outside and every so often I hear a police car or ambulance go by. On the plus side, the toilet flushes. The place has electricity and the water is drinkable albeit with a slight smell of eggs, don't know why. The reason it has two bedrooms is because I have somehow ended up living with my best friend from school, Parker McGregor. The first thing that comes to mind when you look at Parker is...Simon le Bon's slightly fucked up twin brother. Parker is bulging at the seams, broad and a slob. He's like a big green giant. Except he isn't green. His bedroom door is closed. He won't surface until at least midmorning. He's a 'writer.' Which I take to mean, lazy arse. In the two years we've been living here, I don't think I've ever seen him write anything. But he pays me rent, so what the hell, right? *How* he pays is another matter. He's got rich parents, so the pressure's off a bit.

I pull on my shirt (unironed) and trousers (M&S crease resistant) and wander back into the bathroom. I carefully and deliberately apply a generous portion of paste to my hair and pull it as far forward as I can. It's short, I'm not going for any Spandau Ballet thing. I nod at myself and walk out.

When I reach the kitchen, I open the cupboard. Yes, there's only one, and every bit of non-fresh food I own is crammed inside. I pull tins out and rifle around until I find a half-empty box of Special K. That'll do. I open the fridge and peer inside. I won't describe the smell, other than to say it's in my interest to close the door as quickly as possible. Really should Dettol that fucker. Maybe I could leave a note for Parker to do the shoppi- what am I saying? I grab the milk, one of the few items still in date, and pour it over my cereal.

On the plus side, the Nescafe is still in healthy supply. I make a black mug of the strong stuff and wander into the living room with my bowl of cereal. I click on Breakfast TV and watch the presenters being unnecessarily cheerful for the time of morning.

I glance around the flat. Yeah, it's not much to look at. Could be worse, could be living at home.

I prepare to slam the door as I leave. Want to make sure I wake up Tristan next door. He makes a living selling weed to a variety of clients who stop by and always, ALWAYS knock on the wrong door. It gets really boring. Tristan is one of those posh types who fell onto the wrong side of the tracks and has now got himself into that slippery place called 'I owe Wayne more money than I make and I hope what I do give over next time is enough to save my kneecaps.'

I feel sorry for him. But I still think he needs to wake up early, meet the day head on. Get a proper job. I slam the door hard. It bangs and the echo bounces beautifully around the building. Nice.

'OLLIE?' I hear Tristan shout from behind his door.

'YEAH!' I match his yelling with my own.

'FUCK YOU!'

'You too mate. See you tonight.'

'Kiss my fucking arse!'

'Ciao.'

Always good to play with the drug dealers, I think.

The tube journey to work is hellish. I make it

bearable by listening to my iPod. The Northern line is the worst line on the map. Maybe they made it black because it's so bloody filthy. And the people are laughably rude. Well, it would be funny, if I could get on the train. But hey, it's London. Deal with it or leave, right? Not like this city needs me clogging up its arteries like human cholesterol.

I arrive at work at 08:50AM. I stand looking up at the imposing glass fronted building. This is T.B.N. or Television Broadcast News. You want to know what I do? What do you mean, no? Come on, I'm not in the mood to mess about today.

I walk through one of two large glass turnstiles and into main reception. Beyond the glass walls, I can see the newsroom. There are people here twenty-four hours a day and you can tell when you walk through the door because the smell of carpet cleaner lingers in the air. I show my I.D. to the security guard who ignores me as I walk past. I keep going, past a large atrium area and straight over to the glass entrance to the newsroom. I swipe my card and the door releases. I pull it open and walk in.

The 'Morning Programme' is just coming off air. I find my seat on the newsdesk, sit down and log onto the news computer system. I'm a news producer, which is so generic it's almost laughable. My duties basically consist of these things:

1) I am asked to do interviews to go into reporters VT's (a cut news story told with pictures and a voiceover telling you the story).
2) I am asked to do vox pops (interviews with members of the public) to go into reporters VT's.

3) I am asked to doorstep famous people/politicians who haven't agreed to an interview but it's deemed in the public interest for me to stand outside their house at some ungodly hour and freeze my nuts off.

4) Almost anything else the newsdesk wants me to do. I'm essentially the newsdesk bitch.

So that's me. It's a great job and I love it but you have to watch out for new news editors trying to make a name for themselves. Paul Enright walks back to the newsdesk carrying a cardboard box full of coffees. He spots me sitting down opposite him.

'Ah Ollie, glad you're here. Got a job for you,' Paul says. He's a good guy. Despite heading into his twilight years, you can see how much he enjoys his work. Yeah, I know the moustache is a little theatrical but try to look beyond that. Look at his flowing silver hair and unquestionable faith in John Rocha clothing. The bad breath thing is only really noticeable when you're standing close to him.

'Is it somewhere warm? Indoors?' I ask, hope obvious in my voice.

'Sort of,' he says, winking at me. 'Downing Street, cabinet arrivals.' I sigh. One day I want to be doing his job. Probably not as well because no one's as good as Paul, but sometime in the next few years I'll be a news editor in my own right. Then I'll call the shots and tell people to go and stand in Downing Street. That's the plan anyway.

'Where's the Millbank producer?'

'Off sick. Come on, it'll be an hour at most. It's not all bad, Millbank are sending Angelina Segar.'

'Really, well that's something I guess.'

'I was being sarcastic. You get on with her?' He frowns, the lines on his face becoming dangerous caverns.

'Yeah. Why, don't you?'

'She's a pain in the arse,' the phone starts ringing, 'but then, sometimes the good correspondents are, aren't they?' I shrug, considering his words. Paul turns and picks up the phone. 'Newsdesk.'

Downing Street has the usual media suspects lined up opposite the famous black door. I show my press pass to the security guard and, having passed through the metal detector with flying colours, I walk up to our position. Angelina is already there, looking at herself in her compact mirror. She wears a black suit, sports thick cropped red hair and has a figure to die for. Seriously, she must spend all her spare time in the gym.

'Morning,' I say as cheerfully as I can. The clouds look menacing and the wind is already picking up. Downing Street is the worst location for producers and cameramen. There's nowhere to piss, nowhere to get a sandwich and when you're not on air or shouting questions at politicians, there's nothing to do.

'Hello Ollie. I didn't know you were coming down,' Angelina says.

'Yeah well, when they said it was you, I couldn't resist.'

'Ah, that's nice,' she replies, running a brush through her hair. Unsure if I was trying to be sarcastic or not, I opt to carry on.

'So...how's Glen?'

'Urgh, don't ask,' she says.

'Oh. Why not?' I reply. Angelina breathes out.

'Can you keep a secret?' she asks.

'Yeah,' I reply.

'Seriously?'

'Of course.'

'He wants a kid,' Angelina says, in an unenthusiastic tone.

'Oh. Is that not a good thing?'

'Sure,' she says, turning back to the mirror and bearing her teeth to her reflection, 'if I want to give up my career and change shit-filled nappies all day long.'

'Uh, well babies don't have to be about poo-' I pause, spotting the Environment Secretary walking up Downing Street for the Cabinet meeting. 'Do you think the Prime Minister should resign!?' I shout over to him. He ignores me and goes inside. I turn back to Angelina.

'No I know but it's the beginning of the end, isn't it? Look at me, I've got to political correspondent in less than six months, I want to be editor in two years. What happens to that plan if Glen knocks me up?' I look over to some people who have gathered at the gate to Downing Street. It's a protest or something because they're shouting abuse. Can't hear what they're saying.

'What about just taking the pill? Don't tell him.'

'A little bit underhand Oliver, even for you,' I

wince as she uses my full name. 'Guys never get it, I don't know why I even bother talking about it. What about you anyway?'

'What about me?'

'How's that Swedish girl you were seeing?' And there it is. The question I dread. How do I play this one?

'We broke up. About six months ago.'

'You're kidding. She was lovely.'

'I know but well, it didn't work out.'

'Were you a cock?'

'No.' I look down, my face giving me away.

'Oh Ollie. She broke your heart.' I look up to her, straining to stop myself heading down a path where men are simply not allowed to go.

'Nah, you know,' I reply, trying to shrug it off.

'Come here,' she says, offering me outstretched arms. We hug. Don't cry. Don't you fucking cry. The other cameramen and reporters look at us. I want her to stop but she seems intent on trying to make me feel better. She starts rubbing and patting my back. I wonder if she's trying to burp me.

'I'm fine, really,' I say. She releases me and looks into my eyes. I glance away and smile.

'I know it hurts now but one day it won't. Just have to hope that day comes sooner rather than later,' she says.

'Yeah,' I reply. My phone rings. 'Hello?'

'Ollie, it's Paul on the desk.'

'Hi.'

'The Lunchtime bulletin needs a clip doing in the City, can you go?'

'Oh, Angelina and I were just getting to the

good bit in our conversation,' I say, Angelina shoots me a sympathetic face.

'Well maybe you can call her later,' Paul replies, apparently not getting my sarcasm.

'Sure, can you email me the address?'

'Yep, cameraman will meet you there,' he says.

'Okay.'

THREE – THE INTERVIEW

When I surface at Bank tube station I check my emails. Sure enough, there's a briefing from Sue, the business producer. I'm supposed to interview some bigwig about a possible stock market crash. It's a clip to go into a Lunchtime News VT, so should be quite straight forward, if a little dull. I walk along Threadneedle Street, past the Bank of England and- oo look there's the Gherkin. Cool building. Sorry, easily distracted. I don't come to the City that often. Angelina's words echo around my head. *'I know it hurts now but one day it won't.'* I don't really want to talk about it but I genuinely thought Svetla was the girl I would marry. Intelligent, beautiful and always the epitome of calm. I know it's been six months since we split but it still hurts. The thing is...oh, there's the cameraman Phil, loitering outside the bank. Better say hi. I'll tell you about Svetla properly later.

'Hey,' I say.

'Hi, this it?' Phil replies. I detect a grumble in his tone.

'I believe so, yes. Want a hand with the gear?'

'Great, thanks.' I grab the tripod and we walk inside. I glance upwards as we head towards the reception desk. Behind us, above the entrance, are huge letters that read 'United Bank.' This place is enormous. Security guards stand in front of three large double glass doors. I quickly get my phone out, I've already forgotten who I'm supposed to be interviewing. The smartly dressed reception girl finishes her phone call and looks up at me.

'Hello, how can I help you?' I check the briefing email.

'Uh hi, we're from TBN, we're here to interview uhh...' I scroll down the email, where's the name...'Lauren Bates.'

'Okay sir, if I could just get you to sign in here, I'll call up now.' She shows me a security I.D. form.

'Sure.' I grab the pen and start filling in the boxes. 'I'll do yours,' I offer to Phil.

'Thanks,' he replies. I suddenly realise I can't remember Phil's second name. Shit. My pen is poised over the name. Have I ever known what it was? Doesn't matter now, dipshit. I opt for 'Phil – TBN cameraman.'

'Hello it's main reception here, I have an Ollie Hayward and Phil...the cameraman here from TBN,' the receptionist says, reading off the I.D.'s. Now I feel like a douche. I glance at Phil who clearly isn't impressed. I smile awkwardly. 'Okay, thank you. Someone will be down shortly, if you'd like to take a seat.' She indicates a seating area. We walk over and plonk ourselves down.

'First job of the day?' I ask Phil, a crude attempt at small talk.

'Yeah, parking was a nightmare.'

'Really?'

'Yeah, I had to park in the NCP fucking miles away.'

'Oh. Well I can give you a hand after we're done here.'

'Yeah I'll need it, impossible to carry all this crap with no help. We used to have sound recordists but now it's just me lugging shit around all day.'

'Not good.'

'No.' We wait in silence. I elect not to ask Phil anymore questions, he's obviously pissed off.

'Ollie Hayward?' I turn to see a man approaching in a very shiny navy suit. He extends his hand. I shake it.

'Hello I'm James Kennedy, let me show you up.'

'Great,' I reply. I grab the tripod, Phil takes everything else. I glance at James' suit and I swear I can see my reflection. He looks like a walking Blu Ray disc. I decide telling James my thoughts on his attire would probably not be the best way to start things off so I keep schtum. There's a word more difficult to read than to say, eh? Anyway, the double glass doors open and we walk past the security guard into the lift.

'Did you find the place okay?' James asks.

'Yeah, thanks (shiny man). Very easy.'

'Normally Lauren's assistant would come and show you round but she asked me so...'

'Oh, okay.' Who the fuck cares? I nod politely.

He hits thirty-seven and the lift launches skywards. Jesus this thing moves fast, I start to feel sick.

'So you guys got a busy day ahead?' James asks, a smile lacking in sincerity crawling across his face.

'Yeah,' I say. I want to improve on my initial answer but I can't find the words so it comes off as a bit of a 'fuck you' to our polished friend. The lift slows and the doors open.

'This way,' James says. I glance at Phil who rolls his eyes. I smile and follow our guide. We walk out onto a bustling trading floor. Computer screens and monitors are everywhere showing all the main news channels, including TBN. Seems similar to the newsroom on a busy day. We are led past the traders towards two glass offices. I glance to my right, taking in a cracking view of London and the Thames. This is the place to be. Look at that view, Jesus. My attention refocuses to the job at hand and we arrive at the smaller of the glass offices. Inside is a blonde girl on the phone, she has her back to us. James knocks. She turns around. For the tiniest of moments, everything stops. Is this who I'm here to interview? It seems Lauren Bates is a babe. Let me rephrase. Lauren Bates is a mega-babe. She wears a tight-fitting suit with a skirt just above the knee. Her outfit accentuates her perfect hour-glass figure.

'Uh, I have to go, TBN are here...yes...is that what I told you to do? There's your answer Eric...okay, bye.' She hangs up, stands and walks over to us offering her hand.

'Hello there, I'm Lauren.'

'Mm Ollie,' I say, 'and Phil the cameraman.'
She shakes our hands. I glance at Phil who is
thinking the same as me. This day has suddenly
got a whole lot better.

'Thanks, James,' Lauren says. I glance at
James, he's staring at me. Suddenly it's
uncomfortable. What is with this guy? He holds my
stare for a second longer than necessary then
glances up to Lauren and smiles.

'Any time hun, call me if these guys give you
any trouble.' He closes the door and walks away.
Cock. Phil starts setting up the camera.

'So do you want me here or...?' Lauren asks.
What?

'Huh?' I reply.

'For the interview, do you want to do it with
the trading floor in the background or...'

'At your desk is fine, bit loud outside,' Phil
says. Then he stops. 'Unless you're not happy with
that, Ollie?' I shrug and smile.

'Hey, whatever you think, man,' I say. Man?
What, are we in da hood? Fuck's sake Ollie. 'Nice
office.'

'Thanks,' she replies, 'works for me. So will
you take this to Millbank or drive it back?' I frown.

'Oh, how do you know about Millbank?' She
smiles, my heart soars. Don't fall in love Ollie,
don't you fucking fall in love. Millbank is where
TBN's Westminster office is.

'It's not a state secret, is it?' she asks.

'No just, not many people really know or care
to be honest.'

'I'll tell you something though' she says. Oh
yes, here we go. Fuck I wish Phil wasn't here now.

'Oh?'

'I wanted to be a reporter before I got into trading,' she smiles and flicks her eyebrows in a naughty way, like she just told me she enjoys dogging. For crying out loud Ollie. Sorry, sorry. Must stop thinking about sex.

'Ah okay. Didn't work out?'

'Unfortunately not. No money in it.' I nod. (She means reporting, not dogging.)

'So true,' I say.

'But fun. I bet when you get a really massive story all hell breaks loose.'

'Yeah, it gets manic. I love it though, like before I came here, I was in Downing Street. I know I should be all chilled about it but I still get a thrill walking down that road. Apart from when it's raining, cold or I need the toilet. Also you can't get a coffee either without going back through security, which is a real pain but apart from that...' She nods and smiles. I don't know why but suddenly it feels like she's flirting. No Ollie, she isn't. She's being professional and you're being a pervert. Now get your head out of your arse and conduct yourself appropriately.

'I'll bet. Your parents must be very proud,' she says.

'Well my mum is. My dad died a long time ago,' I reply.

'Oh. I'm sorry,' she says. I shrug, shake my head quickly and smile. Hmm, that killed the atmosphere. Why the hell did I bring him into this? I glance at Phil who immediately goes back to adjusting the intensity of the light he was working on.

'So, this is a pretty impressive office,' I say, an attempt at moving things along.

'Yeah. What's the newsroom like, does it have nice views?'

'The canteen on the sixth floor does, but I try not to venture up there unless I'm deliberately looking to use up my supply of Imodium.' She chuckles and I find myself smiling back. Phil moves a chair into position in front of the camera and shifts the light a fraction to the left.

'Right, think we're there. If you could sit in, please,' Phil says, indicating for Lauren to sit down.

'Sure.' She takes a seat as Phil looks into the viewfinder, checking the shot.

'Okay and if you could pull up a chair Ollie and sit here,' Phil says. I do as I'm told, sitting as close to the lens of the camera as I can. I look at Lauren who glances at me.

'So I'm looking at you-?' Lauren asks.

'Yep, look at me, ignore the camera. If you get stuck or you want to do the answer again that's fine. We'll just go from the top, okay?' I say.

'Okay,' she replies. Phil is still fiddling with the camera. Lauren is poised, awaiting the go, staring straight at me. I look back at her. My heart is suddenly thumping. Phil glances to the side of the camera and adjusts a dial. I look back to Lauren who still has her eyes fixed on me. I smile and scratch my head. She is so beautiful. Her blonde hair has a glow when the light hits it.

'Sorry, just need to get another battery,' Phil says. I breathe out. I glance at her, she smiles, my heart thumps faster. Man, I'm never normally like this. My back feels clammy, I shift on my seat.

'I like your shirt,' Lauren says. I glance down at my somewhat creased affair. I should have ironed it. I hate ironing. Maybe she's being i-ronical? Get it? Alright well fuck you, just trying to relieve the tension here.

'Thank you, it's M&S.' Oh for Christ's sake.

'Sexy,' she says. I look up from the shirt, surprised at her compliment. Phil looks up from...battery locating. 'I mean, I was looking for a birthday present for a friend and I think he'd like that.'

'Oh yeah? Well they're pretty reasonably priced,' I reply, glancing at Phil. Hurry up Phil. Hurry up Phil. Phil...hurry up. My eyes connect with Lauren's again and I look down to her tits. Shit, not there...umm, up to the ceiling. No, now I'm overcompensating...uh, the window. Better. Fuck Phil, please...

'Okay, ready,' Phil says. I breathe out again too fast, look back at her and smile.

'Okay. If you could just give me your name and your title for the tape,' I say.

'Lauren Bates, Head of Corporate Finance for United Bank.'

'Thanks,' I say. She swallows, maybe she thinks I'm going to 'Paxman' her. Which, I'm not by the way.

'So what's happening in the Eurozone at the moment and how does it affect Britain?'

She starts giving me her answer and I want to tell you what she said but I'm one hundred percent not listening. Instead I'm watching her mouth move and listening to the intensity and conviction of her voice. She finishes her answer in what I estimate to be around twenty seconds, which is perfect. I need to remember my next question though.

'Uh, if this were to spread further here, could it affect jobs here and if so which industries would most likely be hit?'

Again she rattles off what I'm sure will be the perfect answer for the VT but I pay no more attention to this answer than the previous one. I wonder what it would be like to kiss those lips. That rush of excitement tearing through me. I wonder what the touch of her suit would feel like under my fingers. How would it feel to put my hands under that blouse? My heart thumps as though I've just broken the one hundred metres world record...or had a heart attack. She finishes her answer. I consider what it might be like to be her husband. Like, how that would actually work? We'd have to live out in the suburbs. We'd commute in together, maybe I'd even make her a packed lunch to take in with her. In the evenings we might sit in our garden sipping wine under a fading sun. Then our children might come running out. Horatio and Matilda. Horatio? Fuck, where did that come from?

'Ollie? Is that it?' she asks. I snap out of my daydream.

'Sorry?' I reply, glancing at Phil who's staring at me with a frown and a what-the-fuck-are-you-doing look. 'Sorry. I...well, uh. I glance down at my iPhone for the next question. 'Uh...' Shit, it's gone back to sleep and I can't find the email. She gave a couple of good answers, that'll be okay, won't it?

'That's it.'

'Really?' she asks.

'What?' Phil says, almost straight away.

'Uh, yeah. No, that was great. Really good.'

'That was quickest interview I've ever done,' Lauren says.

'Me too,' says Phil, staring at me with a searching look.

'Well, I've got what I need, so what's the point in wasting your time trying to get you to say the same thing ten different ways.' Lauren shrugs.

'Okay, well if you're sure?'

'Yep, definitely,' I say. Phil starts to pack up the lights. She stands up from the chair.

'So, have you got many interviews to do?' Lauren asks.

'Not at the mo, but who knows what the newsdesk has planned for me. I'll take this to Millbank, feed it and await my fate,' I reply. She nods.

'Well, I hope it works for you. So, do you have a card or...?' Oh my God, she wants my digits. She wants to ask me out. We really are going to spend the rest of our happy lives together. Jesus Ollie, give her the bloody card. Hang on, I don't have business cards. Shit.

'Uh...I don't have business cards,' I repeat my thought verbatim.

'Oh. Well, never mind.'

'I can give you my phone number if you like.'

'Oh,' she replies. Phil glances up from ejecting the SD card from the camera.

'And email and everything else you get on a business card,' I say. You are pathetic, look at this

22

performance.

'Sure, let me get a piece of paper.' She pulls out a Post-It notepad and hands it to me with a pen.

'Ta,' I say. I write my name, mobile number and email address down. I resist the urge to also include my place of birth, bank account number and Gmail password. 'There you go.' I hand her back the pad.

'Thanks,' she says, looking at it then up to me. 'Well, it was really nice to meet you, Ollie.'

'You too,' I say offering her my hand. She shakes it and smiles. I smile back, trying to imprint this meeting in my memory.

'Ready when you are champ,' says Phil. I glance his way and nod.

'Nice to meet you too, Phil,' says Lauren.

'Uh...yeah, likewise,' says Phil, shaking her hand.

'Well, see you soon,' I say. She frowns slightly. 'I mean, not soon. Just...anyway.' I grab the tripod.

'Do you need someone to show you out?' Lauren asks. I frown because I hear the word 'throw' when she says 'show.' Stupid, I know.

'We'll be fine thanks,' Phil says. We walk out of the office, I glance back to her. She's staring after us with a look which I interpret as utter confusion on her face. Man...that really was the worst interview I've ever done.

FOUR – AN UNEXPECTED VISITOR

I get home around six-thirty. As I approach the front door I detect the familiar smell of ganja drifting from Tristan, the drug dealer's, flat.

'Those don't smell like cigarettes,' I say loudly as I pass his door.

'FUCK YOU!' I hear Tristan shout.

'You doing drugs in there again?' I ask.

'Didn't you hear me? I said FUCK OFF!' Tristan replies. I walk on, smiling. I get to the front door, slot the key in the lock and go inside.

As soon as I'm in, I hear the familiar sound of Grand Theft Auto coming from the Playstation. I walk into the living room and dump my bag. Parker sits in his dressing gown engrossed in the game.

'Evening,' I say.

'Can't see,' he replies, not changing the pitch in his voice. I step out of the way. His legs rest on top of the coffee table. Next to them is a plate with toast crumbs and crusts and an empty bottle of Coke. I look at him. His concentration is intense, clicking the buttons on the controller with impressive precision. However, if he walked down Clapham High Road with that face on, I think people would take him for a puppy slayer. He pauses the game and looks up at me.

'What?'

'Just this...' I say, indicating to him. He glances around.

'What?'

'This look, it's not...conveying the impression of a successful young businessman.' Parker looks down at the dressing gown.

'I'm not trying to convey that impression.'

'No I see that but maybe, I dunno. Maybe work might be a good thing?'

'Can't. Haven't got any inspiration.'

'Well occasionally getting out of the flat might help that.' He sighs and tilts his head. I hold up my hands. 'Okay, okay. Just think there's more constructive things you could be doing.'

'Thanks dad.'

'Can you save it, I want to show you something,' I say, going over to my bag. Parker hits save. I pull out a DVD.

'Is this another one of your homemade gay porn films?'

'No, but I think you're going to enjoy it.' I reply, ejecting Grand Theft Auto and inserting my DVD.

'This better be good, interrupting my playing time.' The DVD comes up with a makeshift menu, I take the controller from Parker and hit play.

Up comes my interview with Lauren. Yes I know it's a bit creepy but I wanted Parker to see her.

'What do you think?' I say.

'Fuck me,' he says, sitting up. 'Who is she?'

'Her name is Lauren Bates, she's some hotshot City type. I interviewed her today.' We hear me asking her the first question.

'Is that your interviewing technique?'

'I wouldn't exactly call it a technique.'

'Neither would I, you sound like a girl.'

'Thanks mate,' I reply. We watch Lauren, both suddenly silent.

'She's very nice. You asked her out yet?'

'No,' I say. He looks at me, then sighs.

'It's been six months since Svetla,' he says.

'I know. I need to try something else.'

'She looks very nice.'

'Yeah,' I reply. I think about what I say next. 'She asked for my phone number.' I look at him for a reaction. A sceptical eyebrow rises upwards.

'Yeah?' he asks.

'Well, my card.'

'Oh.'

'Don't say it like that, it's a good thing.'

'Sure mate. I'm sure she wants you. Deluded fucker,' he says the last part quietly, as if only to himself.

'At least try and be supportive.'

'I will, as soon as you man up and get back out there.'

'I'm trying,' I say.

'Do or do not. There is no try. That's from Empire.'

'Yeah I know genius. What's for dinner then?' I ask.

'Whatever you're cooking,' he replies.

'Come on,' I say.

'What?'

'You're the chef.'

'I don't think working at Harvester qualifies me as a chef,' he says.

'More than me.'

'Alright shit-for-brains, what do you want?'

'Pasta?' I ask. He thinks for a moment.

'Yeah, alright,' he replies, standing and picking up the plate and bottle of Coke. He stops to look at Lauren on the screen. 'She's got funny ears.'

'No she doesn't,' I reply, trying not to sound defensive.

'Like, a bit too small.' Off my look he then says, 'I'm just saying.' He looks at her again. 'She's pretty hot though, good luck.'

'Nothing's going to happen.'

'Not with that attitude it won't.' He wanders into the kitchen. I follow.

'I think it's time to try at the relationship thing again, not just sex,' I say.

'You think this girl's just about the sex?' Parker replies, surveying the culinary choices in the lone cupboard.

'I don't know. She oozes sex appeal though. When I was in that room, man…it was tense.'

'Wasn't there a cameraman in there as well?'

'Well yeah, but I think even he felt the sexual tension in there.'

'Because of your homosexual tendencies?' He finds a frying pan, heats some oil, then starts chopping the onions and mushrooms.

'So you think I should just do it? Ask her out

on a date? I'm so crap at stuff like this.'

'Normally people call people up and say something like 'hey there, fancy going out?"

'Not when I do it, they don't.'

'That's 'cos you're an amateur.'

'You're not making me feel any better.'

'No? Get a counsellor.'

We watch Top Gear as we eat our pasta. Parker has these trays with a cushion bit on the bottom so it sits on your lap all snug-like. At first I was like, 'where did you get these from?' and he said 'what do you care, they do the job.' Seemed like a reasonable explanation at the time.

As I put a large forkful of pasta in my mouth, there's a knock at the door. I glance at Parker.

'Well it's not going to be for me,' he says.

'I bet it's Tristan or one of his druggie friends,' I say, putting the tray on the coffee table and standing up. 'What the fuck Tristan...right in the middle of my fucking dinner!' I shout. He'd better be overdosing or dying. I walk to the front door and open it. Standing in front of me is Ashley Morgan, another 'friend' from school. Except she was, on occasion, more than a friend. It's complicated, I'll explain later. My mouth opens. I haven't seen her for, what...two years? Jesus. Her dark brown hair is long and she has it down. She wears grown up makeup and that lipstick stuff that makes lips look wet. The last time I saw her, she was just starting to go out with this real character (I use that word in the loosest possible way) called Gary. We kept in touch on Facebook and as I've said before, we were always...close.

'Ashley?' I ask, still processing the surprise of seeing her here. She smiles awkwardly.

'Hi Ollie. Sorry to just turn up like this but um...I uhh...' She looks down.

'What's wrong?'

'Long story. Do you mind if I come in?' she asks.

'Of course,' I say. My eyes glance downwards and I notice she has a suitcase. A very large suitcase. She steps inside. I hear Parker on his way.

'Who is it?' Parker says. He appears next to me and stops when he sees Ashley. 'Oh. What do you want?' a hostile tone in his voice. Ashley forces a smile.

'Hello Parker. Nice to see you.'

'Well I'd say the same but that would be a lie,' he replies. I shoot him a frown.

'Can I come in?' Ashley asks, looking at me.

'No,' says Parker.

'Yes,' I counter, turning to Parker. He glares at me, shakes his head and walks back into the living room.

'Sorry, I didn't realise you were living with Parker,' Ashley says, picking up her suitcase. I go to help her. 'It's okay, I've got it.' I'm unconvinced because the suitcase is almost as big as she is. However she drags it inside, scuffing the wall a little as she does so.

'Yeah, we've lived here for over two years now.'

'Cool, uh...' she yanks the case again and gives up as it falls on its side. I go to right it. 'Don't worry it'll be fine there, there's not much in it.'

'I disagree, looks like everything's in it,' I say.

'I mean, nothing of value.' I nod slowly, she glances away. 'Nice place.'

'Yeah, it's small but does the trick. You want a tea or coffee?' I ask.

'Tea, if that's okay?' We walk into the kitchen and I fill the kettle. She seems so different to how I remember. Almost, nervous.

'Parker still not forgiven me then?' she says. I shrug.

'Well you did sort of cheat on him.'

'With you, it's not really cheating though is it?' This is a bad situation. You want the details now, don't you? It's not like that. Me and Parker are best friends, have been since school and Ashley and I have always been...complicated. I thought Parker didn't give a shit. They had started seeing each other and he just seemed, almost uninterested in her. I remember commenting about it at the time. He just said she was nice and quite good in bed. That was the phrase he used, 'quite good in bed.' So when he went to university, me and Ashley picked up where we had left off, which was nearly always somewhere physical. I just thought Parker and Ashley had split up. As it turned out they hadn't and he was playing it ultra-cool.

'So, what's going on?' I ask.

'Get straight to it, I get it,' she replies, breathing out. 'I need somewhere to stay. And before you say anything I know...but, I wouldn't ask if things weren't desperate.'

'How'd you even find me?'

'Your mum,' she says, the slightest of smiles on her face. 'She says hi.' I nod. 'She also says a call once in a while wouldn't kill you, she told me to say that verbatim.'

'That's great,' I reply. The kettle boils and I pour the water into the mug.

'Yeah. Look, I'm sorry to just turn up like this...but it wasn't exactly a well thought out plan.'

'She's not staying here,' says Parker, who's appeared in the doorway, wearing his tatty leather jacket. There's a slight pause with no one really knowing what to say before Ashley says,

'Parker, come on-'

'No. There's no room and I know what Ollie's like, he'll just say yes. Sorry but I'm not happy about it and I get a say.'

'Hang on, you do get a say but let's just hear- ' I say.

'Ollie, she can't stay here. That's it. End of discussion. You guys can catch up or whatever but when I get back, she won't be here.' He goes to leave, then turns.

'I won't be back till late, so you have enough time to talk properly, okay?' he says, turning and walking out of the kitchen.

'Parker...' Ashley starts to say. I hear a thump as he trips over Ashley's case. Swearing to himself he opens the door. It slams as he leaves and I hear Tristan shout,

'Can't you guys close the fucking door quietly? Fuck's sake.' I turn to face Ashley.

'Well that went well,' she says.

'He'll calm down,' I reply.

'Maybe this is too complicated,' she says.

THREE WAY

Ashley and I decide to ditch the flat and talk properly, over a pint. We walk into my local, The Old Cock off Northcote Road. Parker says it makes absolute sense that my local has the word 'cock' in its name, what a bellend. I order my usual Guinness, she goes for a glass of Pinot Grigio. The pub is one of those modern gastropub affairs, lots of wooden stools and comfy sofas. We find a spot in the corner and sit down. It's good to see her again. I'd forgotten how well we get on.

'So, what's happened?' I ask. She sighs and sips her glass.

'I split up with my boyfriend. For various reasons. I can't go back home because I'm not talking to my mum and that's it. The end.'

'The end? That's barely the beginning.'

'What?' she says.

'Come on, just be straight with me. You're asking to come and live with me, just tell me what's going on. If me and Parker are going to have a falling out, be good to know the reason.'

'Ollie, Ollie, sensible to the last.' She's still smiling but she's using it as a shield, I've seen that smile before. 'I've been with this guy for over a year and he wasn't the best guy I've ever been with.' My eyebrow rises. 'He was really creative, really driven but he would sometimes get angry and occasionally lash out.'

'Lash out?'

'Yeah.' She flicks her hair to the side, showing me the side of her neck which has a deep scratch mark and a bruise that goes up behind her hairline.

'Jesus.'

'Yeah. It's fine though-'

'It's not fine.'

'No, I don't mean it's fine, just...I've left him and I want to move on.' I look at her, she seems lost. All that confidence and bravado she used to have when we were at school, now suddenly gone. I sigh, quietly.

'I'm not going to beg Ollie, if you can't you can't.'

'It's not that, it's just...whenever we're near each other-'

'No sex,' she interrupts. I stare at her and frown. 'I promise. Just friends. I need to get my life sorted.'

'When has that ever worked?'

'Seriously, having somewhere to live is more important, and aren't you with that Swedish girl anyway-'

'We split up,' I say.

'Oh. Sorry. When?'

'Six months ago but it's...still a little raw.'

'You never said anything on Facebook.'

'Well I'm not exactly going to announce it. It's personal.' She nods slowly, searching my face.

'Shit. Did you love her?' she asks. I sigh.

'I did. I'm trying not to now.'

'How's that going?' she asks.

'Good. Yeah, fine,' I reply. She pulls a face.

'I can see you're lying.'

'No I'm not,' I say.

'This is me, Ollie.'

'Yeah okay.'

'So...what do you think? I promise I won't get in the way or cause problems.'

'What about Parker? I can't screw him over.'

'I'll talk to Parker.'

'Seriously Ash.'

'I am serious. I will make it up to Parker. But you need to say it's okay.' I consider her words. I know how this goes but I can't really tell her to fuck off, can I? She's in trouble and needs my help. She's such a massive part of my life. Well, used to be. 'We're a good team. My life is a bit of a mess and I just need a little help whilst I put it back together.'

'If you can persuade Parker-' I start to say.

'Yeah?'

'Then I guess you can stay-'

'Thank you,' she says, her eyes suddenly watering up. She coughs and looks up, trying to stop herself from crying. 'I really do appreciate this.'

'Well, I'm sure you'd do the same for me,' I reply, smiling. She thinks for a moment.

'I would.'

FIVE – A DAY AT WORK, AN EVENING AT HOME

Thursday. It's a busy day on the newsdesk. Julie, the normal newsdesk assistant is sick so I end up having to be Paul's assistant which involves trying to take as much of the workload off him as possible. It's okay though. You are always the first to know about any developing story on the newsdesk. It's busy, crazy and occasionally bad for your health, which is why I love it.

Today's stories are the usual middle of the running order type affairs. There's a new treatment for breast cancer, in its early stages, but it might eradicate the disease at some point in the future. There's a story about house prices rising to near record levels which the business correspondent is doing. And there's a nice little cutsey wootsey story of a new baby panda born at Edinburgh zoo. So nothing huge to get excited about but that's the sort of day it's going to be.

Annoyingly the phones don't stop ringing

which, when I'm trying to eat my bowl of Corn Flakes, is quite infuriating. With all these distractions around me I'm also finding it difficult to make time to Google 'Lauren Bates.' The phone rings once again.

'Newsdesk?' I say loudly.

'Uh, hello is that the newsdesk?' I hear an old man's voice on the end of the phone.

'Yep, how can I help you?'

'The weather report yesterday was completely wrong, you said there wouldn't be frost last night and what do I find when I go outside this morning...frozen fucking Begonias.'

'Okay, thank you for your comments sir. Let me just transfer-'

'-and another thing-' Click. I transfer him to the complaints department. I know it sounds harsh but the newsdesk gets between two hundred and a thousand phone calls a day and I just don't have time to sit and listen to people's thoughts on the daytime schedule. I'm an arse, that's what you're thinking, isn't it? Maybe I am. I munch another spoonful of Corn Flakes as I ponder on this.

'Right, I can't stand it any more, I'm going to have to get a coffee,' says Paul, 'want one?'

'Yeah thanks, can I give you some money?' I reply.

'I've got it.' Paul stands up and heads off. The phone rings, I pick it up.

'Newsdesk.'

'It's Derek at Scotland Yard. Can I go?'

'Ah Derek, how the devil are you?' He's the overnight correspondent. He's old, stubborn and moany.

'Who's that?'

'It's Ollie.'

'Ollie, are you the news editor?' I love it. I speak to Derek almost every day but when he calls we do this dance like we've never spoken.

'No, I'm the assistant.'

'Who's the news ed?'

'It's Paul but he's just away from the desk, let me check with the Morning Show.' I call over to Carla McCarthy on the Morning Show desk. She decides what goes on air. Under her are a team of overworked, underpaid producers who set up live interviews, cut pictures, write cues and work nights.

'Carla, Derek is asking if he can go?'

'Where is he?' she asks, frowning.

'Scotland Yard.'

'Can you ask him to do a nine and that can be his last.'

'How does a nine o'clock hit sound Derek?' I hear a long sigh then a small grumble.

'Yeah fine.' He hangs up. 'Thank you for using the TBN newsdesk, you have a nice day now,' I say, putting the phone down. Carla laughs.

'I take it Derek was ecstatic,' she says.

'Not entirely, but he'll do it.'

'Nice of him. It's only his job afterall.' My mobile rings, it's Parker.

'Hi mate,' I say.

'Yeah, so funny thing. I get back home this morning and I find a bag sitting in the middle of the living room and Ashley sleeping on the sofa.'

'I said she could stay. Only for a little bit-'

'For Christ's sake Ollie, don't I get a say in this? I said I didn't want her here.'

'I know but come on man, she's got nowhere to go.'

'Yes she does. People always have somewhere else, she just knows she can fuck with you. And me.'

'She didn't know you were going to be there,' I say.

'So she tells you. I'm really not happy about this. If there's a phrase to convey to you just how unhappy I am, then this would be the time I'd be saying it.'

'I know you don't like it but it won't be for long.' Paul comes back with the coffees.

'How do you know that?' Parker asks. The newsdesk phone starts ringing, I can feel Paul's eyes boring into my head. It's a personal call at work, not really allowed. I want to answer Parker's question as honestly as I can but when I think about it, nothing comes out. 'Exactly,' he adds.

'I've got to go mate.'

'Yeah, okay,' Parker replies.

'Bye.' I hang up. Shit, maybe this wasn't a good idea. Parker's really annoyed. Hope he doesn't do anything dumb. Paul places the coffee in front of me, spilling a little on the desk.

'Damnit,' he says.

'It's okay, got some tissues here.'

'Yeah right,' he replies. I detect a hostile tone in his voice.

'Everything okay?'

'Not really. Just had my wife's lawyer on the phone wanting to sort through the divorce. Really don't need that at work.'

'Shit. Sorry,' I say, 'is there anything I can do?'

'No. It's fine,' he replies, sighing. The newsdesk phone is still ringing, Paul turns to me. 'You could answer that phone though.'

'Sorry,' I reply, 'newsdesk.'

'There's smoke coming out of Notting Hill tube station,' the man on the other end says. Shit! I grab my pen.

'Smoke?'

'Yeah, I can see it now. The alarms going off and people are coming out.' I'm writing down everything this guy says.

'What's your name?'

'Brian. Brian Daring.'

'Okay Brian, my name's Ollie.' I glance at the caller ID and write down Brian's mobile number. 'Can you take some photos or video of whatever you can see?'

'Sure.'

'I don't want you to take any risks, just whatever you can get safely. If you send them to my email address which is Ollie dot Hayward at TBN dot com.'

'Uh, okay. Yeah.'

'I'm going to call the fire brigade. Can I call you back in a few minutes?'

'Yep, do you want my number?'

'I've got it here. Speak in a bit.' I put the phone down, look down my list of available camera crews and call Dave Mostow. I tell him to get on his way to Notting Hill.

'What's going on?' Paul asks.

'Possible fire at Notting Hill tube. Can you call

the police?'

'Yep. Need to get a sat truck on its way as well.'

'Yeah, I'm on it,' I reply.

We spend maybe forty-five minutes checking out this story before we discover that it wasn't a fire at all. A tube train had entered the station and knocked some building materials which in turn caused a big cloud of dust. People mistook it for smoke. None of it went to air and as quickly as it had begun, everything returned to normal. Just another day at the office.

I note the silence when I open the front door to the flat. I dump my bag in the hallway and open the door to the living room. Ashley lies on the sofa, a book open on her chest, fast asleep. She's wearing dark-blue jeans, a tight white t-shirt and no socks. I glance around the room, nothing out of the ordinary, other than a switched off Playstation. I step inside and look at the book she's been reading. The title reads 'Conversations with God by Neale Donald Walsch.' I smile and frown, confused at her choice. I quietly walk back to the hallway and see Parker's closed door. As I walk up to it, I hear Coldplay coming from inside. I knock.

'Fuck off,' his muffled voice calls from inside.

'It's me,' I reply.

'Oh.' A few seconds later, the door opens. Coldplay gets louder from his iPod dock.

'You two becoming friends then?' I say. He turns and goes back to his digital piano. He tinkers with the keys as we talk. 'Can we try and make this work?'

'You remember what she did, yeah? What you did?'

'Yes I do, I'm sorry.'

'I just don't get why you would let her in like this. Risk our friendship.'

'She's got nowhere else.'

'Everyone has somewhere el-'

'She doesn't, Parker. She really doesn't. And her last boyfriend beat her up.' He stops playing with the keys and turns to me.

'Beat her up?'

'Yeah, she's got a proper bruise all up her neck.' Parker thinks for a moment.

'Shit,' he says.

'Look, I know how you feel but I can't just kick her out onto the street, you know? You and I go way back. But, so do me and Ashley. We all do.' He listens to me, saying nothing, considering what I've said.

'Just feels like, I dunno, you're rubbing my face in it, that's all.'

'I'm not, and neither is she.'

'You gotta admit, it's a pretty fucked up situation.'

'Yeah but she's our friend. Your friend too and we can't just abandon her because of something that happened years ago.' Parker turns his nose up.

'Easy for you to say.' Off my look he then says, 'alright. I get it, I'm in a minority here. You'd better remember this though.'

'You're not an arsehole, even if you look like

one,' I say, smiling.

'Why are you smiling when you say that? That's not going to persuade me. See, you were getting somewhere and now you've just gone back to the beginning.'

'Alright, alright. I get it.' We glance at each other for a moment.

'This guy seriously beat her up?'

'Yeah,' I reply. Parker thinks for a moment. 'So, you want dinner?' I ask.

'You mean, what am I cooking?'

'No. I'm cooking.' Parker looks at me suspiciously.

'You?' he says.

'Yeah.'

'You're cooking?'

'Yes.'

'Ollie, in the entire time we've been living here, I can count the times you've cooked on one hand.'

'So? I can cook and stuff.'

'Alright, give it your best shot,' he says. I nod.

'Thanks Parker,' I say. 'I mean it.'

'Yeah, whatever.'

I wander out and back along the hall towards the kitchen. I hear a muffled conversation coming from the living room. Ashley is talking to someone on her mobile.

'I don't know...no, it was over when you started throwing things...I'm not going to...no, Gary, I said no. You call me again, I'm going to get my big, scary flatmate to fuck you up.' Silence. Has she hung up or... I try to listen further. When there's still no sound, I quickly turn as the door opens and Ashley comes out. She stops when she sees me standing in mid-sneak. 'Oh...' she says.

'Uh...' I reply, unable to hide a guilty smile.

'Were you listening?'

'Not really.' She tilts her head. 'I'm making some dinner and was going to ask you if you wanted any.' She folds her arms, unimpressed. 'Which big scary flatmate were you talking about just then? Because I can't see Parker beating anyone up.' She rolls her eyes and strides past me towards the toilet.

'Dinner would be lovely Ollie, thank you,' she says as she closes the toilet door. I shake my head. Okay, I shouldn't have listened but come on. I know it was a private conversation but she was saying it loudly enough.

The awkwardness between Ashley and Parker continues throughout dinner. It's my speciality, fish fingers, oven chips and beans. Hey, it's hot and it's not going to kill anyone. I try, as best I can, to make conversation but there is still mild sarcasm from Parker and he ends up leaving with an unfinished plate and heading back to his room. Of course, that could just be my cooking. I glance at Ashley who shrugs at me. She clears the plates away as I sit, lost in thought. I don't know what to do about this.

Ashley walks back in and throws herself onto the sofa, yanking out her 'Conversations with God' book from underneath her and opens it at a folded page.

'Are you seriously reading that?' I ask. She lowers the book to reveal her face and stares at me.

'Problem?'

'No, just doesn't seem very...you.'

'Well contrary to popular belief, I'm not the same girl I was at twenty-one.'

'No, you were like a child who'd down three Redbulls and then move onto a bag of Woolworth's Pick 'N Mix,' I say. She smiles, remembering.

'Woolworths,' she says.

'Shame,' I reply.

'Yeah.' Silence between us. I note that she hasn't raised the book. What's she waiting for? Maybe I should start a conversation. I go to say something but she beats me to it. 'Thanks for letting me stay here, I really appreciate it.'

'No problem. So, before on the phone...was that your ex?'

'Yeah.'

'What a dick.'

'Yeah. Spent a long time putting up with his crap. I never used to be like this.'

'Like what?'

'This. Shy, nervous around people. I used to know where I was headed and nothing would stop me. Now look at me.'

'Hey, at least you left him. That's the important thing. You could still be there now. He could still be hitting you.'

'Yeah, I guess.'

'Took guts to do that. And coming here was pretty brave too.'

'I've always trusted you Ollie. You were always...good news.'

'Thanks. I think.'

'I know what happened before between us. But that was then, and this is now.' I nod slowly and smile.

'I'm glad you came here,' I say.

'Me too.'

SIX – FIRST DATE

Tuesday. I've been at work for just over an hour and a half. Paul is reading the Daily Mail. It's strangely quiet, hardly anyone speaking or shouting. Having just got the team a round of coffees, you'd think one of them would engage in conversation but no. Nothing. They all seem to be miles away. I check Facebook, nothing of note on my news feed. Just for the record, I don't check Svetla's news feed. Except...I do. Don't know why I told you that just then. Sorry. I'm still friends with Svetla. Either she's forgotten to delete me or she wants me to see that her life is perfect and ongoing. On the plus side, it doesn't look like she's found anyone else which is good. I am not a stalker.

My mobile rings, I glance at Paul, checking to make sure he hasn't forgotten I'm sitting opposite him. He's still engrossed in the newspaper. I look back to the phone, the display reads 'Blocked.'

'Hello?' I say.

'Is that Ollie?'

'Yeah, who's this?'

'My name is Lauren, you came by last week to do an interview.' Jesus, the stunner has called me. Right, just need to play it cool. My heart starts thumping like an African drum. I get up out of my chair and head to a quieter corner of the newsroom.

'Hey Lauren, how's it going? Did you see your interview go out?'

'Yes, it was okay. I think I could have given a better answer.'

'Rubbish, you gave some great clips. They were very happy.'

'Well, I just hope it worked for you.'

'Absolutely, really good.'

'Good, oh hang on a second, someone's here. Can I just put you on hold?'

'Sure.'

'Okay, sorry, two ticks.' I can still hear her talking to someone in her office. She obviously didn't press the button properly. 'What...? Then just tell him if he doesn't get Hockney to call me, the contract is void...I had the lawyer go over it with him yesterday...then keep pushing until we close it. I'm not throwing away two million on this arsehole. Greg, get it done, I won't ask again.' Jesus, sounds like she's putting Greg's balls through a blender. There's a slight pause before she says,

'Sorry, you still there?'

'Uh yeah. You sound scary.'

'Oh...you heard?'

'Um, only a little bit. But you sounded like you were kicking arse.'

'Yeah, it's so boring but I just wish people would do their jobs. They're paid well enough.' Why is she calling me? That is the only question zipping through my mind. I opt to try to steer the conversation.

'Was there something you needed?' Professional to the last Ollie, even if it will destroy any chances you have, nice one.

'Uh...well, look I'm sorry if this is a bit weird or... a few of us here are going for drinks tonight, one of the traders is leaving and I wondered if you fancied joining us?' The girl is asking me out. Lauren whatever-her-name-is is asking me out on a date.

'Tonight?' Yes tonight you tosspot, of course tonight.

'Yeah, it's a bit short notice I know and if you can't do it, I understand-'

'No, no, I can. Where are you going?'

'It's a place called Jo Jo's. Do you know it?'

'No, somewhere in the City?'

'Yeah, in Bishopsgate. I'll email you the address. We're getting there around seven if you're up for it.'

'Cool, okay.'

'Great. So I'll see you there?' She suddenly sounds nervous. Do I, Ollie Hayward, make the scary, stunning blonde girl nervous when I speak to her? You know, I think I do.

'Yeah, see you then.'

'Bye Ollie.' She used my name. Maybe she's like, in love with me.

'Bye.' She hangs up, leaving me to ponder my sudden turnaround in female fortunes.

I want to tell someone. I'm almost bursting. I sit back down on the newsdesk. Julie, the newsdesk assistant, sits opposite me. She's new and keen but also young and inexperienced. Her short cropped brown hair doesn't do her any favours.

'What are you smiling about?' she asks. Paul looks up from his paper.

'Well, you know that girl you sent me to interview the other day? In the City?' I reply, looking at Paul. He thinks for a moment.

'No,' he says, eventually.

'Well okay, doesn't matter. Anyway, she's just asked me out on a date,' I say. Julie smiles.

'She asked you on a date?' Paul asks, a quizzical look on his face.

'Yes, don't pull that face, like that's the most unlikely thing to happen on a job.'

'I've been working in this business for over twenty years and no one, no one, has ever asked me out,' Paul says.

'Well I must be a charmer,' I reply. Julie and Paul both laugh.

'Yep that must be it. You think he's attractive, Julie?' Paul asks. She looks at me and shrugs, a smile on her face.

'I don't know. He's not really my type,' I feel like I've been slapped, 'but yeah, he's pretty good looking I guess.' Ah, the youth of today.

'Pretty good looking. I can't tell if that's a compliment or not,' Paul says.

'Me neither,' I reply.

'Well all I can say is she'll more than likely fuck you over. That's what I've found with women.

No offence Julie, but it all comes down to what you don't do. You didn't buy me flowers for no reason. You didn't fix the garage door when I told you. You didn't do that sponsored fun run for the deaf kid at the end of the road,' he says. I glance at Julie who shrugs.

'So the divorce going well then?' I ask.

'What divorce ever goes well, Ollie?' he replies. 'I'll be glad when it's done. Sucking the life out of me and my savings. But I'm sure this girl you've met is the one that's different.'

'We're not all the same, Paul,' Julie says.

'Right. That's what you want us to believe,' he replies. Julie glances over at me, annoyed. I shrug, unsure what else I can add to this conversation.

I don't have time to change, so I jump on the tube and head straight to Bank station. As I try to follow my map directions, I stop and call Parker.

'What do you want homo?' he says, sounding like he's eating and talking at the same time.

'Just to say, don't wait up for me tonight,' I reply.

'I don't wait up for you any night, dick.'

'Well this one especially.'

'Fine,' he says. He's obviously distracted. With what, I don't wish to speculate.

'Don't you want to know why?' I ask.

'Meeting your gay lover?'

'No. I've got a date.'

'Yeah? Your mum doesn't count.'

'Pretty funny. No, really. That girl I showed

you the DVD of.'

'Mate, you're not doing that thing where you stay out half the night walking around in the dark in some vague attempt to prove you're hetro?'

'You can believe me or you can be a dick. I won't be home till late.'

'Are you seriously meeting that girl, what's her name again?'

'Lauren. Yes I really am.'

'Wow. I'd say good luck but I think you're going to need a lot more than that not to fuck this one up.'

'That's great dude.'

'Try not to do anything stupid, like be yourself.'

'Gotta go man, constructive though this conversation is.'

'Have a nice night.'

'You too, with Ashley,' I say.

'Mate, don't even try to-'

'Sorry gotta go.' I hang up and smile. I glance down at my iPhone and reload the map. Says Jo Jo's is just around the corner here. There's no sign or...oh hang on, what's this? I see a small metal sign by a door. Jo Jo's. I stare through the window. Seems pretty full and rowdy. Suddenly I'm nervous. I don't know any of these people. Hope that cock with the shiny suit, James, isn't going to be there. I take a deep breath, open the door and go inside.

Hard-hitting house music pulsates through me as soon as I enter. It's an ultra-trendy bar/club. Well dressed types stand impatiently waiting to be served. The bar area disappears into the distance to my left. People stand chatting and shouting at each other over the din. I scan the crowds for Lauren. I spot her coming out of the Ladies and move to intercept. She sees me.

'Hey. You made it,' she says, leaning in to kiss my cheek. She's wearing a grey trouser suit. Her long blonde hair is pulled back tightly into a sexy ponytail. She looks stunning.

'Hi, uh yeah,' I reply, my dufus gene kicking in at the perfect moment.

'I hope you don't mind me calling, I just... I don't know, thought it might be fun.'

'Yeah no, absolutely,' I say. Perhaps we can move on to two or more syllable words now Ollie, what do you think?

'You want to meet everyone?' she asks.

'Sure,' I reply. Yeah, I want to meet 'everyone'. Smooth, she'll definitely want to have sex with me after that line. Are these people going to be a bunch of wanker bankers? She takes my hand and leads me through the throngs of people to a table with maybe fifteen well-dressed types sitting around it. I note they are all about five years older than me. I spot shiny suit man doing the entertaining. Great.

'...which is why my team closed the sale and everyone keeps their jobs,' James finishes saying as Lauren and I approach. He looks up, others follow his gaze. Now I really do feel like a douche.

'Everyone, this is Ollie from TBN. He was the one that came and interviewed me the other day.' Some people nod, others glance at one another. I put up my hand and mouth hi.

'Shuffle round,' Lauren says. They do,

somewhat reluctantly.

'So no one being fired today then?' one of the guys asks James.

'No, they're safe for today,' he replies, taking a sip of his pint. The conversation fragments and soon people have split into smaller discussions. The guy next to me turns and offers his hand.

'Hi, I'm Mark,' he says.

'Ollie, nice to meet you,' I reply. Mark looks like one of those clichéd well groomed city men. Good looking, olive skin, immaculately dressed and something about him that reminds me of George Michael.

'So you work for TBN? That fun?' he asks.

'Yeah, you know, it has its days like any job but it's interesting and every day is different.'

'You're a reporter?'

'Producer. Which basically means, I do all the work and get none of the credit,' I reply, an attempt at a joke. Mark smiles but doesn't chuckle.

'I can't get my head round this, you do interviews that someone else uses?' Lauren asks.

'Yeah. Some days I'll do interviews, like the one I did with you. Other days I'll be sent down to court to break the result or be sent to a breaking news story like a riot or anything really.'

'Sounds really interesting,' Lauren says.

'It's not always that exciting,' I reply.

'No sure, but when a big story breaks, I bet everyone goes nuts,' she says.

'Yeah they do, but must be the same where you work?' I say.

'Oh no, we're completely calm all the time,'

Mark replies. Lauren shoots him a look. 'I'm just fucking with you. It gets pretty nasty sometimes but that's the job, right?'

'Sure,' I say. I don't know what to make of this guy. Seems friendly enough, if a little into himself.

'You'd better not be talking about me,' says James, across three people. Mark and Lauren look over to him.

'Why would we be talking about you?' Lauren asks, smiling. 'Ollie's far more interesting.' James pulls a face and whispers something to the voluptuous girl sitting next to him who giggles as she sips her cocktail through a straw.

'You want a drink, Ollie?' Mark offers.

'If you don't mind, beer would be great,' I say.

'Boss?'

'Same again please,' Lauren replies. Mark turns to the rest of the group.

'I'm not buying all of you drinks unless someone comes to the bar to help me.' He stares at James.

'I can't get out mate, I'd love to,' says James.

'You're coming. Come on,' Mark says. James rolls his eyes.

'Fuck. Sorry guys, excuse me,' James says. People shuffle to allow James out. They walk off together.

'So are you working tomorrow?' Lauren asks.

'Yeah fraid so.'

'I hope you don't mind me calling you like that. Just sort of out of the blue.' She stares at me, her eyes sparkling in the low light.

'I was surprised to hear from you. Although when I heard you ripping that guy a new arsehole I thought, man you're scary.' She puts her hands over her face.

'God, so embarrassing, what must you think of me?'

'What had he done?'

'It was more about what hadn't he done. It's fine. He did what he needed to and now everything's as it should be. Don't you ever shout at people where you work?'

'I guess, sometimes.' I glance over to the bar, James and Mark are doing rock, paper, scissors. James loses and he doesn't look happy about it. Ha!

'So whereabouts do you live?' Lauren asks. I turn back to her.

'Clapham,' I reply. She nods. She knows where Clapham is, that's good I guess. 'You?'

'Pimlico,' she replies.

'Nice,' I say. She shrugs. There is something crackling between us under the surface. I feel it charging through me. It's all I can do to keep my heart from jumping out of my chest.

'So do you have a girlfriend?' she asks. I look at her.

'No. You?' I ask.

'Girlfriend? No.' She smiles, her eyes never leaving mine. The intensity between us is suddenly overpowering. The rowdy bar has all but disappeared. Just the two of us, caught in each other's headlights. 'I'd be lying though if I said I hadn't experimented,' she says, winking. What's that now? She what? This girl has just admitted to me that she-

'Here you go,' Mark says, putting the pint

down in front of me which immediately breaks the spell with Lauren. I look up at him.

'Thanks,' I say. I want to explore the lesbian angle Lauren just dropped into the conversation but now Mark's here it feels somehow inappropriate. 'That was quick.'

'Yeah, the barman knows me. We're in here a lot,' Mark replies.

'You mean, you're in here a lot,' Lauren says.

'So? It's a cool place, right Ollie?'

'Yeah, cool,' I say.

'Just don't get a round in, it costs a small fortune,' he says, smiling.

'Mark, why don't you sit here and I can chat to Ollie,' Lauren says.

'Uh, sure. Whatever you say, boss,' he replies. Lauren stands up and shuffles past Mark. She sits down and smiles at me. I smile back. Everyone's happy. Mark starts talking to the girl with the huge boobs next to him.

'So...' I say.

'So,' she replies, taking a sip of her drink.

'What is it you do again?' I ask.

'I'm in charge of all the trading managers at United. I make sure they don't do things they're not supposed to.'

'Right. Cool.'

'So what about you, have you ever met the Prime Minister?' she asks.

'Yeah.'

'What's he like?'

'Honestly, he's a bit of a prick. On camera, he's one person, off camera he's someone else.'

'Oh. How disappointing.'

'Yeah.' A pause settles itself between us. Then I say, 'So tell me about these past experiences then?'

'Past experiences?'

'Yeah, what we were just talking about before, you know?' I say, smiling. She purses her lips, her eyes flirting with me.

'Right, right. In order for me to tell you about that, I'm going to need a lot more alcohol-'

'Easily sortable,' I say.

'And I need to be able to trust you.'

'You can trust me,' I say. She stares at me, searching my face for untruth.

'Hmm,' she says, smiling, 'we shall see.'

The evening moves onwards and before I know it, it's chucking out time. Everyone stands outside, saying goodbye to one another and working out who can share cabs with who. Mark and one of the other girls climb into a cab together. James has already left with two other guys. I'd tell you their names but I can't remember.

'Lauren, you coming with us?' Mark asks, one leg inside the cab, the other outside.

'Yep, hang on two secs,' Lauren says, before turning to me. 'Well, that was nice.'

'Yeah. Thanks for inviting me along.'

'Anytime. We should do it again sometime,' I say. She smiles.

'We should.'

'So, yeah. Bye.'

'Bye,' she replies. We stand awkwardly. Am I supposed to make a move? In front of Mark and everyone? I'm unsure, and in that moment of indecision she turns and walks over to the cab.

THREE WAY

She gets inside and slams the door. They drive off,
I wave as they go. Damn.

SEVEN – THE EMAIL

On the way up to the flat, I spot Tristan's hall light on. A familiar and banned smell wafts from his apartment. I turn the key in the lock slowly. I'm aware it's past one in the morning and I'm keen not to wake anyone up. I open the door to a dark hallway. Carefully, I close the door and peek inside the living room. Ashley is lying on the sofa, asleep. Her light is still on, her God book draped across her chest. I go to leave.

'How was your date?' she asks, her eyes still closed.

'Good,' I whisper, 'get some sleep.'

'Did you have a nice time?' she asks. It sounds like a loaded question.

'Yes, thanks. I'll see you in the morning,' I reply.

'You don't have to tiptoe around me.' She opens her eyes and looks at me.

'I had a nice time,' I say.

'I'm glad,' Ashley says.

'Nothing happened,' I start to say, then stop

myself, suddenly realising I don't need to justify myself.

'Then, when you see her again, make sure it does,' she says with a cheeky smile. I don't know why she says it like that but somewhere inside it feels uncomfortable. I chuckle, covering as best I can. I try to form a sentence in my mind. 'Night,' she says. I open my mouth to say something but nothing comes out.

'Night,' I reply and walk out. I get to my bedroom and close the door, throwing my coat on the bed. I try to make sense of the evening. Lauren is definitely interested. She made all the moves which is strange because I'm normally on my knees when a girl finally gives me the green light. I don't think I've ever had it the other way round, apart from Ashley, of course. But then she's not like other girls. Even if she is wounded at the moment, I'm sure it's only a matter of time before she gets her mojo back. I hope so anyway.

As I replay the evening in my head, the fear begins. I start to wonder what a girl like Lauren could possibly see in me? Gorgeous, successful, on top of her game, what is it that I bring to the table? Then it hits me, my job. She's a high flying trader type and it doesn't do her any harm to be on the arm of someone that could potentially further her career/beef up her profile. She did ask me a lot about my job. But I guess they all did, and what better way is there to break the ice? Mark seems like a cool bloke and although he's a little arrogant, I could see us being friends. I guess if I do end up going out with Lauren, that might be a possibility. James is still a twat, hope I don't see too much of him. I undress and get into bed, turning out the light. Memories whip around my head, my mind focusing on the smallest of details. Lauren's blonde hair. Mark's cool clothes. Ashley.

'The next station is Waterloo,' the computer voice on the Northern Line says. I only hear this in a very distant way. The message swims around my head. I'm asleep. I had so little sleep last night, I nodded off almost as soon as I got on at Clapham Common. Now, as consciousness returns, my neck feels a little stiff. I open my eyes and quickly realise that my head is resting on the shoulder of the person sitting next to me. Ah. Problem. I carefully try to raise my head but it's then I note that said person has their head rested on top of mine, effectively trapping me in place. Awkward. How exactly to play this? As I ponder on how to extricate myself the stations zip past and before I know it, we're approaching Goodge Street. Nothing for it but to move my head more forcibly. The person next to me, realising what's happening, is off me in a flash. I sit up and rub my neck. I see who's shoulder I've been resting on. It's a man of around sixty and I'm unsure if he has a permanent residence. The clues are:

1) He smells.
2) He needs a shave.
3) His fly zip is undone or jammed. I can't say which and I'm not going to study it further.
4) Between his legs he has a 'Bag for Life,'

which does indeed look like he's had since he was born.

I smile, embarrassed.

'Sorry,' I start to say, immediately regretting engaging in conversation.

'What yer sorry for?' he replies.

'Just...you know, leaning on your shoulder.'

'Hmm. Give me money and I'll forget it ever happened,' he says, hand outstretched. The doors open, the computerised voice stating,

'This is Goodge Street.' I jump up, fumbling in my pockets. I pull out the first thing that comes out, which happens to be a ten pound note. Damnit. He stares at it. I have no time. I shove it into his hand and bolt for the doors as they ring. I make it just in time. The train pulls away, I spot the man staring at the ten pound note then over to me. He gives me a smile, followed by a thumbs up as the train disappears into the tunnel. Shit. That was my lunch money. How the hell did that happen? Who falls asleep on the nearest hobo? Don't answer that.

By the time I get to work, I've tried and failed to forget my monetary loss. How could I be so...? Calm Ollie, just let it go. I swipe my ID card and wander into the newsroom. Paul sits on the newsdesk, feet up on the table, Daily Telegraph in his hands. Julie is staring intensely at her computer, a frown on her face.

'Ah morning Ollie. There's nothing for you at the mo, so if you want to get some breakfast-,' he says.

'What happened to you?' Julie asks. I walk

around to her side of the desk and pull up a chair next to her.

'Late night,' I reply.

'Oh yeah, with a girl?' she asks, smiling.

'Well, yeah I guess it was,' I reply.

'Ooo, tell me. Was it that girl you interviewed?' she asks. I glance at Paul, who's not listening. I lower my voice, just in case.

'Yeah.'

'How'd it go?'

'Good, I think. I mean, they're bankers so…spawn of the devil and all that but, she's great. I still can't get my head round the fact she called me.'

'Why? Girls ask boys out sometimes.'

'Do they?'

'Well sometimes they do. So what's she like? Did you…?'

'I'm not going to tell you anything but no we didn't. It was quite difficult to talk with everyone else there. She's a bit older than me-'

'How old, forty?'

'No, maybe thirty?'

'That's not old.'

'I didn't say it was, I said she was older than me.'

'Yeah by like a couple of years, that's nothing. I went out with a guy once who was forty-five.'

'Well, that's not that old.'

'It is when you're nineteen.'

'Ah yes, okay.'

'Cool, so you seeing her again?'

'I dunno. I guess.'

'Ollie, you can't trundle through life hoping

good things will just happen. You have to take the initiative and make them happen.'

'I only went out with her yesterday.'

'She'll expect to hear from you today. Maybe send her an email.'

'You think? Doesn't that look needy and desperate?'

'Sure it does but you are needy and desperate, no point trying to hide it,' she says, chuckling. I nod and flick my eyebrows.

'Thanks for the advice.'

'No worries. You're not doing anything now, why don't you log in and send her something?'

'Okay but if this goes wrong, I'm blaming you.'

'Why would it go wrong? It's an email.' Hmm, I guess it couldn't hurt.

'How's Josh?' I ask.

'You don't care about Josh.'

'Yes I do, come on.'

'I think he's going to ask me to marry him but keep it to yourself, okay?'

'Wow, that's amazing.'

'Amazing someone would want to marry me?' she asks, blinking in that slightly strange way she does.

'No, amazing you're going to get married. I mean, you're still quite young.'

'Shh,' she says, looking around. 'I don't know anything for sure, just feels like he might.'

'I'll tell no one,' I say.

'Go write your email.'

I do as I'm told and try to compose something that doesn't make me sound like a bellend, dick, prick, schmuck, retard or slimeball. I admit, it's harder than it sounds. After forty-five minutes of fannying around, this is what I come up with:

'Hi Lauren, it's Ollie.

Just a quick email to say how much I enjoyed last night. Hope you got home okay and if you're up for it, maybe we could meet up again sometime soon. I'm around on Friday if that works, or I guess Saturday or Sunday if that's better. Seem to remember you said you might be busy but basically if you're around anytime in the next month then I'm sure I can work around it. Hopefully see you soon,

Love always, Ollie.'

There, I think that should do it. Okay, it's not perfect but hey, it's a first draft. My mind suddenly flashes an image of Svetla and my gut drops to the floor. I close my eyes. Come on Ollie. First stage of moving on. What harm can it do? Just an email, right? Julie has been glancing at me as I write and edit. Her face conveys a certain degree of concern but I'm sure her mind will be put at ease when she reads this. I send the draft to her.

'I've sent you something, let me know what you think,' I say, looking over to Julie.

'Haven't got anything,' she says. I stand and walk around the desk, looking over her shoulder to Outlook. She's telling the truth, no email has appeared. Hmm.

'Patience. Probably just TBN's shit servers,' I say, concern apparent in my voice.

'Still nothing,' she says. 'You sure you sent it

to my work email?'

'Of course I'm sure,' I reply. That's a lie. A worried feeling is now permeating through me. I go back to my computer and click 'Sent Items.' The email at the top has the correct Heading but my heart skips a beat when I realise I've sent it straight to Lauren. How? Oh God no.

'Oh God no,' I say out loud. Julie is standing behind me in a second.

'What? You didn't send it to her, did you?'

'I might have,' I reply. Julie bursts out laughing.

'What did you write?' she asks. I double click the email and she reads it. I hear a giggle, then a snort. 'Oh Ollie.'

'What? Is it bad?'

'No, it's not bad. It's probably the most terrifying email I've ever read.'

'No. Stop fucking with me.'

'I'm serious. If a boy sent me that, I'd be on to technical support to retain it for evidence.'

'Are you serious?'

'...basically if you're around any time this month. And you've even signed off with 'love always'...Ollie,' she can't stop laughing.

'This is not making me feel better.'

'What are you two doing?' Paul asks from behind his paper.

'Ollie's just sent a girl a stalker email,' Julie says.

'Great, let's have a read,' Paul says, standing up and walking around. I click back to the news program to cover it up.

'No. Come on,' I say.

'Seriously, I want to read it,' Paul says.

'No,' I reply, frowning. Paul stares at me and somehow I find myself saying, 'alright fine.' I click back to the email. Paul reads, then ever so slowly, a smile forms on his face.

'Oh dear. Do you find the stalker thing works?' he says. Julie laughs again.

'Brilliant. Just brilliant.'

EIGHT - TALK

Thursday. Day off. I have no plans and it feels great. I'm going to lie in, have a late breakfast and spend the rest of the day doing nothing but watching TV. Except, of course, none of that is anything remotely like what actually happens.

From somewhere deep in my subconscious I hear the toilet door bang shut. I'm awake, staring at the inside of my eyelids. I hear someone straining and obviously having difficulty, judging by the huffing and puffing now emanating around the flat. Parker. I hear him whisper the word 'Christ' followed by more huffing. I pull the pillow over my head, not wishing to be any more involved than I already am. Definitely quieter under the pillow. Then a noise that sounds suspiciously like my door opening. I wait, my heart suddenly pumping hard. Nothing. I push the pillow to one side and look over to the door. The silhouette of Ashley fills the doorframe, her hand on her hip.

'What?' I say.

'Do I seriously have to listen to that?' she says.

'Urgh, what do you want me to do? The guy's got to take a shit.'

'Not like that he doesn't.' I huff and pull the cover off. I'm wearing only a shrunk-in-the-wash pair of boxers but modesty is the last thing on my mind. I walk past Ashley, wiping some sleep from my eye and head to the toilet. I knock on the door.

'Parker?' I say.

'What?' he replies, surprise and mild indignation in his voice.

'Can you just...try and keep it down?'

'I'm taking a dump,' he says, as if no further explanation is necessary.

'Yeah I know, but so do next door so, could you just, try and do it...a bit quieter.'

'Fucking hell man, what is this Nazi shit? Can't a guy unload any more without an interrogation by the Hayward Gestapo?'

'No, I'm just saying-'

'Uh hold on...' he says. I glance at Ashley, she's scrunched her face up and looks suitably disgusted. I shrug and head back towards my bedroom.

'Uh God,' Parker says.

'Oh man,' Ashley says and walks back to the living room, shutting the door behind her.

'Can we talk about this later, please? I really need to concentrate,' says Parker.

'Definitely. Forget I said anything,' I reply.

'What?' he asks.

'I said don't worry about it,' I say, louder. I shake my head and go back to bed. Well, Ashley's perked up a bit and all it took was Parker going to the toilet. Saying that, there are many things I don't want to be woken up by and this is definitely near the top.

I manage to go back to sleep. When I do finally surface, the time is just past eleven. I get dressed and walk into the living room, Ashley isn't there. Parker sits on the sofa watching TV, still in his...I wouldn't call them pyjamas...night clothes? He cradles a cup of coffee.

'Morning,' I say.

'Hi,' he replies 'want some coffee?'

'Nah.' I slump down on the chair. 'Where's Ash?'

'Said she had to go to work,' Parker replies.

'Work?'

'Yeah.'

'Where's that?'

'How the fuck should I know? What am I, her diary PA?'

'Easy.'

'My guess is she sells her body,' he says. I glance at my watch.

'Bit early.'

'Maybe she enjoys her job.'

'Careful now,' I say. We sit watching yet another repeat of Top Gear. I'm not in the mood. 'You done anything constructive today?'

'I'm psyching myself up to it,' Parker replies.

'How'd it go with that girl?'

'Okay, yeah.'

'Okay? Just okay? What happened, you find out she meant another Ollie Hayward?'

'Funny. No, I...sort of wrote her an email.'

'Sort of wrote her an email? And?'

'Well, let's just say I don't expect to hear from her again.' Parker laughs.

'You're such a fuck up.'

'I know, it's pathetic.'

'Next time you want advice about girls, ask me.'

'Or I could try not asking you and see if that works out better.' Parker ignores me and carries on watching. I stand up.

'Well this is dull, I'm going to the supermarket. Want anything?' I ask.

'How about a flatmate that doesn't talk to me during my favourite show?' he replies.

'You are such a shitkicker, it's not even funny,' I say, grabbing my coat from the door. 'If I'm not back in five minutes, just wait longer,' I say, a vague attempt at movie quoting. Parker ignores me. I walk out, mildly disappointed.

As I reach the end of my road I start to regret not wearing my rain jacket. It's July, it should be hot and sunny. Instead it looks like it's going to hurl down. Saying that, however, it feels good to be out in the fresh air. Or as fresh as air gets in South London. I walk briskly towards Northcote Road then turn left.

I make my way towards Clapham Junction as the first spots of rain start to patter on my shoulder. I cross Falcon Road and wait for the lights to change. It's at that moment the deluge starts. What started as a few drops quickly becomes a cascade. In the Amazon I'm sure the locals would have glanced up and thought 'huh, minor shower.' In London, people run for cover. It feels apocalyptic. As I watch people scurry to find shelter, I quickly realise I'm not one of them and I'm getting drenched in the downpour. My brain shifts into gear and I sprint across the road and straight into the Snail and Tomato pub. It's quiet for a weekday afternoon but people are muttering and staring at the rain. An old man in a tweed coat takes one look at me and says

'Bet you wished you brought an umbrella. You're drenched son.'

'Thanks for that, old man I don't know,' I reply. Except, of course, I don't say that. I think it and, with a big smile say, 'Yeah.'

I glance at the window, the rain isn't going to stop any time soon. I turn around and walk to the bar. The barmaid has her back to me, loading bottles of beer into fridges. I cough. She finishes the box , stands and turns around. It's Ashley. Her eyes widen when she sees me.

'Ollie? What are you doing here?' she asks.

'Ash? I was on my way to the supermarket. This is where you work?' I reply. She glances down.

'Just until I get back on my feet, I want to pay you rent and I can't do that sitting in the flat.'

'You don't have to pay rent, you're a guest.'

'No. I'm not going to just take a handout. I want to pay my way. Look, it's not bad, I meet lots of sexy guys.' I smile.

'Really?'

'No. They're letchy and obnoxious. But it's money and that's what I need right now.'

'Fair enough.'

'You get caught by the storm?'

'No I fell into a swimming pool,' I reply, glancing down. Her eyebrows rise at my sarcasm.

'You want a coffee or something? Warm you up? I can sit with you for a bit, I'm due a break anyway.'

'Okay, yeah sure.'

'Take a seat.'

I squelch over to a table and sit down. I watch Ashley move swiftly as she prepares the coffees. It looks like she knows where things are. I wonder how long she's been working here. Her hair is tied back in a ponytail and she wears a white apron. Her blouse is undone revealing a little cleavage and she is wearing more makeup than normal. She looks good. Sexy. She glances over to me, I look down and pull out my phone pretending to check my email. I hear china cups placed on saucers and look up. She lifts her tray and walks around the bar towards me. She places the tray on the table and sits down opposite.

'Day off today?' she asks, taking one of the cups and passing it to me.

'Yeah.'

'So you thought you'd come see me. That's nice.'

'Yes, this was definitely a well thought out plan.'

'I can understand why you sought me out. I am pretty amazing,' she says, tearing a sugar sachet and pouring it into her cup. So the date went okay?'

'I wondered how long it would be,' I say.

'I watched the DVD, she's hot.' I nearly spit coffee all over myself.

'You watched the DVD of my interview. MY DVD?'

'Yes. It was just lying there, I thought it was one of my music CD's. Sorry, I didn't realise it was a secret.'

'It's not but...doesn't matter.'

'I have to say burning a DVD of an interview with a girl you've just met is a bit disturbing but she is stunning.' I don't say anything, maybe the shock of her finding and watching my DVD. 'So did it go okay, the date?'

'It was more like a work gathering that I was invited to.'

'Oh.'

'But yes it went fine. I think I've sort of fucked it up though. I sent her an email the other day which, God... it's just embarrassing.' She smiles.

'Yeah? What did you write? Not 'I love you."

'No, I basically said I was available any day for the next month.' She starts laughing.

'Oh dear.'

'And I signed it 'Love Always.'''

'Oh Ollie.'

'I know. She hasn't responded. So that's another one down the toilet. I'm such a fuckup when it comes to women,' my voice falters slightly. She stops laughing suddenly when she picks up my tone. Her hand moves over mine.

'Hey. You're not a fuck up.' She reaches over and pushes my chin up gently so my eyes meet hers. 'So it didn't work out with the Swedish one, just have to get back on the horse.'

'I know. I need to get over her.'

'What actually happened between you?' she

asks. I sigh heavily.

'I dunno. I took her for granted. Wore her down. And one day she said she'd had enough. Enough of my selfishness. Of my moaning. Everything. I don't know why I behaved like that. I loved her, we were together for two and a half years. The only girl I ever really loved.' I look up and see a flash across Ashley's face. 'I mean, I love you Ash, but you know.'

'I know what you mean.'

'She moved all her stuff out. She cried. I cried. I tried to convince her to stay, told her I'd change and all that. She knew though. She knew I was desperate to hold on to her. And that's what it was, I guess. I just wanted to keep her mine. I look back now and I can see there were so many things wrong with our relationship. Things I stopped her from doing. From being herself. She just went along with it most of the time. Didn't complain. I guess she just got to the point where she couldn't compromise herself any more. Don't blame her really.'

'Have you seen her since she moved out?' I shake my head slowly, sit back and sniff the emotion back in, a vain attempt at pretending it doesn't mean anything. 'Sounds like you were a real dick,' she says, softly. I look up, sudden annoyance in my heart from her lack of compassion. She stares at me with a serious face. I realise she's just being honest. I look down.

'I was,' I say.

'So, next time, don't be. Be someone else. Be the person you want to be. And don't be that moany, selfish fucker. Don't let him out.'

'Yeah. Sorry I... you're working.'

'I think you should call this girl and ask her out.'

'After that email? She'll think I'm stalking her.'

'I doubt it. She called you first and that's a sure sign she's interested. You'd have to really fuck it up.'

'I probably already have.'

'Don't be so down on yourself. Just give it a go.' I nod and sniff again. 'Hey?' I look up, our eyes meet. She stares at me, then nods slowly. 'She really got to you, huh?' I try desperately not to let myself go. I can feel strong emotions swirling around inside my chest and it's all I can do to stop myself from breaking down. I swallow and clear my throat looking at Ashley. Then something rises through me, a distant, familiar connection between us. I give her a simple smile. Slowly she leans in and kisses me. I'm suddenly right back in school. The ease of the kiss hits me instantly. Like home. Her lips, just as they were. Warm and good. I breathe in her smell, it fuses through me. Our kiss gets more intense suddenly. It's no longer a feel-better kiss. Something more urgent is fighting its way through. I slow it down and pull my lips away carefully. We stare at each other, neither saying anything at first.

'Well...you can still kiss, there's hope for you yet,' she says. I smile. 'There's a smile as well, see it's not all bad.'

'No, not all bad,' I reply. She glances over to the bar where a couple of drenched customers are waiting, wondering why they're not being served.

'Better get back. Stick around if you like,' she

says, standing.

'I'd better head off, I was supposed to go shopping.'

'Can I give you some money?' she asks, walking over towards the bar.

'No. We're good,' I reply.

'Hang on, I've got some here,' she says, then turns to the waiting guys, 'be with you in two ticks gentlemen.'

'It's cool,' I say, holding up my hand, 'see you back at the flat.' I head for the door and turn as I get to it.

'Ash?' she looks over to me. 'Thanks.' She smiles then turns to the first guy and asks him what he wants to drink. I open the door and head back out into the rain.

NINE – SHOPPING AND PLAYING

As I walk to the supermarket, Ashley's words whistle around my head. She had said it so casually, 'sounds like you were a real dick.' I was and I know I was. So how do I use that information to move on with my life? Lauren could prove a welcome distraction. Assuming, of course, I haven't scared the bejesus out of her with that shamefully amateur email.

I reach the supermarket quicker than I expect. As I start to walk down the fresh produce aisle, I'm struck by a sudden urge to take control of my life. I get out my iPhone and find Lauren's number. Fuck it. I hit the call button. My heart is suddenly thumping hard. It rings once. Then again. And a third time. Fuck, she's not going to even-

'Lauren Bates.' I hear her voice on the other end of the phone.

'Hi, Lauren?' I say, my voice unsteady.

'Yeah, who's this?'

'It's Ollie. Hayward.'

'Uh...' Christ, she's forgotten me already. 'Ollie

from TBN?' And there it is. She remembers my job. Ever so subtly, my heart sinks. I'm memorable for my job, for television news.

'Yeah,' I reply, unable to hide the slight dejection in my voice.

'Hey, I was just thinking about you,' she replies. Yeah? Just thinking how you could get yourself on the evening bulletin?

'Really?' I say.

'Yeah, I was just reading your email again. So cute.' Oh God. I want to die. That email.

'Umm, yeah sorry about that.'

'For what?'

'I dunno, just...maybe it came out wrong.'

'What? The fact you want to see me?'

'Well, yeah.'

'That's a good thing.' See, she says it's a good thing. I knew I wasn't a total fuck up.

'I guess.'

'So...you're around on Friday?'

'Yeah.'

'There's a place near here called the Proxy Bar. On Curtain Road. Eightish?'

'Sounds good to me.'

'Great, see you then?' she says.

'Yeah, cool. See you then.'

'Okay, bye Ollie.'

'Bye.' I hang up and lean against the wall. I have a date. A proper date this time. With a beautiful girl. Cool. My heart's thumping through my chest like I just drank three Red Bulls.

Slowly I calm down and as I stare at the assortment of fresh vegetables in front of me, I start to wonder what Svetla is doing right now. Is she back in Sweden? Did she ever get that job at BoDune Industries she wanted so badly? Does she still think about me? Has she found someone else? Someone better? God, I miss her. I don't know why today is turning out to be such an Svetla day. It should be a Lauren day. I've got myself a date with a stunning girl. Why am I still thinking about Svetla? Life is trying to pull me in a new direction, which I'm game for. I really am. Just...I miss the old me. The old life. Svetla was so beautiful. Such a deeply caring, lovely person. Okay, get a grip Ollie, starting to get emotional at the Asda food counter. I step backwards and breathe out, making my way to the milk and cheese aisle. Two pints of milk, some mozzarella, Flora. Svetla always made me buy the light stuff. She's not here any more. I could buy the full fat. I take the full fat Flora and chuck it into the basket. I begin to walk away and suddenly I start to feel guilty. Like I'm betraying her. I stop and glance back at the shelf. What the fuck are you doing Oliver? What am I doing? I don't owe her the light stuff but it's not bad tasting and it is better for me. Jesus Christ, move on.

I arrive back at the flat with less than half the items I wanted to get. Must start writing a shopping list. As I'm hauling the shopping up the stairs I spot Tristan smoking on his balcony. A joint. Of that, I have no doubt.

'Hey Ollie, that looks heavy,' he calls.

'Yeah it is,' I reply.

'Maybe you should try Tesco delivery. Then the guy lugs the shit up for you.' Maybe you should fuck off Tristan. Get a proper job, stop dealing to teenagers. Hmm? Try that.

'Yeah maybe.' I drop the shopping outside the front door and knock. Parker better be in. I wait, glancing briefly at Tristan who waves and pulls an exaggerated comical smile. I nod back, smiling politely. Where the fuck is Parker? I bang again. 'Come on,' I say quietly.

'You forget your keys?' Tristan asks, inhaling a deep breath of military grade ganja.

'No, just...Parker's supposed to be in,' I reply. I can't believe this, he's there all the bloody time and the one time I need him to be in...fuck it, just do it myself. I fumble through the absurd number of pockets in my jacket before eventually finding my keys. I open the door and nearly fall in. Tristan laughs at my misfortune. What a cocksucker. I start lifting bags from the hallway into the kitchen. This is far too much work. Why the hell am I doing this? I have two flatmates, both of whom don't pull their weight around the place and here I am, Captain Muggings, doing the shopping for the two of them. I don't care if Ashley is a good kisser, she still has to do her part.

'Parker?' I call. Nothing. Brilliant. I carry the last of the bags into the kitchen and sigh. I walk down the hallway to the toilet when I notice Parker's bedroom door closed. I walk slowly up to it and listen. Silence. I say a quick prayer that he's not engaged in some form of self-abuse, then I knock. Nothing. 'Parker?' I say again, opening the door. He's not in there but the fool has left his novel up on his computer. Now, should I? I know what you're thinking, it's personal, it's a first draft, he wouldn't be happy about it. All good reasons, I grant you. But fuck it, if the roles were reversed,

Parker wouldn't even be hesitating. I scroll up and start to read. Here's a sample:

'Her eyes glared at me like she was gonna kick the living crap out of my arse. I wanted her bad but somehow I also knew she wanted to play the game.' –Punctuation, grammar and general rules of English thrown mercilessly out of the window - something about a time machine. Blah-blah, hang on let me get to a good bit...ummm. Okay- *'the guy had no idea what was coming. With her devastatingly fast moves she had him in a headlock before he knew what had happened. The blood started to drain from his head and he started to feel dizzy. Her grip was locked tight. A hyena couldn't have escaped that grip* (???) *Slowly he came to the realisations* (how he spelt it) *that he was indeed doomed.'*

'Shit,' I say out loud. What did you think? A budding Charles Dickens in the making or could Parker be about to find out that his choice of career is a massive mistake? Could it be edited to be better? Sure, if we started with a blank page. Oh Parker. He's hung his dreams on this? Fuck. Now what? Do I tell him, devastate the guy? Or pretend I haven't and make subtle hints? I wish I'd never seen the thing now. How is he ever going to pay his way, long term, if this is the sort of drivel he's churning out? Not good. Not good at all. I walk back to the kitchen, unload the shopping and make myself some lunch.

Ashley comes home at five, still wearing her pub uniform.

'Hey,' she says, walking into the living room. I've got my feet up, watching TBN. I know I'm sad for watching the news on my day off. Can't help it, I quite enjoy it.

'Hi. How was work?' I ask. She collapses onto the sofa and pulls her shoes off.

'Interesting. Some guy started telling me all this personal stuff and by accident we ended up snogging,' she replies, smiling.

'Really? That's terrible.'

'I know. But see, the thing is, he's not over his ex and he's trying to move on with his life but every so often he takes reminiscent step backwards. And he's been so good to me I want to try and help him move forwards.'

'I see. Did he listen?'

'He did after I stuck my tongue down his throat.' We both chuckle. I look at her, a moment of genuine affection between us. 'We used to be a good team, Ollie.' I nod, the smile fading.

'Yeah we did. Until we started going out,' I reply.

'Yeah, things went a bit weird. Why was that?'

'I don't know. Never figured it out. Better with the physical stuff, I guess.'

'Yeah,' she says, a cheeky smile forming. I chuckle. The atmosphere has become charged, I'm breathing quickly. She moves closer to me, suddenly running her finger over my chest. I glance down then back to her.

'We shouldn't really...' I start to say. She shakes her head.

'No, we shouldn't.' We stare at each other, the tension overwhelming. Our lips move almost closer.

'This is not a good idea,' I say with no real

conviction in my voice.

'No,' she says. I move in and kiss her. Urgent. Passionate. She responds, moving her arm around my waist. All the pent-up tension forcing its way out of both of us. My fingers move over the familiar curves of her body, she feels the same as when we were at school. She pulls off my T-shirt. I unbutton her work trousers and yank them down. I feel her pulling at my jeans and suddenly my abdomen feels cool as the denim is removed. Before I even know what's happening, we're making love on the sofa, half-naked. Energy moves from me to her and back. She pulls my hair and scratches my back. I move between her legs roughly, little yelps escaping from her. Parker could come back from wherever he is...where did he go anyway? Who cares, Ashley feels so good. We were just made for each other. I can't remember how many times we've done this but every time feels like the first. I slow down, the energy changing and suddenly we stare at each other. Neither saying anything. Peering straight into each other's souls. I see who she is. I feel it and I know she sees me. She comes, shaking softly as she does. I come. Eyes closed, feeling the utter ecstasy of the encounter flooding through me. And then, silence. Nothing and everything. Slowly, I'm aware of my breathing, and before long I'm aware of hers. We're back in reality. Back in the present. I open my eyes, there she is. Her blouse is ripped under her armpits and her makeup smeared. She looks at me and smiles. 'Oops,' she says. I smile.

'Yeah, oops,' I repeat.

TEN – SECOND TIME LUCKY

Friday. I sit at work, thinking. Always thinking. Mostly about Svetla. A little about Ashley and some about Lauren. What am I doing? Somehow, while being fucked up about Svetla, I've managed to book myself on a date with Lauren and fooled around with Ashley. Total confusion reigns. Should I even go on this date with Lauren when I'm feeling like this? Surely someone's going to get hurt, most likely me but there's a possibility it could be Lauren and I would hate that. She seems like a nice girl. Do I want to load her up with my baggage? Of which, there is a considerable amount. What to do? Could do with some advice. I look around. It's a quiet day today, not much news around. Julie sits reading the Guardian. Such a liberal, doesn't make her a bad person or anything. I walk over to her and sit down.

'Hi,' I say.

'Hi Ollie, how's it going?'

'Not bad. I have a little dilemma.' She turns towards me and folds her newspaper.

'Oh? I love dilemmas. Tell me.'

'Okay well. You know that Swedish girl I was going out with?'

'Svetla, yes we all know about her Ollie.'

'Ah,' I reply. I hadn't realised I'd bored everyone with my tales of the Swedish one.

'What about her? Don't tell me you're back together?'

'No. Just...I'm going on a date tonight,' I say. She inhales excitedly.

'With the girl in the City?'

'Lauren, yeah. But the thing is, I sort of...fooled around with an old school friend who happens to be staying with me.' Julie's expression shifts from excited to a small frown. 'We're not going out or anything but we have this sort of, complex relationship.' Her expression changes again to what I would describe as disappointment. 'We went out in school but it was a bit of a disaster and we nearly lost our friendship, so we worked out some rules. Bearing in mind this was a few years ago, I'm assuming those rules still apply.'

'So these rules say you can shag her but not go out with her?'

'Well, yeah I guess. God, you think I'm evil don't you?'

'No, just a man,' she replies, sighing. 'Maybe you shouldn't be shagging your school friend when you're going out with Lauren.'

'Yeah,' I say. A pause before I then continue with, 'I'm just worried I'm going out with Lauren for the wrong reasons and maybe I'm still fucked up about Svetla and using Ashley to make myself feel better.'

'So you're shagging one, dating another while secretly pining for the third?' Julie says, staring at me. Well jeez, when you put it like that...

'I am such an arsehole, aren't I?' I say. She shakes her head.

'A little bit, yeah.' Her words sting with the bitterness of truth. 'Look, what do you want?'

'You think I should cancel the date?'

'No,' she replies, thoughtfully. 'Just, don't string her along. I guess you don't owe her anything but it could get really bad, really soon. Especially if you carry on with your school friend.'

'Yeah,' I reply, taking in what she's said.

'So, she lives with you, this friend?'

'Yeah, her boyfriend was being an arse, she had nowhere else to go.'

'She just showed up?'

'Yeah.'

'Man, she is so in love with you.'

'No, it's not that sort of relationship.'

'I know you think that but trust me, she wants your babies,' she says.

'This is not helping. How's Josh anyway, has he asked yet?' I ask, deftly changing the subject. Julie sighs again.

'No and I'm getting...it's fine. I'm not expecting anything.'

'But if he doesn't ask you to marry him the next sixty days, he's toast, right?'

'Right,' she says, automatically. 'No! I just...look, the ball is in his court. That's all I'm going to say.'

'I'm sure he'll do it soon.'

'Yeah. Exactly,' she says, looking back at her

paper.

How do I describe the Proxy Bar? A little bit too fashionable? The customers inside look like they all own swimming pools and Segways. There isn't a man in there that isn't wearing a tie and jacket even though there's no official dress code. The best word I can find to describe this place is poncey. Marginally too up-its-own-arse. I peer inside, looking for Lauren. I can't see her. Do I want to go in, sit at the bar like a loner boy? Or should I stand outside looking like a homeless person on the scrounge? I opt to head inside, it's too cold outside anyway even if it is July. Blue LEDs light the top of the bar. The aluminium bar stools are buffed to a high shine. The noise is incredible. People have to shout above the din. Although I would never choose to hang out in a place like this (my wallet could never take the damage) I have to admit it does have a certain energy. The place feels comfortable in its style, abundant with primness and patrons.

Taking a deep breath, I walk over to the bar. I glance over at the sea of customers impatiently waiting to be served. Well, at least I can kill some time while the staff supply the rest of these people.

'Yes sir?' the barman says. I glance over at others who'd been waiting longer.

'Oh…uh,' I reply. I haven't even chosen what I want. I look at the line of draught selection, all premium beers. All, no doubt, painful on the wallet. I can't decide. The barman's expression shifts from expectant friendliness to annoyed irritation.

'Uh, uh...Leffe, I'll have a Leffe,' I blurt out. Man, that was surprisingly hard work. I glance around again, looking for Lauren. No sign. I look at my watch. Five past eight. It's fine, she probably couldn't get away from work. The barman places a beer mat down on the bar and positions my pint on top.

'Six pounds fifty please.' My mouth hits the floor. I almost say 'Fuck me.' That is an insane amount of money for a pint, don't you think? Christ, that must be in the running for most expensive pint in London. Six pounds fifty! I begrudgingly hand over the money, shaking my head as I turn to look for somewhere to sit. The place is heaving, there's no way we're sitting in here. I feel a hand on my shoulder and turn to see Lauren standing behind me. She looks breathtaking. Wearing a power suit and white blouse, the whole ensemble looks fantastically sexy.

'Hi,' she says.

'Hi,' I reply, unsure whether to go for a kiss on the cheek. Fortunately, she leans into me and kisses my left cheek. It sends my nerves tingling. I smile. She glances down at my pint.

'Leffe? Good choice, I love Leffe.'

'Let me get you one,' I reply, turning to the bar. Of course, now he's serving someone else and I just know I won't be that lucky again.

'You look very nice,' Lauren says, putting her hand through my arm.

'Thanks, so do you,' I reply, knowing how lame

it sounds.

'Sorry I'm late, had a few bits to clear up at the office.'

'No worries.' I'm strangely nervous, not sure what to say. I turn back to the bar, a vague attempt to catch a barman's attention. We stand, slightly awkwardly, neither saying anything.

'So busy day?' I say, still having no luck with the barman.

'Always. You?'

'Not really, not much going on,' I reply.

'It didn't look like there was much news around today.'

'No. Bit dull,' I reply. I turn back to the barman who catches my eye, I smile at him.

'Yes mate,' he says, suddenly spotting Lauren. I see him do a double take. Yeah fuckhead...she's with me. Don't know why I called him fuckhead but it feels right somehow.

'Another pint of Leffe please,' I say. He nods and glances at Lauren. Or was it at her tits? Unsure. Let's not go there. I turn back to her. 'Sorry about that email.'

'Why?'

'I dunno, just could have written something... better, I guess.'

'Ollie, seriously, don't worry about it. If I thought you were a psycho, I would have given tonight a miss.'

'Fair enough,' I reply. I don't know what else to say other than the obligatory 'Will you have sex with me?' which I know I can't say out loud but...any thoughts would be great at this point? Anyone? No? Brilliant.

Luckily, the barman brings over the pint and asks for another eye-watering sum of money for it. At this rate, I'll be out of money before we've even eaten. She takes the drink and sips the beer.

'Damn that's good,' she says, 'those Belgians really know what they're doing when it comes to beer.'

'Yeah,' I say. Lame-arse. I look around the bar. 'Nice place.'

'Yeah, it's okay. It's a bit pretentious but it's close to work so, convenient.'

'Should have booked a table, sorry.'

'I'll just ask someone to move,' she says.

'Yeah right, good one.' I say, chuckling. Turns out, she's not joking. She heads over to two guys sitting at a large double table that could easily accommodate more if they were pulled apart. I watch her talking to them. They are eager to please, their expressions give them away. Men are so easily influenced. I observe this knowing full well I would be doing exactly what they are doing, which is moving their chairs closer so we can pull one of their tables away. Lauren beckons to me to come over, which I do, like the obedient dog that I am.

'Wow, good job,' I say, pulling off my jacket and hanging it over the chair.

'Just have to ask, most people are very accommodating if you ask with a smile,' she replies, taking her seat.

'Well, they're accommodating for you, Lauren. Doubt it works for everyone.'

'Why's that?' she asks.

'Well, because you're...'

'What?'

'Pretty.'

'You think I'm pretty?'

'Come on, you know you're gorgeous.'

'I think I'm not bad. I wanted to see what you thought.'

'Well I don't really think it's up for discussion.'

'Thank you.'

'You're welcome,' I smile and take a sip of my beer.

'So, how did you get into being a news producer?' she asks.

'I used to be a runner for music videos, commercials. Making tea and coffee and stuff. And I was sending letters off to people asking for jobs and one was TBN who came back to me saying 'thank you for your letter, we'll keep it on file, blah blah' and then six months later I got a phone call asking if I wanted to come in for an interview. So I did and they gave me a job as a news runner, running scripts to presenters and helping graphics with the background images behind the newsreader. So I sort of worked my way up from there.'

'Sounds like a lot of fun.'

'Yeah, it was. Nice team. Although when I screw up I get shouted at in front of the whole newsroom but...'

'Really?'

'Yeah. Luckily I don't screw up that often, so it sort of works out,' I say. She nods slowly.

'How long have you been there?' she asks.

'Maybe, four years now.'

'Do you still like it?'

'Yeah I really do. Like any job it has its dull days but every so often I get to do something or see something that no one else gets to do and on those occasions I feel pretty lucky.'

'Does it get busy often?'

'All these questions...' I say, smiling. 'I haven't asked you anything.'

'Sorry, it's just...I love journalism. It's so interesting.'

'Well the reality and the perception can be quite different sometimes.'

'I'll bet.'

'What about you? How did you get to be where you are?' I ask, picking up my beer.

'I slept with every boss I've ever had,' she replies. I gulp my beer down, and stare at her. I chuckle, unsure if she's serious. Her face betrays nothing.

'Really?'

'Would that offend you?' she asks. I frown slightly.

'No. I don't believe you.'

'Believe it,' she says, still deadpan.

'Okay,' I reply, slightly unnerved. Suddenly she bursts out laughing.

'Ollie! Of course I didn't!' she says, touching my arm.

'Oh, okay,' I reply, relief in my voice. 'Very good.'

'You are going to be so easy to wind up.'

'Yeah,' I say. This girl is weird.

ELEVEN – DECISIONS, DECISIONS

We're onto our third pint by nine-thirty and I think the alcohol is starting to go to my head. I consider whether drinking with no food is a wise idea but hey, I'm here now. I'm still trying to figure Lauren out. She seems like a fun girl but she asks me about my job a little too often which fuels my fear that she's just here to raise her profile. What the hell. I guess it's just a first proper date, doesn't have to turn into love, marriage, babies, houses, affairs, divorces, midlife crisis'. That's not how I look at life, by the way. Anyway, where were we?

'I'm having a nice time, Ollie,' she says, placing her beer down, slightly off the mat.

'Me too,' I reply.

'You ever had issues in the bedroom?'

'What?' I say, chuckling. I'm slightly taken aback by the directness of her question.

'Have you?'

'Don't beat about the bush, just come out and

say what you're thinking then?'

'I am,' she says, a slight smile on her face. She waits for an answer.

'Right well, uh have I ever had bedroom issues? Well. Sure, everyone has at some stage haven't they?' She nods slowly. 'Or has every boyfriend you've had just been able to perform perfectly, like some sort of rabid lion?' She bursts out laughing, it's a strange sound, bit like a snort. I laugh with her.

'Rabid lion?' she says, still laughing.

'Yeah, I dunno.' I shrug. We laugh again.

'You're strange,' she says.

'Me? What about you with your 'crap-in-bed' issues.' Her mouth opens again. I smile cheekily at her.

'You want this beer over you? Huh? So rude. I do not have 'crap-in-bed' issues. I was asking if you ever had those sorts of problems.'

'No I know. Sometimes, but it hasn't happened for ages. If you're concerned about being disappointed, don't worry. I rarely disappoint. Except that one time when she wanted to try it up the bum and I couldn't muster the penile energy,' I say. She laughs again and covers her shock by putting her hand across her mouth. She shakes her head.

'Gross. But you're funny, so I forgive you,' she replies.

'Funny ha ha? Or funny weird?'

'Funny weird. Definitely funny weird.' Her expression changes, the smile disappearing from her face. 'But I like funny weird.' We stare at each other. My heart is suddenly pumping full stretch like it's going to burst from my chest at the sudden intensity of the moment.

'Uh oh,' I say.

'What?'

'This is going to be trouble.'

We stumble out of the Proxy Bar into the chilly night.

'Where shall we go?' Lauren asks, threading her hand through my arm.

'Isn't Yogi's just up here?' I suggest. She wrinkles her nose.

'Oh no, tell me you don't go there? I was starting to like you as well,' she replies, a drunken smile on her face.

'No, I was just saying it's up there. My sad flatmate used to go there sometimes. What's your suggestion then genius?' She exaggeratedly places her index finger on her lips and looks up, thinking.

'I know. Come with me.' Taking my hand, she leads me through Finsbury Square and over London Wall to Old Broad Street. The City feels alive with Lauren next to me. She tells me she loves the City, with its tall glass skyscrapers comfortably sitting next to medieval stone buildings. So modern and yet, at the same time, so steeped in history. We round a corner and press on.

'Where are we going?' I ask.

'Because I am fortunate and cool I will take you to somewhere very few people ever go,' she replies.

'Ooo, sounds exciting,' I reply.

'It is exciting.' We walk on, the sound of her heels clip-clopping on the pavement. 'I like your aftershave, what is it?'

'Uh, Armani,' I reply, unsure if I put any on before I came out. Either way I guess it's a compliment. Suddenly, an image of Svetla hits me like a slap across the face. At some point during our time together, Svetla and I have walked down this street. In this exact way, arm in arm. The details are hazy but it feels like yesterday. I pull up suddenly, the copycat image of Svetla and I doing this same thing unsettling me. Lauren looks at me, frowning.

'What's wrong?' she asks. Svetla. Lovely, lovely Svetla. What the hell am I doing here? I glance at Lauren, who stares at me with a quizzical look. 'Ollie? What? What is it?' she smiles, briefly.

'I...' I struggle to express a form of words to describe what's happening.

'You're not going to go all weird on me now, are you?' Lauren says, the smile dying.

'No. Sorry, I just remembered something,' I reply, my voice unconvincing and distant.

'Okay. You wanna talk or..?' Pull it together Ollie, right now, or this is going down the shithole.

'No. I'm fine. Sorry, I don't really know what happened there. Maybe I'm just overwhelmed by your beauty.'

'Yeah right, that's exactly what it looked like,' she replies. I smile and we walk on but something deep inside me has changed. I'm now starting to look carefully at the situation I'm in. What exactly do I want from this? Another date? Sex? A relationship? I quickly realise I don't know. Which then begs the inevitable question, why then, am I doing this at all? I don't have the answers and somewhere deep down I know I need some to continue what has begun here. Stop it Ollie. Stop questioning everything you're doing. She's a nice girl, you're having fun. As you said, this is one date. Come on, pull it together. Yes. Good.

'Hey, you still with me?' Lauren asks. I suddenly realise I've been internalising and haven't engaged in conversation for almost half a block.

'Yeah, sorry.'

'We don't have to go to this place if you'd rather not?'

'Well I was just thinking, I've got to be up early.'

'Okay. You work Saturday's?' she says. I nod.

'Yeah. Sorry.'

'Not a problem. Just need to say, that's all. We haven't got to the point here where I can read your mind,' she says, smiling.

'Sorry.'

'Stop saying sorry.' I nod, uncomfortable. She looks at me with a concerned expression. She knows something is wrong. Fuck it! She turns and looks around for a taxi. Spotting one, she holds her hand up.

'Taxi!' she calls. The black cab pulls over and we jump in.

TWELVE – THE PHONE CALL

I glance at the clock again. It's four in the morning. I've been sitting here on the edge of the bed for the best part of an hour. Slightly drunk, confused and a little down. I'm sure it's the alcohol aggravating the feelings but things feel wrong. What happened with Ashley, the abruptly halted date with Lauren and my entire relationship with Svetla. I miss her so bloody much. Must try not to go down the road of self pity. Just keep it together. The purpose of the exercise is to try and rationalise things in my head. I stare at the carpet, dark feelings seeping in and out of me. The thing is, I know I shouldn't but I just want Svetla back. Could I...? Is that even possible? I don't even know where she is. I hear a soft knock at my door and look up surprised. Was it a knock, or just the wind? I listen. Nothing. I stand and walk over to the door. I open it, as quietly as I can. No one there. I look out, down the corridor and just catch the living room door closing. Ashley had come to check on me. I consider going after her but something in me can't face it. I close the door carefully and walk to the centre of the bedroom. I catch my reflection in wardrobe mirror. I stand and stare at myself. Who the hell are you? I sit back on the bed and throw my feet under the covers. I turn out the light and stare into the nothingness. I hear a brushing sound coming from under my door. I sit up and switch the light back on. A piece of paper sits under the door. I get out of bed, walk over and pick it up. She's written me a note. It reads 'Always here if you want to talk, Ash xx.' Was I being loud? Don't think so. Maybe I woke her when I came in? Who knows? I'm touched by her note though. I already feel a little better and this time I go straight to sleep.

I wake up a few hours later, my alarm smashing through the peaceful serenity of perfect deep sleep. I don't want to work today. I get up and grudgingly pull on some clothes. I head into the kitchen and start making myself some coffee. I feel a presence behind me and turn around. Ashley is wearing a very short nightie and not much else. She yawns wide.

'Morning,' I whisper.

'Hi,' she says, half asleep. Her hair is splayed in random directions. 'You making coffee?' I look at the kettle, the pot of Nescafe and the empty mug. I turn back to her.

'That's right.' She smiles and pushes me.

'I'm so tired,' she says, yawning again.

'Why are you up, it's early?'

'Couldn't sleep. You okay?'

'Yeah,' I reply, getting another mug.

'Yeah?' she tries to make eye contact with me.

'I'm fine, really. Thanks for your note.' She leans against the worktop and stretches almost to the point I can see everything that I, as a man, would ever want to.

'You're welcome,' she says.

'You hot or something?' I ask, looking down at her bare legs which are visible almost up to her-

'What?' she replies, glancing down.

'Doesn't matter.' The kettle boils and I pour some water into the mugs.

'So did the date not work out?'

'Now why would you think that?'

'You wouldn't be here if it went well,' she says. Her logic is sound but I counter with,

'Oh she wanted me, there's no doubt. I just decided to take it slow.'

'Right. Slow. You wanted to take your time.'

'Exactly.'

'So you're out with a beautiful, stunning girl and you wanted to...wait.'

'It's not like that.'

'Got to take the reins, move with purpose.'

'Is that from your God book?' I ask, spooning some sugar into the mugs. I then add a dash of milk.

'No,' she replies. She waits for a moment then says, 'so you gonna see her again?'

'I don't know Ashley.'

'Christ, you're an amateur.'

'Why are you so desperate for me to see her anyway? Jealous?'

'Yes, so jealous that I'm actively encouraging you to see her again.' I hand her the mug of coffee.

'I think it's just a cunning way of hiding your undying love for me,' I say. Ashley fake-laughs loudly.

'Shhh,' I say, 'Parker's still asleep.'

'Parker isn't here.'

'What?'

'He didn't come back last night.'

'Again? Where is he then?' I ask, frowning.

'Hang on, let me get my crystal ball. Oh no, wait a minute...they don't exist.'

I arrive at work ten minutes late. I hate the Northern Line. Have I mentioned that before? Well I do. I hate it. I can see why they coloured it black on the tube map. Christ, I've said that before as well. Let's just...move on, shall we?

'Hi Paul, sorry I'm late,' I say, walking in a little flustered. Paul looks up from his paper.

'I hadn't realised you were late, but now you're here you can make yourself useful and get the coffees in.'

'What's that about coffees? Are you getting some?' Julie says, from behind her desk.

'It appears I am, yes,' I reply.

'Mine's a latte, thanks Ollie,' she says. I nod. 'Do you want some money?'

'No, it's fine. Penance for being late. What do you want Paul?'

'My divorce papers to come through but short of that...double shot Cappuccino please.'

'Right,' I reply, unsure how to respond further.

I head upstairs to the canteen. This place is a real hoot. It's like the contractors running it regret ever tendering for the contract and now actively try to provide the worst possible service they can. The only upside is the view of London from up here. About the only thing worth buying is the coffee. Just. As I head towards the coffee lady, my phone rings. I whip it out and stare at the display. My world is suddenly turned upside-down. 'NEVER CALL THIS NUMBER...is calling.' Oh. My. God. Suddenly I'm having trouble breathing. Calm. Deep breaths. And...calmly answer.

'Hello?' I say in a tone that says, 'I'm so over you but I'm mature enough to be able to take your calls because you mean nothing to me.'

'It's Svetla,' she says, her familiar voice and accent makes my heart ache with pain.

'Hi?'

'Hi. Sorry to call you but you know I left some things at your flat and I wonder if I can have them back?' Her accent plays on my ear like a soft harmony.

'Oh. That was like, six months ago.'

'I wanted to wait. I didn't need them until now.'

'You want the old photos and books?'

'Yes and my CD's as well. If you still have them?' Why wouldn't I still have them? You think I burnt them, Svetla? You think I had a CD bonfire and I burnt your poxy Phil Collins Greatest Hits? Well I didn't, because I am an adult.

'Right. Yeah.' Long silence before she says the inevitable.

'How are you?' I'm devastated you Scandinavian bitch. Heartbroken. I don't think I'll ever be happy again. With anyone. You ripped my fucking world apart. I'm with two girls now, that's how fucked up you made me.

'Okay. Not bad,' I say. 'How are you?' Wrecked? Destroyed?

'Well it hasn't exactly been easy,' she says. Why would it? You're attempting to get over me, most never do. 'But I think, slowly, I'm getting there.' What? How can you be 'getting there?' Getting where? It's only been six months. How can you be 'getting there' already? What the hell? Am I that forgettable? We were together for two and a half years, and you get over me in six months...I mean Jesus.

'Good. That's good,' I say.

'Yeah.' Another long, awkward silence. 'So is there a good time to pick up the stuff?'

'Just the books and CD's?'

'There's some cutlery and plates that I need as well. And the Playstation.' Abso-fucking-lutely not.

'Oh come on, you want the Playstation? Give me a break.'

'No, you bought that for me for Christmas. It has a Blu Ray player. I've got all these discs and nothing to play them on.' This sucks. So she breaks my heart, rips it from my chest, nukes the shit out of it with her stupid pink retro microwave and now, on top of all that, she wants the fucking Playstation?

'No,' I say, a slight menace in my voice.

'No? No what?'

'I'm sorry Svetla, but you can't have the

Playstation. I don't mind giving you everything else but you're not having that.'

'Ollie...'

'I mean it. I use that almost every day.' Parker uses it every hour.

'But you bought it for me,' she replies, a little too quietly. For a second, I almost feel guilty but I'm on a warpath now, nothing is going to stop this freight train.

'Yes well, that was when you loved me.' Stunned silence.

'I...we don't work, Ollie. We didn't work for a long time. I should have done something about it sooner. I never stopped loving you, but surely at some point you've got to say enough is enough.'

'You can't have the Playstation,' I say. I hear her sigh.

'I really didn't want a big fight. You want to keep the Playstation then fine, keep it. But I want the rest of my stuff left in a box outside your flat and I'll come and pick it up.'

'You want me to pack your shit up so you can just take it away? Fuck you.' Another silence. I've gone too far, I know I have. I should apologise. Go on then, say sorry. I can't bring myself to do it.

'I thought we might be able to behave like adults about this. But I guess I was wrong,' she says.

'I guess you were.'

'Keep the stuff, if you want it so much. I just thought...doesn't matter.' I have nothing to say. I swing between venom and regret. I want to tell her I know I'm being an arse. Can't she see what this is really about? I'm on the fucking edge here.

Because of her. 'I have to go.'

'Wait, Svetla...I'll pack the stuff. Pick it up on Wednesday, okay?'

'Okay. Thank you. But do me one favour?'

'What?'

'Don't be there. Just let me pick it up. I think we've had enough dramas.'

'What dramas?'

'Please, Ollie,' she says. I breathe out, a crap attempt at calming the shitstorm pelting down on me.

'Okay,' I say.

'I'll be over on Wednesday morning.'

'I'll leave the box outside.'

'Okay. Thanks. Bye.'

'Bye.' She hangs up. I think that went well, all things considered, don't you? What? Oh, you think I'm going to do what she's asked? That I'm not going to lie in wait for her? You are so wrong. So, so wrong.

THIRTEEN – THE SWEDE RETURNS

After an unfulfilling day, I arrive back at the flat around six-thirty. The shock of speaking to Svetla on the phone still pulsates through my soul. She sounded so...normal.

The flat's deserted, no one in the living room. Ashley must be at work. I look down the corridor to see Parker's door is ajar, no one home. Nice. For once, I have the place to myself. I walk into the living room and collapse on the sofa. I can't even be bothered to take my jacket off. I flick the TV on and channel-hop, looking for something to watch. My mind replays some of the conversation with Svetla. I know she said she had moved on and everything but she still sounded like she missed me. I don't blame her, I am pretty missable.

Not sure what I do about Lauren. I like her. I mean, she's stunning to look at and I'd be up for something physical but do I want to head down that alley? Am I being responsible or is she just a distraction from Svetla? What do I want? That's the question that has become a recurring theme. I hear the front door open and voices echo around the corridor. Parker and...another female. I sit up, suddenly interested. The door to the living room opens.

'...exactly which is why I said to her-' Parker stops in mid flow. 'Oh...I thought you were seeing that girl.' Behind Parker stands a girl I have never seen before, wearing a light grey pleated coat. She has long dark hair, naturally long eyelashes and thin lips. In summary, she's pretty but not like amazing. I look at her then over to Parker who's already rolling his eyes.

'Nope, that was last night. I'm sorry, we haven't been introduced,' I say, standing up and offering my hand to the addition to our little family. 'I'm Ollie.'

'This is Nicola,' Parker says. She smiles but doesn't say anything as she shakes my hand.

'Nicola, nice to meet you,' I say.

'And you,' she says. Suddenly everything feels awkward. Parker apparently wasn't expecting me to be here and now appears to be unsure what to do about it.

'Maybe we should...go to my room?' Parker says, glancing at her. She nods and looks over at me.

'So, how do you two know each other exactly?' I ask.

'I'm an old school friend,' she says at exactly the same time as Parker says,

'We used to work together.' They both glance at each other.

'Right,' I say.

'Shall we..?' Parker indicates for Nicola to

leave.

'It's funny 'cos, I was at school with Parker and I don't remember you at all.' Look, I know I'm bad but I'm enjoying this.

'Well, I went to a different school and we'd meet up after,' she says, more confidently. I frown.

'Ah. So are you two..?'

'None of your fucking business,' Parker says.

'Parker!' Nicola says. He looks at her then to me. I am beaming at this point, a big smile right the way across my face.

'Sorry,' he says. 'We're now going to go to my room. So, I'll see you later, yeah?'

'Sure buddy. Hey, nice to meet you Nicola.'

'You too,' Nicola replies, walking out. Parker gives me his evil stare which tells me I'm dead, then follows her out. I hear his door close. Blimey. Where did she come from? I thought Parker just sat in his room all day writing poor prose and masturbating. Instead he's got a bit on the side that I knew nothing about and they seem to have known each other for a long period of time. Parker obviously wanted it kept secret and now I've just managed to torpedo the whole charade. Brilliant. I can't wait to interrogate him when she's gone. Awesome. What a tossa.

I'm halfway through another repeat episode of Planet Earth when I get a text from Lauren. It says 'Hi there, wonder if you fancied coming to a BBQ on Sat PM? Few people from work, could be fun, what do u reck? L x.' Hmm, BBQ eh? Another one of those work things where the only person I know is her. If that cock James is there I'll probably have to make chit-chat with him. Can I be bothered? It

would be another 'date' with Lauren I guess.
Maybe we could sneak off and mess around in the
bushes somewhere? I'm guessing the place will be
large enough for such a venture. I suppose it could
be fun. I click reply and say, 'Hi L, BBQ sounds
fun. Where/when? Maybe we can get into some
trouble? The Olster x.' I send it and throw the
phone back on to the table. Before I turn the
sound on the TV back up, I suddenly hear a female
voice. I listen, straining to hear. Nothing. I wait,
convinced I heard something worth listening out
for. Then I hear her again. A moan. Oh Christ,
Parker and Nicola are having sex. Another moan,
then again.

'Ooo yeah,' I hear them clearly.

'Shh,' Parker's unmistakable tones. My hand,
clutching the remote, hovers in the air. I'm unsure
if I want to listen to this but morbid fascination
stops me turning the TV back up. The room has
gone quiet again. Then,

'Oh fuck! Right there, don't stop you fucking
arsehole!' I hear Nicola say. Jesus. Nicola didn't
like it when Parker used the 'f' word before and
now she is either suffering from tourettes or the
man is screwing the swear words out of her. 'God,
don't stop...don't you ever stop...oh no...Parker
come on!' I can't help it, I'm laughing now. My
hand is over my mouth. 'You're kidding me?' then I
hear Parker say,

'I'm sorry darling but you said...(something
unintelligible)...and you know when you do that,
five minutes is my record.' Oh this is classic. The
ridicule is going to last for years. No wonder he
never brought her back here before.

'It's on my jumper, have you got a towel or something?' Oh guys, really? Come on.

'Yeah, hang on.' I quickly hit the volume up button. David Attenborough's voice suddenly fills the room. It couldn't be more obvious if I'd tried. I hear Parker walk into the kitchen, then the tap starts running. That is so nasty, I've got a good mind to tell him so. In fact-

I jump up from the sofa and walk into the kitchen. Parker turns from the sink. He's wearing a light pink dressing gown. It looks...silly.

'Having fun there?' I ask, smiling.

'Don't say a word. I don't want to hear a fucking word from you.' I hold my hands up.

'Hey, big guy. I never said nothing.'

'Yeah, keep it that way.' He's holding a small tea towel under the tap. He turns the tap off and squeezes the tea towel.

'What's that for?' I ask, smiling.

'Please fuck off, Ollie. Please.' I nod.

'Sure. Yep. I hear you. No more questions from me.'

'Great.' He goes to leave.

'If it's wool, you might have to put it on a delicate wash if the tea towel doesn't do it.' Parker stands, frozen. His back turned towards me. I wait for his reaction and some possible form of physical harm to come to me. Instead he just walks out and back down the hallway to his room. I'm trying not to laugh but it I can't help it. Absolutely brilliant.

I hear my phone bleep again and walk back into the living room, wiping a tear from my eye. Lauren's replied. 'Hi The Olster?? trouble sounds like fun. It's at James Kennedy's apartment in

Rotherhithe next Saturday. I'll email you the address. Looking forward to seeing you. The Batester x.' Fuck yeah.

Of course, before the BBQ, I have another little matter to take care of. Svetla.

Wednesday comes around fast. I have to call in sick as it's not my day off. Paul is dubious about the cold/flu I have suddenly developed but doesn't question it. I have packed all the items Svetla wants into a box which I carry into the living room. Ashley sits, watching the TV in her pub uniform. Parker's not around, I assume he's off with Nicola, the sex-swearing fiend.

'Thought you were working today?' she says.

'Uh, no. Day off,' I reply, putting the box on the table.

'Yeah? You have more time off than Santa Claus, you know that?'

'Thanks for that.'

'It's true. I marvel they actually still employ you.'

'So do I mate.'

'You know about Parker's bit on the side?' she asks.

'Nicola? Yeah. How do you know about her?' I reply.

'I was doing a bit of spring cleaning, which doesn't happen often enough,' she says. I nod in agreement. 'Anyway, I was replacing the bin liner in the bathroom and I saw a used condom. Figured it couldn't have been you. But I admit, it was...disturbing.'

'Yeah. I imagine it would be. That'll teach you to start cleaning.'

'Rookie mistake,' she says, glancing over at the box. 'What's in the box?'

'Uh, just some stuff I'm getting rid of.'

'Can I have a look?' She gets up and walks over to me. Before I can respond she says, 'unless...you don't want me to?'

'No, no, it's fine. Just charity crap.' She starts going through it and soon pulls out a CD.

'Lionel Ritchie?' she asks, holding it up.

'I'm getting rid of it.'

'How do you even own this?'

'It was Svetla's,' I reply, almost without thinking. Ashley's smile disappears and she looks into the box again.

'Is this...all Svetla's? You're giving it away?' she asks, staring at me. I open my mouth but I can't slot the words together. She sees my hesitation. 'She's coming over, isn't she?'

'No...why, would you think that?' I reply. Ashley tilts her head. 'Alright yes she's coming over.'

'Ollie...' she says.

'What?' I reply, trying not to sound defensive.

'Do you like pain or something?'

'I said I'd leave it outside for her to take.'

'Yeah? How come it's in here then?'

'Because...look I don't have to justify myself to you,' I say. She gives me a simple smile. 'What's that look for?'

'It's going to end in tears,' she says, glancing over to the clock. 'Shit, is that the time? No good me chatting away like this, some of us have got to work.' She grabs her bag and turns to face me. 'Hey...good luck,' she says, patting my shoulder.

'Thanks,' I reply. I'll need it.

She smiles, turns and walks out. I hear the door open then close. I don't know what to do now. Maybe I should just leave it outside and not engage with Svetla. That would be the honourable thing to do. Thing is, I'm not honourable.

I sit on the sofa waiting. I look at the clock. 11:03. I have no idea when she might get here, she did say morning. I look through the box to make sure I've packed everything she asked for. I pull out a pink, fluffy scarf and run it through my fingers. Soft. I smell it. It still has the faintest trace of her smell. I close my eyes. I pull out a framed photo of Svetla posing with uh...oh god what's his name? That celebrity on...you know, the one that does Match of the Day. Forget it. I look at Svetla's eyes. So happy, so sexy.

I hear a car pull up outside. I quickly put the photo and scarf back into the box. I locate the Lionel Ritchie CD and place it next to the photo. I close the box and walk over to the window. Outside, her distinctive red VW Polo is parking up. I wait, keeping close to the wall. I hear the car door open and glance out. There she is, dressed in a black suit. I've never seen her in a suit before. Damnit, why'd she have to look so stunning? Her hair is tied back and her high heels clip-clop on the tarmac. She gets to the stairs and starts walking up. I grab the box and walk to the front door. I see her hazy figure through the frosted glass. She's obviously looking for the box. I open the door. She's bent over, searching next to the door. Quickly, she straightens up. We stare at each other.

'Hi,' I say. A hand moves onto her hip.

'Hi,' she replies, 'I thought you were just going to leave the box.' I nod slowly.

'Yeah, I couldn't help it. I wanted to see you.' She looks at me, her eyes unsure what to say. 'You look good.' She looks uncomfortable.

'Thanks,' she replies, looking down at the box in my hands, 'is that everything?'

'Yeah, you want me to put it in the car?' I say. She thinks for a moment then seemingly gives in.

'Sure.'

I follow her downstairs and over to the car. She opens the boot and I place the box inside. I step back and she closes it. Our eyes meet, she looks away.

'So, are you doing okay?' she asks.

'Yeah, you know. Things are good.' She nods slowly.

'What about you? You get that job?'

'Yeah. It's going really well.' Her accent faintly slurs the words, the familiarity of it suddenly makes my heart sink.

'Good.' A long pause before I say, 'I've missed you.' She looks at me, forlorn eyes.

'We can't do this, Ollie.'

'I know, I know. I just...wanted you to know,' I say.

'It's not easy for me. I loved you, you have no idea how much -' she replies.

'I do-'

'No you don't. You threw it all away. Such a

waste,' she says, shaking her head.

'Maybe we could-'

'Don't you dare. Don't you dare say that. Bad enough I have to come here but to see you, speak to you as well?' She sighs. 'I have to go.'

'Wait, look, let's give it another try. I know I was arse, I know I was selfish and took you for granted but these last few months have been literally the worst of my life. I can't think without you. Can't do anything worth anything.'

'It's too late Ollie. It's all too late.'

'Svetla, please.'

'I have to go.' She places a hand on my shoulder, leans in and kisses me on the cheek. 'Take care of yourself, okay.' I want to be dignified, strong in this moment but I'm panicking.

'Svetla please, don't go okay? Why don't we just go for a chat somewhere? Talk through the things we need to get sorted.' She sighs, opens the door without looking at me and gets in. I stand there, not wanting her to leave but unable to throw away any remaining pride. She closes the door. 'I love you,' I say. She looks at me, shakes her head, a vague disappointment in her eyes, then starts the engine. There's nothing more to say. I can only watch as she drives to the end of my road, indicates left and is gone. I stand, staring after her, hoping that I might see her little red car drive back. It doesn't.

FOURTEEN – THE DOG THAT BARKS IN MY HEAD

The rest of the day moves achingly slow. I keep replaying the conversation with Svetla in my head. She really is moving on. I know I need to do the same but there's a need, a desperation in me that I just can't let go. I want her to be happy. I just happen to think she'd be happiest with me. I was a dickhead during the last few months of our relationship, but I really think if we were to get back together now it would be a completely different story.

I sit on the sofa, leaning forward, staring at the floor. I run my hands through my hair and cover my face. I breathe into my palms and close my eyes. Fuck me, this is hard. I need someone to talk to. I think I could do with some sense being knocked into me. Ashley is the best person for that. My hands drop from my face and I sigh heavily. My eyes wander to the window, the sun is partially blocked by a cloud floating in front of it.

The sky looks like a Turner painting, almost as if The Divine is trying to tell me to get it together. I take the hint. Right.

I stand up and pull on a coat. It's not cold out but it's not hot either. I grab my keys from the table and head out. I walk along Northcote Road with purpose. Lots of people out today, buses rev loudly past me. Every so often someone beeps at the person in front of them. Ashley will give me good advice. If I'm honest, I know what she's going to say. I need to move on, get on with it, go out with Lauren etc. but I still need to hear it.

I round the corner and cross the road, narrowly avoiding a double-decker that races passed me. Fucking bus drivers and he has the gall to give me an evil. What a cock. I get to Ashley's pub, open the door and walk inside. It's quiet again. The old man in the shabby black coat, who spoke to me the first time I came in here, is sitting at the bar, reading a newspaper. He must live here. A tourist couple sit in the corner looking at photos on their camera. I walk in slowly and approach the bar. A tall bodybuilder type barman is polishing glasses. He nods at me as I approach.

'Hello mate, what can I get you?' he asks, in a surprisingly cheerful voice.

'Uh, just a Coke please,' I reply. He puts the empty glass down.

'Is Pepsi okay?' he asks. I frown. No, if I wanted Pepsi I would have asked for fucking Pepsi. I want Coke.

'Sure. Is uh, Ashley here?'

'Yeah, she's out back with Norman,' he replies, filling the empty glass from the Pepsi hose.

Norman? Who's he, the manager? Something inside me suddenly feels uncomfortable. 'Here you go, one pound fifty please.' I pay him. 'You want me to get her?'

'It's okay, if she's busy. I'll just be over here,' I reply, walking over towards a booth. As I put my glass down on the table, I glance to the left and see Ashley in the shadows, mid-snog. The subject of her affection is a middle-aged guy wearing thick-rimmed glasses and a tank top, last known whereabouts, nineteen sixty-two. I look away, hoping she hasn't seen me and feeling strangely embarrassed. Unfortunately, she has.

'Ollie? What are you doing here? Are you stalking me?' I turn and smile.

'Hi. No. Sorry, I didn't realise you were...busy,' I say. They both look down. She turns and walks over to me. The guy, who I assume to be called Norman, takes his cue and walks through a door that reads 'Staff Only.'

'You saw, didn't you?' she asks.

'Uh...saw what?' I feign. She shoots me a disbelieving look and I say, 'Okay yes.' She sits down opposite me.

'It's not what you think.'

'Ash, I don't care who you do, or uh...see.'

'It's just a stupid thing,' she replies. 'He's old enough to be my dad.'

'Hey, stop justifying yourself. I don't care, as long as you're happy,' I say. She shakes her head and sighs.

'How'd it go with the Swedish one?' The question throws me suddenly and I fluster for an answer.

'It...went okay, you know. As good as could be expected I guess.'

'She didn't want a reconciliation then?'

'No.'

'That sucks.'

'Yeah.'

'You okay?'

'Not really. But hey, nothing I can do about it, right?'

'Fraid not. What a pair we are.'

'So are you like, going out with that guy?'

'Norman? No, we're just...' she shakes her head, trying to think, 'I don't really know what we are.'

'Can't believe you're seeing a guy called Norman.'

'Why is that funny?'

'Norm? Ash, please.'

'I didn't christen him,' she replies. I shake my head.

'Man, my opinion of you has really dropped.'

'Yeah, because you have such high standards.' I look at her, considering how to respond. 'Look, he's probably just a stopgap after Gary. Bit like you.'

'Me?'

'Well, we seem to have ended up in bed since I started living with you.' I nod slowly and smile.

'Hmm, yeah well...so have you and Norm-'

'None of your business, Hayward.'

'He's a large man.'

'Stop right there.'

'I'm just trying to work out the physics with the glasses.' She tilts her head, her expression suddenly annoyed.

'Hey, play nice, okay,' she says.

'Sorry.'

'What about that Barbie doll you're seeing? She can't exactly be top of the gene pool.'

'Lauren? Well, she runs a bank, she's not stupid.'

'High maintenance though. Looks like a princess to me.'

'She's not really. At least, not from what I've seen.'

'Uh huh. You wait. Auntie Ashley is always right.' We sit quietly for a moment before I say,

'Norman,' I repeat, smiling. She looks at me and smiles, rolling her eyes.

Ashley is eventually called away to do some work. I wait patiently in the hope she might get a little more time. But every time I see her she's busy. I decide maybe I should just speak to her at home and grab my coat.

'Hey, I'll see you later,' I call. She waves.

'See you back there,' she replies.

'Ciao,' I say, waving. I open the door and step outside.

I do some window shopping on my way home. There's nothing I want or can afford. Within twenty minutes I'm back at my place. I see Tristan having a smoke. Refreshingly, it looks like a cigarette this time, rather than hemp.

'Your dog's barking,' Tristan says.

'I don't have a dog,' I reply. This small detail

confuses him. He frowns, trying to work out whatever it is he's thinking.

'No you have a dog and it was barking its nuts off.'

'Mate, I don't have a dog.'

'Well what the fuck was all that barking?'

'Could have been Parker. He's got a new girlfriend.' Tristan eyes me suspiciously then nods slowly.

'Yeah. Parker,' he says, slowly. I put my keys in my door and open it.

'Those things will kill you,' I say, glancing at the cigarette.

'Yeah well, so will AIDS,' he replies. We stare at each other, neither really having a response to that one. I opt for going inside.

I walk into the kitchen and set about making myself a coffee. I hear talking outside and stand in the kitchen listening.

'...what dog? Wait a minute, you saying my girlfriend's a dog?' I hear a muffled unintelligible response.

'Right. Mate, I really don't have time for this, cheers though,' Parker's voice is clear. I hear the front door open and go back to making the coffee. The door slams. 'You here, bitch?' he calls.

'Yep, in here,' I reply. Parker walks in wearing a comically tight T-shirt that reads 'Off The Market.'

'Man, what the fuck is Tristan's problem? Did you hear what he just called Nicola?' I feign ignorance and shake my head. 'A dog. I nearly decked him. Cocksucker.'

'I wouldn't pay much attention to Tristan to be

honest, he does drugs.'

'Yeah right. You making coffee?'

'No, I'm building a rocket.'

'Why do you have to be such a shitkicker?'

'I dunno, it's the only thing I'm really good at.'

'Can I have a coffee as well, please?' Parker asks. I sigh and open the Nescafe jar again. Parker is quiet for a bit then says, 'So, what'd you think?'

'About what?'

'Nicola.'

'Oh. Yeah, she seems nice.'

'Yeah. Sorry I didn't tell you about her before. Just, you've been a bit down about Svetla and I didn't want to rub your nose in it.'

'You wouldn't. How long have you two been together?'

'Few weeks. It's nice. Really working well.'

'Good man. That's great. But she's not a school friend.' I say. He sighs and shakes his head.

'I don't even know why she said that. We used to work together when I was at the pub. Maybe she took the whole 'let's go out in secret' thing a bit too seriously.'

'No worries, all good.' I boil the kettle again and pour water into Parker's cup.

'Yeah. The only thing is she uh…I dunno.'

'What?'

'Probably shouldn't tell you.'

'Come on dude, give me some credit,' I say, giving Parker his cup of coffee and taking a sip from mine.

'Well, okay. She farts.' My eyes dart up to him and I burn my upper lip on the coffee.

'What?'

'She farts. Like, all the time.'

'So what? So do you.'

'I know but, she's a girl. Girl's aren't supposed to fart, not this early into the relationship anyway. It's like she doesn't care.' I laugh. 'What? Come on.'

'Seriously, everyone farts. Even girls.'

'I know but they really smell. I don't know whether it's her diet or what but they make me feel sick.'

'Shit man, that's uh...that's an interesting problem.'

'Yeah great, now what do I do about it?'

'I dunno, maybe talk to her?'

'Oh yeah right, 'hey baby, listen can we have a chat about your farting?' I'd be dumped in a second.'

'She doesn't do it during sex, does she?'

'So far no, but can you imagine?'

'Yeah, that would be bad.'

'No shit,' he says. We stand sipping our coffee.

'I don't know man, I got nothing,' I say.

'Fucking useless.'

FIFTEEN – MARCH TO THE RIGHT

Thursday. The newsdesk sends me down to a far right demonstration at Kings Cross. I love these things. My cameraman is called Martin and he's more used to working in war zones, so this should be a walk in the park. The sun is out and although this part of London is always slightly shabby, the morning light makes the place more pleasant than normal.

I walk down towards the House at Home pub where the police have told me the demonstrators will gather. I hear them before I see them. Turning the corner into Caledonian Road, I see a number of men with shaved heads, English flags draped around them. Some of them hold pints of lager. They are shouting football slogans at a line of blue-capped policemen. I stand with Martin as he knocks off a couple of shots. They're loud but not violent. I stick close to Martin, just behind him, watching his back as he films. The police then herd the protestors into a group and they start marching towards...uh, hang on let me check the map on my iPhone. So Kings Cross is here. Ah, they're heading to Aldgate. Should be fun. The march is rowdy but peaceful. The looks on people's faces as they spot the march for the first time is classic. A mixture of horror and the occasional surprised smile.

Finally we get to Aldgate where the organisers have set up a makeshift stage and speakers. There are a lot of police - a line of regular police in uniform. Behind them, a line in riot gear and helmets. The next line is police dogs with handlers and just for good measure they finish their deployment with a row of police on horseback. All in all there must be about two hundred police and around fifty demonstrators. Oh, and there's a police helicopter circling as well. The dogs bark at the protestors with real ferocity. The guy on the mic ignores them and gets started.

'We're here to exercise our democratic right to stand in the middle of our city, in our country and say whatever the fuck we want!' he shouts. The crowd goes nuts. Martin moves to get a better shot. We carefully make our way through the crowd towards the stage and film some shots of the crowd from a slightly higher vantage point.

'Happy?' I ask Martin. He nods. We jump down and Martin starts filming more shaved-headed people. The man on the stage continues his rant. I look to my right and am struck to see a gorgeous girl. Long brown hair, slim build and tight hot pants. I look at her, she smiles. I smile back, slightly embarrassed. Is she a reporter? Not in those pants, she isn't. Bloody lovely though. She mouths 'I love you' and smiles again. My heart soars. Jesus, this can't be happening. Who the hell is she?

'We don't want the fucking immigrants over here taking our jobs. It's hard enough for regular English people to get a job and now the government wants to make the borders even easier for the foreigners to get in!' the guy on the mic looks like he might burst a blood vessel. The crowd shouts in outrage. The girl smiles at me again then turns and shouts with them. And the pieces of the puzzle suddenly slot together. This stunning, sexy girl swings way too far to the right. How disappointing. She claps with the crowd then looks back to me, smiling again. This time, I don't smile back. Martin starts moving through the crowd again, I follow him.

'Fucking media scum,' I hear one person say as we move past. I ignore it. The atmosphere has changed slightly.

'Watch it, reporter man!' another shouts.

'That's a nice camera,' says a man with a large swastika tattoo on his right arm. He looks like a bear. Martin glances up to him.

'Time to go,' I say.

'Oi mate, who'd you work for?' asks tattoo man.

'TBN,' I reply, friendly.

'You the bloke that did that report last week about us being a bunch of fucking racists?'

'Nope, nothing to do with me,' I reply, nervous now.

'Bet it was him,' says another. 'Look at him,

fucking mummy's boy.'

Suddenly one goes to grab Martin's camera. He yanks it back.

'FUCK OFF!' Martin says. Before I know what's happening I feel an elbow smash into my left cheek. The force sends me to the floor. The police move in. A bottle is thrown, I hear the glass smash. My face is thumping. I try to stand, Martin grabs my shirt. His nose is bleeding.

'Time to get out of here,' he says. I push through the crowd making my way towards the police line.

'GET BACK,' shouts a riot policeman, holding his nightstick aloft. I pull out my press card.

'TBN, let me through. He's injured.' The policeman steps aside and lets us through, the line closing behind us. I look at Martin.

'You okay?' I ask.

'Yeah,' he replies touching his nose, 'that was fucking awesome. Let me get my nose sorted and we can get back in there.'

'No way. That's it, we're done.'

'It's still going on, we need to film this,' says Martin.

'No one gives a shit about these guys, they'd have to set fire to half of London before we gave this lot any coverage. We're leaving.'

'What happened to you?' Paul asks when we get back to the newsdesk.

'Your Nazi friends decided to tear me a new one,' I reply.

'They're not my Nazi friends,' Paul replies.

'Are you okay?' Julie asks, walking around the desk to get a closer inspection of the damage.

'Yeah, looks worse than it is. Just a bruise,' I say. She peers into my face, frowning and bearing her teeth.

'Ouch. That looks sore,' she says.

'It is sore, Julie. My date on Saturday is going to be all the more special looking like the elephant man,' I say, glancing at Paul.

'Sorry Ollie. Did it kick off?' Paul asks.

'Not really, just me and a couple of the Hitler Youth playing fisty cuffs.'

'Go and clean yourself up, I may have an interview doing in Oxford later,' he says. I stare at him.

'Are you serious?' I ask, an incredulous tone creeping into my voice. Paul shrugs and frowns.

'What?' he says.

'Paul, I've just has three types of shit beaten out of me. Maybe I could...I dunno, get my cheek x-rayed or something?'

'Sorry mate, there's no one else to do it,' he says. I shake my head. Unbelievable. The fucker is going to deploy me again. Most bosses, when you've gone through something like this, would have said 'hey Ollie, looks like you just went through a real shit time, take the rest of the day off.' Not Paul. Nope, just suck it up and get back to work. Julie gives me a sympathetic look. I nod, accepting no one is going to get me out of this.

'What's the interview?'

When I get home from Oxford (late because the trains are screwed), it's gone eight. Parker and Ashley sit in front of the TV, eating pizza. They both look up when I walk in.

'Jesus, what happened to you?' Parker asks. I throw my bag down.

'Fucking Nazis is what happened to me. I was sent down to a far right march and this was their equivalent of a goody bag and a thank you for coming present.' Ashley stands up and walks over to me, she tries to touch my cheek. I back away.

'That looks sore,' she says.

'Yeah it is, I might even say it hurts,' I reply. I look at the pizza, most of it gone. 'Any left for me?' Ashley and Parker look at each other.

'Uh, you can have the rest if you like,' Parker says. I look at the half-eaten piece that remains then back at Parker.

'So you want me to finish your leftovers? That's my dinner, is it?'

'Dude I know you've had a bad day but there's no point taking it out on us, I don't know when you're coming back. You never let me know when you'll be home any more.'

'You guys are like an old married couple,' says Ashley.

'He's older than me,' says Parker, a vague attempt at a joke. I nod my head, resigned.

'Well, it's good to see you guys not at each others throats,' I say. They glance at each other again.

I walk into the kitchen and over to the freezer. We have an oversupply of frozen peas. I yank two packets out to see what else might be available.

'Do you want me to make you something?'
Ashley says, coming up behind me. I turn to face
her.

'No, it's fine cheers,' I reply. I pull out a bag of
oven chips and some frozen chicken nuggets.

'So what happened?'

'Guy elbowed me in the face. Cameraman got a
busted nose but he wanted to go back in.'

'What?'

'Yeah I know. Don't get people like that who
just want to get in there for the thrill of it. I like my
face.'

'You have a nice face,' Ashley says, 'just a bad
day.'

'Yeah. I'm sure Lauren will really dig this look.'
I turn on the oven.

'She might. You've got a cool story to go with
it. Girls like guys who get into trouble.'

'Nazi trouble?'

'Were they really Nazis?'

'Far right. Debatable.' I pour the chips and
chicken nuggets onto a baking tray and pop it in
the oven. 'At least you and Parker seem to be
getting on better.'

'Yeah, we had a little chat. He asked me about
Gary. It was...surprisingly nice. I've sort of missed
him.'

'Good, I'm glad. How was the rest of your day?
How's Norm?' She shoots me an evil stare.

'Norman,' she says.

'Right, Norman.'

'He's good, we might be going away this
weekend. He wants to take me to Cromer in

Norfolk.'

'Sounds nice.'

'Yeah. I know he's older but he's kinda...cool.'

'As long as you're happy. So, no more shagging, right?'

'Well, it's not that serious,' she says. I frown.

'Ash-'

'What? We're just going away, I'm not marrying the guy. If I still want to fool around then I can.'

'Sounds dodgy to me. Not sure Lauren would be too happy about me 'fooling around' with you.'

'Well, what she doesn't know...'

'Uh huh.'

'Speaking of which, those chips will take half an hour,' she says, smiling.

'You are bad,' I say, chuckling. She moves towards me, putting her arm around my waist. I hear Parker heading towards us from the living room. I move Ashley's hand away from me and quickly turn towards the sink. Parker walks in, puts his plate down and heads out. I glance at Ashley who smiles, I shake my head.

'You started it,' she whispers, smiling.

SIXTEEN – ROTHERHITHE BARBEQUE

Saturday. When I exit Canada Water tube station, I'm hit by a blinding sun and a balmy seventy-two degrees. I'm wearing a white Calvin Klein slim-fit shirt and stonewashed navy-blue jeans, although now I'm out in the sun, I wish I'd worn shorts. I've also got a plastic bag with a six-pack of Fosters. I get out my iPhone and look up the address. James Kennedy lives about five minutes east of here, I start walking. The sun is hot on my neck and I arrive in a partial sweat. The building is a modern apartment block close to the river. I find the intercom on the door and buzz the top floor. A male voice answers.

'Hello?'

'Uh hi, is that James Kennedy's place?'

'Yeah, you here for the barbeque?'

'Yeah.'

'Top floor.' The buzzer sounds and I open the door. The first thing I look for is a lift which either doesn't exist or is hidden so well I can't find it. I begin the ascent up the stairs. When I get to the top, I'm panting. I knock on the door. I hear someone coming, the door opens to reveal James Kennedy wearing a white shirt open three buttons down. He's on his mobile.

'...thank you babe. I, uh...' he looks at me and frowns. 'Hang on a second. Uh, hi?' he says, frowning.

'Hi. Um, Lauren invited me?' I say. The look on his face tells me everything I need to know. It would appear that although Lauren invited me, she had apparently failed to tell James this small but important fact.

'Oh. Right,' he says, glancing down at my attire.

'I bought beers,' I say, holding them up, eager to please.

'Well, come in. What happened to uh..?' he asks, referring to my face.

'Long story,' I reply. He shrugs, takes the bag with my Fosters and walks ahead of me into the kitchen. Maverick Sabre's soulful voice wafts from the stereo system in living room which, by the way, is enormous. He also has an outside area where everyone is hanging out.

'You want a cold drink?' I hear James ask.

'Uh sure, if you don't mind,' I reply. He appears a few seconds later, phone still clamped to his ear and gives me a cold bottle of Peroni. 'Why would I mind?' he asks. 'Sorry darling, yeah so you were saying about the HSBC thing?' I watch him walk back towards his guests, leaving me stranded. Man, that guy is a cock. 'Why would I

mind?' his sarcastic words replay in my head.
What a shitty little...calm Ollie.

I follow in James' wake, taking note of the
huge plasma screen to my left as I head towards
the outside living space which is like a balcony on
steroids. It's huge and can seemingly accommodate
many, many people. Jesus Christ, this place is
incredible. Everything is ultra-modern and shiny.
Sort of like its owner, I guess.

I spot Mark and a couple of other people I
recognise from pub. Jeez, they all look like they
know one another, this is going to be awkward.
Why didn't Lauren tell him I was coming? I knew
this was a mistake. I can't see her. Shit, do I go out
there and start mingling? I stop, indecision getting
the better of me. Suddenly, I feel two hands move
across my eyes, cutting my vision. I immediately
feel a stab of pain in my cheek.

'Guess who?' Lauren says behind me.

'Ow,' I say. She immediately withdraws her
hands and looks at me.

'Oh my God. What happened?' she asks. I turn
to face her. Wow is the only word that comes to
mind. Her hair is down but brushed straight,
salon-style. She wears a white, flowing summer
dress with little flowers dotted around it. In
short...she looks staggering.

'I...I got sent to a far right march and got a
little pushed around.'

'Jesus,' she replies, going to touch my cheek. I
flinch at the prospect of her touch. She withdraws
her hand.

'I know. I look terrible but I'm told it will heal.
One day.'

'No I'm...just glad you're okay. Someone punched you?'

'Yeah, something like that. It's fine. Happens sometimes.'

'Maybe you should take a security guard or something next time.'

'Yeah, it wasn't supposed to be that sort of march. Anyway, how are you?'

'Good. It's good to see you,' she replies, staring at me with a big smile on her face.

'You too. James, didn't seem to know I was coming.'

'He did, I told him last week.'

'Oh. Okay.'

'I see you've already got your drink sorted,' she says, looking at my Peroni.

'Uh yeah, you want it?'

'Just got one,' she says holding up her bottle. I nod, nervous, not sure why. I suddenly have nothing to say. Small talk, quick.

'This is an amazing place,' I say.

'Yeah, James earns way too much. As his boss, I will be looking into that,' she replies. I smile. Man, she does look stunning in that dress. First time I've seen her out of a suit. Smokin' and I don't mean the barbeque either. 'I like your shirt, Calvin Klein?' Her comment causes me to pause in my current gulp of beer. 'It's written on the back.' I swallow.

'Ah yes. You look...wow, really nice,' I say. I know I'm crap but I'm nervous. I already told you I don't know why.

'Thanks. You okay?'

'Yeah, oh definitely,' I reply. She smiles.

'It's really good to see you. I've...sort of missed you this week.'

'Yeah, sort of missed me?' I ask, unsure how anyone could miss me. 'I guess I sort of missed you too,' I reply. I promise our dialogue will get better, just stay with me.

'You don't have to say that.'

'No, I really did.' I swallow and take another sip of beer.

'You want to meet some people?'

'Sure.' She takes my hand and leads me over to the outside area. The view is astonishing. Canary Wharf is directly ahead of us with the river running past the apartment building. To the left is the Shard, the buildings of the City and St Paul's Cathedral. To the right, more Docklands buildings and East London. The Superbalcony, as I shall now refer to it, extends up to another level where James and Mark are cooking on a large expensive-looking barbeque. Other people sit at a big round table under an enormous umbrella. Two girls sit on the step up, talking with glasses of Champagne in their hands. The smell of meat and smoke fills the air.

'Hey Lauren, you going to help James with the barbeque?' asks Mark, stepping down and over to us.

'No, that's what guys do at these things, isn't it?' she replies. 'You remember Ollie?'

'Yeah, hey man, good to see you,' Mark replies, shaking my hand. If he notices my bruise he says nothing. 'Fuck, I'm sweating like a dog.' He wipes his forehead with his arm. 'You guys okay for beers?' I nod.

'Yeah, thanks,' I say. Lauren nods.

'Cool, escuse moi.' He moves past us, and into the flat.

'Hi there,' says a woman's voice behind me. I turn to see a pretty brunette. She's slim, wears a tight-fitting red dress and holds a glass of half-drunk Champagne. 'And who do we have here?'

'Sarah, this is Ollie,' Lauren says. 'Sarah's with James.' I nod and shake her hand. 'Nice to meet you,' I say.

'You too. So you're the famous Ollie,' Sarah says.

'Uh oh, sounds like I've been discussed,' I say.

'In explicit detail,' Lauren says. Sarah laughs. She has an infectious laugh which makes you smile the moment you hear it.

'Don't worry, I know nothing,' says Sarah. 'You're the one that works for TBN?'

'For my sins, I'm afraid it's true,' I reply.

'I think that's really interesting. So have you been in a warzone recently or something?'

'No, some protestors took issue with his haircut,' Lauren says.

'What?' Sarah says. I nudge Lauren playfully.

'No, I was out on a far right demonstration and it broke into a few scuffles, that's all.'

'He's very brave,' Lauren says, putting her arm through mine. Sarah smiles.

'You have a dangerous job,' Sarah says.

'Nah, just sometimes...so, what do you do?' I ask her. She takes a sip of Champagne.

'I'm a counsellor, well just starting out. But I had my first client last week.'

'Really? A counsellor.'

'Yeah, I've been studying like forever but I finally got my degree so-' she looks up to James, distracted by the barbeque fire that appears to be getting out of control.

'Holy shit!' I hear James shout. 'Mark! Water now!'

'James, what are you doing?' Sarah says. 'Excuse me, sorry.' She leaves to attend James' unfolding barbeque disaster.

'No worries,' I say. I turn to Lauren. 'You look amazing, did I say that already?' She smiles, staring at me. We say nothing for a moment, just looking at each other. 'What?' I ask. She shakes her head, her eyes not leaving mine.

'You look very smart in that shirt and the bruise makes you look dangerous,' she says.

'Yeah, dangerously ill-prepared for a fight.'

Barbeque disaster is averted when Mark runs out and moves some of the meat James was cooking to a cooler side of the grill. James, it appears, thought that adding more lighting fluid was the answer to non-cooking food. A fire brigade situation is avoided by Mark's quick thinking thus saving the flat and all the wealthy people. Yay.

I'm introduced to another couple from United Bank, Karen and her fiancée Billy who seem very nice. Everyone settles in for a relaxing evening. Lauren helps Sarah with the drinks leaving me to talk to a guy called Darren who, if I'm honest is really dull but luckily it isn't long before Lauren finds me again. We find a spot away from the others and sit down, looking out at the remarkable view. I have a chicken leg in one hand and, I think, my third Peroni in the other.

'So,' I say.

'So,' she replies.

'You ever...been in love?' I ask. Her smile dies and she becomes reflective.

'Yeah. Many times. Maybe that's my problem, I think I fall in love too easily. Normally ends up in a car crash.'

'Yeah? Been hurt?' I ask. She looks at me then back to Canary Wharf ahead of us.

'Of course. Who hasn't? But that's life, isn't it?'

'I guess.'

'You?' she asks. I nod slowly. 'Recently?' I look at her, my eyes giving me away. She sighs. Suddenly, a simple conversation has taken on a new darker edge. 'Who was she?'

'Nah. Look this is supposed to be a fun thing, right?'

'Are we heading into rocky shores before we've barely set sail?' she asks. I look at her, the sudden poetry in her words surprising me.

'No. We're good. We're better than good,' I say, as convincingly as I can.

'It wasn't this girl that gave you that shiner, was it?' I chuckle and shake my head.

'No. But it has happened before. I think I must have a very punchable face.' She laughs her little snort laugh which, in turn, makes me laugh. Suddenly she leans in and kisses me. Carefully, she moves her hand to the back of my head, which I replicate by running my hand through her hair.

'Oh jeez, you two! Get a room,' James shouts from the barbeque. Our lips part and Lauren turns to James.

'Just cook the meat, Kennedy. Less shouty shouty, more cooky cooky, yeah?' she calls back. James smiles and turns back to the barbeque. She turns to me. 'Let's just be careful with each other's hearts?' She stares at me, a serious look on her face. I nod slowly, swallowing. Guilt rises through me, causing my heart to start pounding. 'Another beer?' she asks, looking at the empty bottle in my hand. I nod. She stands and heads off towards the kitchen, leaving me to ponder what the hell I'm getting myself into.

Afternoon soon becomes early evening. Lauren and I talk for what feels like hours. I find out all sorts of things. She's incredibly driven, makes a lot of money and seems to have had her heart broken a few too many times. I detect a little high maintenance in some of her comments but then, who isn't? I know I am sometimes. Eventually we split up when James and Mark corner her into a conversation about some banking stuff to which I can make no real contribution. I head towards the toilets. As I walk past the kitchen I see Sarah taking a tray of party food out of the oven.

'Hi,' I say.

'Hey Ollie, how you doing?'

'Good, thanks. This is a really great party.'

'Thanks. It's easy in a place like this, a lot of space.'

'Yeah. It's amazing,' I say. She turns the pigs in blankets or whatever they are, then shakes the tin. 'So how long have you and James been together?'

'Over a year now.'

'Cool. How did you meet?' I ask. She smiles

uncomfortably, her eyes thinking of her response.

'We uh, at a club. A little bit of a rollercoaster to get where we are now. But he's a great guy.'

'Yeah,' I reply. Maybe it was the way I said it but she picks up on my tone immediately.

'I know. But, a lot of it is just bravado. Underneath it all, he's actually a good guy.'

'No sure. He seems nice.'

'Sometimes he's a cock. Especially to people he doesn't know very well and if he's a bit strange with you, there's a bit of a past with Lauren.'

'What?' I say, unable to disguise the surprise in my voice.

'Oh no, I only mean...they dated for a bit. It's over now. She's lovely.' My heart is thumping again. James and Lauren...what on earth could she see in him?

'Yeah, she is,' I say.

'Maybe I shouldn't have told you that.'

'It's cool. We've all had ex's,' I reply. She puts the tray back in the oven. 'Don't you find it weird, James and Lauren working together?'

'No. I know I'm the one he wants. Don't get me wrong, Lauren is beautiful and smart but I think we're a better fit. At least I hope we are. I try not to stand next to Lauren too often. She puts us all in the shade a little,' she says, chuckling. I smile politely. 'So, you like your job?'

'It's okay. It's different every day and I like the challenge of it,' I reply. She looks at me and tilts her head.

'Yeah?' she replies. I frown.

'Yeah. Why, you don't believe me?'

'Sorry, doing the psychologist thing. Must

remember not to analyse my guests,' she says, slapping her forehead. I chuckle. Suddenly my need for the toilet strengthens considerably.

'Toilet's over there,' she says, pointing.

'Wow, you're good,' I say. She smiles.

SEVENTEEN – DARK SPACES, STRIKING VOICES

I walk back outside and sit down at the table,
a new beer in my hand. I watch Lauren talking
then laughing with James and Mark. I feel weird,
not jealous exactly, just not part of the group. I
look out towards the fading sunlight. Canary
Wharf is already half lit. The river is at high tide
and calm. I take a sip of beer and my thoughts
start to wander to Svetla. I wonder what she's
doing right now. Maybe she's found someone else?
I didn't detect that when I saw her but then, why
would she tell me? I miss her. What am I doing
here? I like Lauren but she's trouble, I can feel it.
And do I want anything more than just a casual
thing? Is it wrong to even think that? She seems
keen and I guess I should be grateful. It's not like
I've ever pulled anyone remotely that stunning in
the past but something in me feels...what's the
word? Unexcited. Am I unexcited by the prospect
of being with Lauren? Am I wasting not only my

time but hers as well? I see Lauren turn and look for me, her eyes scanning the Superbalcony. She sees me. I take another sip of beer, watch her say something to James and Mark and step down from the higher level. She walks over to me and pulls up a chair.

'Hey there, you okay?'

'Yeah,' I reply.

'Sorry, I'm neglecting you. Just trying to sort out a deal we're doing next week.'

'No worries.'

'Are you up for a little misbehaving?' she asks, smiling. I raise an eyebrow.

'What do you mean?'

'It's a big apartment. Maybe I could show you around?' The moment she says that, my mind kicks in with 'yeah there's a reason you know every nook and cranny in this place.'

'Sure,' I say, my stomach doing backflips. What the hell is wrong with me? She takes my hand and we head back inside, through the living room and into the hallway.

'This is the hallway,' she says, giggling. I chuckle.

'Yeah, I see that,' I say, smiling. She pushes open a door to another room. Looks like a bedroom. It's dark. She closes the door behind us and leans against it, bending one leg and putting her foot against it. Suddenly the atmosphere is charged and electric. She raises her arm above her head.

'Kiss me,' she says. I move up to her and kiss her neck. Her skin is warm and soft. I move slowly, kissing her cheek then her lips. Excitement hurtles through me, the kiss becoming more passionate, more urgent. My tongue touches hers as I run my hands along her hips and up to her breasts. A moan escapes her, then hushed uneven breathing in my ear as my hand moves under her dress. The door bangs slightly as we move against it but neither of us cares. I feel her fingers move to my groin and then tug at my jeans. The cold air hits my skin then I feel the warmth of her hand. Jolts of pleasure ripple through me. I want her, right now. I grab her waist and turn her around, pulling up her dress and her G-string to one side. We're away. It's raw, animal and fervent. She slams her hands against the door which makes an almighty bang.

'Oh,' she whispers. I hold her shoulders, moving in and out. Then I grab her hair and pull hard. She lets out a tiny yelp. I consider the possibility I've yanked a little too hard and quickly loosen my grip. 'No, pull harder,' she whispers. I do as instructed.

The feeling is coming, either I slow down or this is coming to an end. I don't care, not about lasting forever. I just want her. I move faster, harder. Driving almost to hurt. She reacts by dropping her head, her hair swaying to the movement. I come. And suddenly everything stops for the slightest of moments. We are one. I hold onto her as the moment peaks and slowly begins to melt away. All that's left are the two of us, panting. I move away allowing her to stand and turn around.

'Jesus,' she says, adjusting her dress.

'Yeah. Not sure what came over me there,' I

say, pulling up my jeans and buttoning them.

'Whatever it was, we definitely need to explore that some more.'

'Yeah. Definitely.'

'Phew,' she says suddenly laughing, 'that was hard core.'

'I'm not normally like that.'

'Really? I don't believe it for a second,' she says, smiling.

We get dressed, sort ourselves out and sneak back, red-faced and looking like we've just run a Nike 10K. If anyone heard us, no one says–

'Where have you two been?' Mark says as we walk into the kitchen. Shit.

'Lauren was just giving me a tour,' I say quickly. Mark raises an eyebrow.

'Oh yeah? Of James' bedroom?'

'Mark,' Lauren says with a scolding tone. He smiles.

'I'm just pulling your chain. I'm on beer duty, anyone?' Mark says. I glance at Lauren.

'Sure,' I say.

'That would be nice,' she says. He wanders off, chuckling. I watch her, watching him with a look in her eye that says 'don't mess with me.' She turns to face me.

'I bet you're well scary as a boss.'

'Nah, it's all show,' she says. We stand looking at each other.

'Well. That was...interesting,' I say.

'Yes it was. We should do it again sometime,' she replies, smiling.

'Yeah,' I reply. We head back to the Superbalcony and find a spot to sit. We talk until the early hours, getting to know each other. She still asks me about my job but then delves more into my parents and how my dad died. We talk a lot about him. Do I miss him? Do I wish he was still around? What's my relationship like with my mum? Eventually we move on to questions like what I do for fun which I deftly sidestep. Can't exactly say, 'I love playing Portal on the Playstation,' to a babe like Lauren. Before long, my head is swimming with alcohol and it's time to head home. Although secretly I'm waiting for Lauren to ask me back to hers, she doesn't. We say our goodbyes to James, Sarah and Mark and walk outside together.

'Maybe you could come round mine for dinner or something?' I ask. She smiles and nods.

'I'd like that,' she says.

'Cool. So, I'll see you soon?'

'Yes,' she replies. I lean in and kiss her, she closes her eyes. Energy races between us, I pull her to me, breathing her in. Then, carefully our lips part.

'Until next time,' I say.

'Until next time, Mr Hayward,' she replies.

In the taxi back to my flat, thoughts whizz around my head. That was a strange, yet rewarding evening. Lauren's incredibly hot and the bonus is she wants to see me again. Which is good. I find myself surprised by how I feel. I want to see her again. In fact, I want to see her very, very soon. I text her to say, 'Loved seeing you tonight, let's do it again soon, Ollie xx.' I don't get a text back, which I try not to misinterpret. Probably just went to bed. The taxi dumps me outside my flat around half two. I'm drunk but not paralytic.

As I reach my flat, I spot Tristan's light is on and I hear the faint tones of Bob Marley coming from his place. That guy is a walking (or no doubt at this time of night, lying) cliché. I turn the key in the lock, open the door and go inside. It's dark. Everyone must be asleep. As I creep towards my room, I suddenly hear Parker playing his piano in a way I've never heard before. I move cautiously toward his room. The sound is stunning. A slow, melancholy song. Then it gets faster, still holding the sad theme. More and more dramatic. I lean against the bathroom door in the darkness, mesmerised. Parker is an amazing piano player. Except...suddenly I hear a voice singing along to the theme and quickly realise it's not Parker playing, it's Ashley. Parker must be staying at Nicola's.

And it's a lonely heart.
A lonely heart in my soul.
Tears and rain
Cannot keep you from me
But it's jealousy
Jealousy that beats inside

Now she slows the rhythm right down. She hums along, her soft voice echoing around the flat. It's achingly beautiful.

And I kiss you
I kiss you

She finishes the song with a final few sad notes and the music ceases. I wait transfixed, hoping she will play something else. Suddenly the door opens, the light hitting me from inside.

'OO! Jesus!' she says, jumping. 'Fuck Ollie, what are you doing out here?'

'I was listening to you,' I reply. 'Where did you learn to play like that?'

'Nowhere,' she says, walking towards the living room.

'Ash. Ash...' I say, moving to stop her. She turns. 'I'm not kidding around, that was amazing. You should be doing that sort of thing professionally.'

'No I shouldn't. I didn't know you were listening. Are you high?' she asks. I frown, confused for a moment.

'No...well I'm a bit drunk but I was listening and I think-'

'I'm tired Ollie, I'm going to bed.' She goes into the living room and closes the door. I'm not sure exactly what happened there. Okay, I can see she was annoyed someone listened to her song but it's not like I had to make excuses about how shit it was. It wasn't. It was incredible. Like listening to someone on the radio. She may not think she's any good but now I've heard her, I'm going to make sure others do as well.

I wake up around eleven. I glance at my iPhone and collapse back onto the bed. Parker is home, I hear him playing on the Playstation in the living room. I feel mildly hungover and in desperate need of a drink of water. I smell my armpits, yep could do with a shower as well. I walk into the bathroom in my dressing gown.

'You up, shitkicker?' Parker calls.

'Nope,' I shout back.

'Great,' he replies. I jump into the weak electric shower and wash myself. My mind drifts back to last night. Lauren. Am I starting to feel something for her? She's beautiful and smart. So, why not? I could do a lot worse, I guess. Fuck Svetla, I don't need her. I don't need to be constantly thinking about her. The whole thinking about her drives me nuts. Probably drives you nuts too. I'm sorry I keep going on about her, just need to think about something else. Someone else. Lauren maybe? She would be a new direction in my life. I need to work out what I'm going to cook her for our date. It has to be something that will knock her out. Svetla always liked my Thai curry. Just so we're clear, it wasn't my Thai curry, it was Sharwoods. Not sure if Lauren even likes Thai. Who cares what Svetla liked anyway, this is a new page. A new chapter. I do need to figure out what I'm going to cook though. I step out of the shower, pull on some clothes and walk into the living room. Parker pauses Grand Theft Auto.

'So I have a question for you,' he says.

'Yeah?' I reply, noting the serious expression on his face.

'Have you been going in my room?' he asks. Shit, Ashley must have left evidence.

'No. Why?'

'Things have been moved around, there's stuff on my piano that wasn't there before. Someone's been in there, and if it wasn't you, it must have been Ashley. I'm going to fucking crucify her.'

'Well what if it was Nicola or someone?' I say. I know, it's lame but I don't want to get Ashley in trouble.

'What? Don't be a fuckwit. Nicola doesn't go into my room unless I'm there.'

'Hmm, yeah okay,' I say. Maybe I should take the rap. Parker and Ashley are only just starting to get on, don't want this to screw that up.

'Okay it was me,' I say. Parker tilts his head.

'What the fuck man?'

'I know, I know. I lost something and I thought it might be in your room.'

'What?' he asks. Shit. Umm, what could I have lost...quickly...

'Uhh, my ID for work. Sorry dude.'

'Why would your ID be in my room?'

'You're right. I'm sorry, I won't go in there again.'

'Good. Don't. If you've lost something, just tell me and I'll help you look for it but don't go wandering into my private space without asking. Those are the rules, yeah?'

'Yep, got it. Sorry,' I say. We sit for a moment, neither saying anything.

'I didn't find any porn if that's what you're worried about.'

'Why would I be worried about that, no one has physical porn any more. That's what the internet is for,' he replies, resuming his game.

EIGHTEEN – PERSONAL PHONE CALL

'I see your face is healing,' says Paul. I nod, in agreement. 'Need you to go to Bicester.'

'Oh, I was just going to get the latest details on Ollie's love life,' says Julie. I stand up and grab my coat.

'Sorry mate, guess it will have to wait. What's the job?' I ask.

'Is it going well?' asks Julie, winking.

'Julie please,' says Paul. She holds up her hand in apology. 'Need you to interview a doctor about the dodgy botox story.'

'Dodgy botox?' I ask.

'Front page of the Mail, here,' he throws me a copy. I look at the headline which reads 'NHS Bill For Deadly Botox.' Some company manufacturing botox injections was seemingly using cheap ingredients and has now gone bust leaving people in limbo about what to do about it. Says in some cases the injections could cause cancer.

'Okay, who's the interviewee?'

'One of the doctors who's going to report to the Health Secretary on Wednesday.'

'Great. I'm on my way. Catch up later, Julie?'

'Definitely,' Julie says.

'Anything from, you know who?' I ask. Julie shakes her head. God, she looks like she might cry. What the hell is this Josh guy playing at? Look I don't know the fundamentals but Julie's a nice enough girl, if a little kooky, she deserves a proposal. I'm sure it's only a matter of time.

I head down to the garage to meet the cameraman. It's Phil, the guy whose second name I can never remember. The garage is filled with estate crew cars and the odd satellite vehicle.

'Hey,' I say.

'Alright,' he replies, 'where we going?'

'Bicester,' I reply, getting into the passenger seat.

'Great, I love Bicester.'

'Really?'

'No, it's a pain in the arse and I should be on lunch but apparently (he puts on a whiney voice for the next bit) there wasn't anyone else that could go.'

'Ah well, at least you've got a nice producer.'

'Yeah, great,' he replies, getting in and slamming the door shut.

We drive out of the garage and head west. Phil doesn't say much and my mind is blank for small talk so we sit and listen to the radio. This could be a perfect opportunity to catch up on some sleepage. I feel the need to call Lauren. Is that wrong? Needy? I want to arrange another date.

Fuck it. I whip out my iPhone and call her. It seems to ring for ages until

'Well hello there,' she says.

'Hi,' I reply, 'how you doing?'

'Yeah not bad, I just had to sneak out of a meeting.'

'Oh sorry.'

'It's okay. What are you doing?'

'On my way to Bicester to do an interview, what are you doing?'

'Losing money left, right and centre.'

'Oh dear, doesn't sound good.'

'Nah, we'll be fine, just one of those days.'

'Yeah, right.'

'So...are you going to invite me round for dinner then?'

'Uh, yeah that's actually why I was calling. What date's good for you?' I ask, leaning forward to open my bag. Where the hell's my diary. I locate it and flip it open.

'I'm free this Friday, the seventh, any good?' she asks. Frankly I'm free everyday but I don't want her knowing that so I do a bit of umming and ahhing. 'Or the eighth?'

'Yeah, eighth would be better,' I reply.

'Excellent, the eighth it is. That's this Saturday coming.'

'Yeah I know,' I reply, smiling.

'Alright, just want to make sure I don't turn up to find out you've forgotten and we end up getting fish and chips or something.'

'You don't like fish and chips?' I ask. I'm rather enjoying this little flirty conversation until, that is, Phil clears his throat indicating his disapproval. 'Uh, well anyway Saturday's good. Better go, things to do, important people to interview.'

'You're so cool,' she says, playful sarcasm in her voice.

'I know. I'll see you then.'

'Okay. Bye hero.'

'Bye.' I hang up, smiling. I sit, replaying the conversation in my head, enjoying the sound of it. Damn, she's keen. If only Svetla could see what Lauren looks like, she'd be so narked.

'So who was that, your mother?' Phil asks, his face serious.

'Uh no. Actually it was that girl we did that interview with in the City. Lauren?' Phil frowns, he clearly has no recollection of the event I'm describing. 'You know, blonde girl at United Bank. The manager.'

'Nope,' he replies.

'Seriously? You don't remember her?'

'No.'

'The stunningly gorgeous trading manager who was flirting with me.'

'Flirting with you?'

'I forgot your name at reception.' Slowly. And I mean painfully slowly, Phil's expression changes. A shadow of a memory passes over his eyes.

'Oh her. You're going out with her?'

'That's right. Cool huh?'

'How?'

'What do you mean?'

'How does someone like you get someone like that?' Phil asks, he glances at me. It's a serious question.

'I honestly have no idea. Maybe it's my job.'

'Right,' Phil replies, nodding, 'yep, that's it.'

The way he says it with such certainty makes me feel uncomfortable.

NINETEEN – V.I.P. STATEMENT

We arrive in Bicester and navigate to the address. Our interviewee is a professor normally working out of Oxford University. Whoever set this up obviously asked if it was okay to do the interview at his home. I help Phil with the gear, carrying the tripod to the front door. I knock. An elderly woman opens the door.

'Yes?' she whispers.

'Hi there, we're from TBN. We're here to interview Professor McGain.'

'Oh yes. I'll just call up to him,' replies the old woman. She leaves the door open, I'm about to go in when my phone rings. I carefully place the heavy tripod on the floor and yank the iPhone out.

'Hello?'

'It's Paul.'

'Hi.'

'Need you to go to Chequers, PM is going to make a statement on North Korea.'

'I haven't done the interview with the doctor yet.'

'Forget the doctor. Downing Street wants to do this within the hour.'

'Fuck's sake,' I say under my breath. 'Okay, can you email me the postcode? How far is it from here?'

'About forty-five minutes, so get on your way. I'll brief you when you're moving.' Paul hangs up.

'Right, we've got to go to Chequers for a PM statement on North Korea,' I say to Phil.

'Oh brilliant,' Phil says. I turn towards the house and step inside. It has a musty smell and there are holes in the carpet.

'Hello?' I call, 'I'm really sorry but...'

'Are you Ollie from TBN?' a tall, distinguished looking man is suddenly standing next to me.

'Uh, yes,' I reply.

'I'm Professor McGain,' he says.

'Hi professor. Listen, I'm really sorry but the newsdesk have told us we have to do a Prime Minister statement at Chequers so I'm afraid we'll have to cancel.'

'Oh. But I've just driven here from a meeting.'

'Oh no. I'm really sorry.'

'Right.' The man is not happy but I haven't got the time.

'Phil we've got to go.'

'Very sorry sir,' I say as we head out of the door. Now I feel like an arsehole.

I check my phone as soon as we've loaded the gear back in the car. Paul has sent me an email with the details. It reads:

THREE WAY

From: Paul Enright-News
To: Oliver Hayward
Subject: PM statement

Ollie,

PM will come out to you at 1500. He will do a pre-recorded on-camera statement about North Korea's nuclear threat towards South Korea. You need to do the statement and feed it via the sat vehicle which should be there not long after you. It's a POOL statement so the other broadcasters will get it.

Call me when you get there.

Paul

'I've got the postcode,' I say. Paul turns on the sat nav and taps it in.

'Gonna be tight, says fifty minutes,' he says, indicating the sat nav.

'Fine, let's go.'

We head out of Bicester. My heart is thumping now. The Prime Minister. This is big. Never been to Chequers before. Must make sure everything goes smoothly. Phil drives fast, I don't dare look at the speedometer but I can feel it's over the limit. I load up the TBN app on my phone and read up about what's been going on with North Korea in case there's an opportunity to ask a question.

We arrive with five minutes to spare. I see the satellite vehicle already there, the dish on the roof just going up. I get out of the car and run over to it. The side door is open and two middle-aged guys sit inside what looks like a mobile control station for a nuclear bunker. So many buttons and switches I don't have a clue what any of them do. Four small screens and a mixing desk. All fitted into a DHL delivery truck. Clever what they can do nowadays. Anyway...

'Hey guys. It's a pre rec statement, so me and Phil will do it and I'll give you the card to feed.'

'Sure. We won't be ready for five minutes anyway,' says the engineer with a scraggly beard.

'Cool,' I reply. I walk back over to Phil who's setting up the camera. A car is driving towards us along the private road leading from Chequers. It pulls up next to us and a black man in a dark suit gets out. He looks like James Bond, almost a bit too glam for someone that works in Downing Street.

'Are you from TBN?' he asks.

'Yeah,' I reply.

'I'm Marcus from Downing Street press office.'

'Ollie,' I reply, shaking his hand.

'Phil,' says Phil who also shakes Marcus' hand.

'How long before you're ready?' Marcus asks. I glance at Phil.

'Ready now,' Phil says.

'Okay,' Marcus replies. He pulls out his phone and makes a call. 'They're ready here.'

'Can you give me a white balance?' asks Phil, handing me a sheet of paper. I hold it in front of the camera. 'Thanks.' I feel the expectation in the air. From the road you can't see the Prime Minister's official country manor house, just the grounds.

'So just to confirm, this won't be live. Just a

pre recorded statement,' says Marcus. I nod.

'Yep,' I say.

'Good.'

We wait. I walk back to the satellite vehicle.

'You guys ready?' I ask.

'We're always ready,' says glasses engineer, think his name is Henry. I've worked with him before, just can't remember his surname.

I walk back to Phil. We both look back down the private driveway. I breathe in, trying to calm my nerves. Mustn't screw this up. I walk back and forth along the road. Five minutes go by. Then another five. The clouds are starting to look threatening.

'How long?' I ask Marcus.

'Soon,' he replies. I nod and start pacing again. Suddenly, I see two Range Rovers and a Jaguar driving towards us.

'Here he is,' I say. The Range Rovers get to the end of the driveway and stop. Four big guys in suits get out, then I see him. The Prime Minister and a female press officer who looks tired and stressed. The PM is shorter than I remember from our last encounter but has the air and authority of the most powerful man in Britain. His hair is slicked back and his suit is perfectly pressed. The bags under his eyes make him look older than he is. The strain of the job, I guess. They walk up to us. Marcus does the formalities.

'Prime Minister, this is Ollie from TBN.' The PM offers his hand. I shake it.

'Nice to meet you,' the PM says. Not sure why but I'm disappointed he doesn't remember me. Suppose it's a bit much to expect him to remember everyone he meets. I was only with him for five minutes, I guess.

'You too. If you don't mind standing just here, sir,' I indicate where he should stand. He looks distracted or maybe he's just focused on what he's going to say. I stand as close to the camera as I can, looking at the PM. The female press officer is not far away, making sure she hears every word he says. The PM looks at me as Phil gets ready.

'Okay, we're rolling,' says Phil.

'Prime Minister, what's your reaction to today's events in North Korea?'

'Well the first thing I want to say is we believe North Korea should stand down its nuclear missiles on the border and re-engage with the talks that myself and the US President attended only last week. And...uh...shit can we go again.' I glance at Phil then over to the female press officer.

'Of course, no problem,' I reply. Phil puts his hand in front of the camera then says,

'We're still rolling.'

'When you're ready,' I say. The PM clears his throat and licks his lips, repeating to himself quietly what he wants to say.

'Okay,' the PM says, 'Ready.' Phil nods.

'What's your reaction to today's events?' I say.

'North Korea has to stand down its nuclear missiles and reengage with the talks that the President and I attended last week. This act of aggression will not be tolerated and I urge Kim Jong Un to come to his senses and enter full negotiations with us and the South Koreans to prevent this situation spiralling out of control. They have a choice, more isolation from the international community or reengagement with us. It's in their hands. I hope they make the right decision. Thank you...okay?' I look at Phil who checks the recording back.

'Yep, good,' Phil says. The PM shakes his head and turns to the female press officer.

'Next time can we make it a little snappier, I'm not going to learn these massive paragraphs you come up with, I'm not an actor Anna.'

'Of course sir,' she replies. He walks back towards the Range Rover, Anna in tow.

'Thank you, sir,' I call. He turns back to me and waves, insincerity painted all over his face. What a piece of shit. That ladies and gentlemen is the man leading our country, God help us all. The motorcade moves off back towards the house.

'Okay, thanks guys,' says Marcus. He walks over to his car and drives back down the driveway towards Chequers. Phil hands me the SD card with the interview on it. I take it to the engineers.

'Here you go guys. We'll need to play this out on a clock start so everyone gets it at the same time.' I take out my phone and call Paul.

'Newsdesk,' Paul says.

'It's Ollie, we've done it and it's ready to go. Playout in ten?'

'Yep, what did he say?' My mind goes blank. What did he say? I was so busy concentrating that I didn't hear what he was saying. Something about North Korea reengaging?

'He said he wanted North Korea to reengage with South Korea and the West and to stand down their nuclear missiles to prevent the situation spiralling out of control.' I hear Paul typing what

I'm saying. 'It wasn't very long maybe, twenty seconds?'

'Okay, playout in ten. Good job Ollie.'

'Thanks.'

The guys on the truck cue up the SD card.

'There was a false start so make sure you just feed the second answer,' I say. Henry nods. We wait for the clock to hit three-twenty exactly then, making sure all the other broadcasters can see the paused image of the PM, we hit play. The clip starts playing, well done me. Except...for some unknown reason I realise it has jumped to the very beginning and starts to play the PM's first answer. The one where he says 'shit!' Oh fuck no. TBN, SKY, BBC all cut to the feed live as it comes in.

'NO! That's the wrong clip!' I shout. Too late, every broadcaster has cut to our feed transmitting the PM saying 'shit, can we go again.' I close my eyes. My phone starts ringing. It's a car crash and I'm in so much trouble.

'You have any idea the shitstorm that rains down because you can't cue up a tape and press play at the right time?' says Jonathan Crawley, Head of Home News. He's wearing an expensive suit and looks like the Fat Controller. I stand in front of his desk, head down.

'I'm sorry, we did cue the card correctly but the machine reverted to the beginning and by the time we realised, it had already played out,' I say.

'By the time you realised? You should have pulled it off the air the moment it started playing.

If I wanted a fuck up, I'd have sent my four-year old son. We send you because you're supposedly one of our best producers. All of us here expect simple things like this to go smoothly. When they don't Oliver, I get fucked up the arse. And I hate getting fucked up the arse by anyone except my wife. I don't send monkeys, I send producers who are supposed to know what the fuck they're doing.'

'You're right, it's my fault. I can only apologise.'

'Are you a monkey Oliver?'

'No.'

'You sure? People will understand if they thought a monkey was sitting in that sat truck pressing play at the right time. Because monkeys are a lesser species, incapable of organising pool playouts. You sure you're not a monkey?'

'No,' I reply, looking down. Jonathan huffs.

'You know why it took so long to call you in here? Because I couldn't get Downing Street off the fucking phone. I had to sit and listen to that prick Adrian Short give me lecture after lecture on how biased TBN is towards the opposition and how this episode proves it. How we deliberately stitched up the Prime Minister to make him look like a dick and how they will make sure we pay. They've been chewing my arse for two hours, I've got nothing left to sit on.' I nod slowly and go to respond when suddenly the mobile on his desk starts to ring. He picks it up and looks at the display and rolls his eyes skywards.

'Fuck me,' he says, showing me the display. 'My wife. And here I was thinking the day couldn't get any worse. Get out of my sight, Hayward.'

'Sorry,' I say. He waves me away in disgust.

'Darling, it's daytime, this is an unexpected pleasure...' he says.

I open the door and step out, red faced. I breathe out and walk towards the newsdesk. I feel the whole newsroom watching me.

'You okay, Ollie?' Julie asks.

'Not really,' I reply.

TWENTY – DINNER DATE

Saturday. I've had time to recover from the bollocking of a decade and I want to move my life in a more positive direction. No point in dwelling on the negative even if every newspaper did splash my screw up all over the front pages the next day. Nightmare. Anyway, let's just pretend that it never happened and that my prospects for promotion haven't just been dealt a fatal blow. What the hell, at least I still have my health, right? Although that mole on my hip looks like it's getting bigger...

So it's dinner with Lauren tonight at mine. I tell Ashley and Parker not to be in, which is a better conversation than I expect. Ashley is seeing what's-his-face. Damn, what is his name? Norman, that's it. Norm. Brilliant. Anyway, Parker wasn't originally seeing Nicola but when I told him to not be in this evening he gave her a call and now they're going to Pizza Express - he's even printed off a voucher. He's so classy, I totally get what she sees in him.

So first things first, I need to decide what the

hell I'm going to cook tonight. As I've said before, cooking isn't exactly my strong point. Not sure what is but it's not cooking. I'm standing in the Asda cooked meat aisle, staring at a long chorizo sausage, unsure of what I'm doing. Maybe I should have looked up a recipe. Yeah, that would have been better.

I walk round looking for inspiration. Pasta? No, too simple and I don't know any pasta recipes other than spaghetti bolognese and I have to do better than that. I don't know what to cook. I whip out my phone and call Parker. It rings then,

'What do you want, dickhead?' Parker says.

'I need a recipe for tonight. What's easy to cook but will be, you know, impressive?'

'Why don't you just take her for a McDonalds, that's more your speed, isn't it?'

'Funnily enough we did actually talk about fish and chips-'

'Christ, you are such trailer-trash.'

'Not in a serious way, dickwad. Come on, I need help here.'

'Okay...what about Chicken Cordon Bleu.'

'Cordon what?'

'Fuck's sake. I'll email you a list of ingredients. What are you doing for a starter?'

'I was going to do garlic bread.'

'No. You're going to do scallops and chorizo.'

'Ooh good, I'm standing right next to the chorizo,' I say.

'That's great, Ollie. And for desert...uhh, I dunno, homemade brownies?'

'Sure, sounds good.'

'Ok, check your email in a couple of minutes

and I'll tell you what to get. Amateur.'

'Thanks mate, really appreciate it.'

'Yeah whatever. Bye.'

'Bye.' I hang up and await Parker's email which is in my inbox faster than a Cheetah on speed. I move around the supermarket picking out the ingredients as I go. Of course, I get lost and I can't find breadcrumbs to save my life. Eventually however, I source them all. I am the epitome of male hunter/gatherer.

I get back to the flat around one. I see Tristan outside, smoking another (perfectly legal) cigarette. I can barely move for the amount of shopping I'm carrying. Tristan merely watches me unswayed (again) by the load I carry.

'Don't worry, I've got it,' I say. Tristan looks at me.

'Should have taken my advice about Tesco delivery.'

'Why would I need that when everyone pitches in and helps?' I reply.

'I don't lug other people's shit.'

'Right, okay,' I say, getting up the final step and pushing past Tristan as I go. I dump the bags outside the front door and try to find my keys.

'What you making?' Tristan asks, glancing down at the bags.

'Chicken Cordon Blue,' I say.

'Cordon Bleu,' he replies.

'What?'

'It's Cordon Bleu, not Blue,' he states, inhaling on his cigarette. I stare at him.

'Thank you for correcting me on that.'

'Welcome,' he replies, with zero irony in his

voice. I locate my keys and open the door, pulling in the bags. I glance up at him and frown. He gives a little wave as I close the door. Tristan definitely does not know more than me about cooking. It's not possible. Unless you count hash cakes. His words unsettle me nonetheless.

I drop the bags onto the kitchen floor and set about putting things away. Ashley walks in.

'Hey,' she says.

'Hi,' I reply, placing the loaf of bread next to the sugar jar.

'I can't believe you're cooking for this girl.'

'I cook and stuff.'

'I think you've cooked once the entire time I've been here.'

'Well you haven't been here very long so...' I say. Ashley watches me unpack the food from the bags. I look up at her. 'You going to watch or do you want to give me a hand?'

'Sure,' she says, bending down to help me.

'Aren't you supposed to be at work?' I ask.

'Day off,' she replies.

'Huh,' is all I can think of in response.

'So what are you making her then?' Ashley asks. I pull out some chicken breasts.

'Chicken Cordon Bleu,' I say, correctly this time.

'Nice.'

'Hopefully,' I reply, placing the chicken breasts in the fridge. 'So you seeing Norm tonight?'

'Norman, his name is Norman,' she says, repeating the name deliberately slowly.

'Sorry Norman.'

'Yes, he's taking me out to Giovanni's on

Lavender Hill.'

'Nice.'

'Yeah.'

'How's it going with the Nor-man?' I accentuate his name.

'Good. Yeah. He wants to introduce me to his mum to which I just said no.'

'Why?'

'We only just started going out. And it probably won't last anyway. Rebound guys never do.'

'Is he a rebound guy?'

'What do you think, he's called Norman for God's sake?'

'Right,' I say, chuckling. I catch her watching me in a funny way. Suddenly the atmosphere feels mildly awkward. 'So, you going to start playing the piano in public?'

'No.'

'Why? Seriously, what I heard was really good.'

'I just do it for fun. Not really a career choice.'

'You wanna work in a bar for the rest of your life?'

'No,' she replies.

'If you're scared about what other people will think-'

'I'm not scared. It's my choice.'

'Well, then it's a waste of a great talent, which is even worse.' I place the apples next to the sink. She thinks for a second then says,

'I need to get ready, we're going out early for drinks.'

'Go, thanks for your help,' I say. She walks to the door, stops and turns, leaning against the frame.

'You really think I was good?' she asks. I stop unpacking and look at her.

'Yeah, I really do. It sounded like a professional song. I'm not just saying that either, it really did.'

'Hmm,' she replies, taking in my words. She pushes herself off the door frame and leaves.

Lauren arrives bang on seven-thirty which on any other day would have been perfect. With my cooking as it is, however, it's the last thing I need. I run to the door and open it. She stands in front of me, wearing a tight-fitting black dress and strappy high heels. Her hair's in ringlets which changes her appearance dramatically. Honestly, she looks like a model and I suddenly feel that familiar feeling of intimidation. She carries a black holdall bag, I guess she's staying over...which is nice.

'Hi,' I say.

'Hi,' she replies, smiling. She takes a step in, hands me a bottle of wine and kisses me on the lips. In her heels, she's almost as tall as me.

'Thanks,' I say.

'For the kiss?'

'No...well yes, and the wine.'

'It's one of my favourites.'

'Come in, come in. Let me take that,' I say, taking the black holdall and nearly doing my back in. 'Jesus, what's in here?'

'Everything a girl needs for the night,' she replies.

'Are we going to be weight lifting?'

'You're a funny guy,' she says, smiling. I close the door as she walks past me. I tidied up as best I could but I'm still self-conscious. I lit some candles to distract from what I'm sure she regards as a dated paint job and wallpaper effect. We walk into the living room. I head over to my iPod and hit play. Adele's tones immediately fill the air and soften the atmosphere.

'So, this is the living room,' I say.

'Nice,' she replies.

'Shall I give you a quick tour? Won't take very long.'

'Sure,' she says. We walk back to the corridor.

'I know it's small and nothing like James Kennedy's place-'

'It's really nice, Ollie,' she says.

'Yeah well...it's a foot on the ladder anyway,' I say as we walk into the kitchen. 'Here's where the magic happens.'

'Ah yes. And I was thinking it only happens in the bedroom,' she says with a naughty smile. I smile back, embarrassed.

'Well anyway,' we walk back to the corridor and past the bathroom. 'Bathroom is there. Parker's room,' I say, pointing out the closed door. 'He's out with his girlfriend tonight.'

'Ah, so we have the place to ourselves?'

'Oh yes, and uh...this is my room.' We walk in slowly, I place her bag down on the floor. She looks around, spots the double bed in the centre and the floor to ceiling wardrobe.

'Very nice,' she says. She presses the bed. 'How much action has this seen?'

'Oh every weekend. And normally it's someone new each time, I'm just that good,' I say. She chuckles and walks towards me placing her arms around me. 'Well if the barbeque was anything to go by, I don't doubt it.' I lean over and kiss her, breathing in her perfume. I feel her grip tighten around me. She breaks the kiss. 'Maybe we should have some dinner before we…move on,' she says, smiling. I nod.

'Yeah, good idea.' We make our way back to the kitchen. I find the printout of the recipe Parker sent me and I get to work. Lauren watches me.

'So, what are we having?' she asks.

'Chicken Cordon Bleu,' I reply.

'Nice.'

'Yeah,' I reply, distracted. 'Sorry, this won't take too long, just need to make sure I get it right.'

'You carry on.' She walks out and into the living room. The chicken is sorted, now for the starter. I grab the chorizo sausage and the packet of scallops and get frying. Then I pull out a bottle of Champagne from the fridge and two glasses. Okay yes, it was on special at the supermarket but I can't afford what she's used to, which is probably Dom Perignon or Moet. I put the (perfectly respectable) Champagne in an ice bucket and walk into the living room. I find her looking at my photos on the desk. She turns as I walk in.

'Who is this?' she asks. She's referring to a picture of me and Svetla. Shit, I should have put those away.

'Uh, that's Svetla. My ex,' I reply. She nods slowly.

'She's pretty.'

'Yeah. But we weren't right for each other,' I say, placing the Champagne on the table.
'Champagne?'

'Lovely,' she says. I tear off the foil and pop the cork. Except me being me, the Champagne fizzes up and I get half of it on the table.

'Shit!' I say. I manage to pour some of it in the glass.

'Oops. Shall I get some kitchen roll?' she asks.

'No, I got it,' I reply, heading for the kitchen. Real smooth Ollie. I walk back with a roll of kitchen towel and start mopping the table. I fill two glasses and hand her one.

'Cheers,' I say.

'To us,' she replies.

'To us,' I repeat. We take a sip. I'm not normally a Champagne guy mainly due to the exorbitant cost but it's very nice. Lauren stares at me as we drink, I find it vaguely intimidating.

'You're looking very dapper, Mr. Hayward.'

'Thanks. You look...wow,' I reply, with the vague thought I could be a little late in saying that. Better late than never?

'Thanks. Do you like my hair like this?'

'Yeah. It looks quite different but I like that,' I say. She smiles. The air crackles between us, I force a breath out. 'Better just check on the starter.' She nods. I make my exit. I serve up and dust the plates with a little chopped parsley, exactly as Parker told me and walk into the living room, placing the plates down on the table.

'Here we go,' I say. Lauren walks over and sits down at the table. I pull out my chair and sit down opposite her.

'Mmm, this looks nice,' she says, sliding a scallop and a slice of chorizo onto her fork. I stare at her chewing and suddenly realise I'm watching her so intently I've forgotten to eat anything myself. I quickly remedy that. 'Very good.'

'Thank you,' I reply.

'So. Do you still have a thing for your ex?' Lauren asks, taking another bite. I nearly choke but I control the urge and swallow my scallop.

'No. Why do you ask that?'

'No reason. Just what you said at the barbeque and having pictures still out. There's one by your bed as well. It's just a bit weird.' Shit! I am such an amateur. Why didn't I just throw those bloody things away? Silly, silly boy.

'We were together for a long time and when we split up, it hurt. A lot. But...' I want to say I'm over her. I barely think about her any more. Svetla who? The thing is, I don't like lying. 'I don't know.'

'What is this?' she says, her arm gesturing between the two of us.

'We've just started seeing each other. You're gorgeous. I think we get on really well. We live in different worlds but I find that quite interesting. Can I promise that I'm a hundred percent over my ex and everything that happened? Not really. But we hit it off and I just thought, why not give it a shot. If that's not what you want to hear-'

'No. Don't misunderstand me, Ollie. I'm not giving you the fifth degree. We have only just started seeing each other. And I appreciate your honesty,' she says. She looks like she wants to say more but instead opts to take another bite. Then, she puts her knife and fork down and stares at me.

THREE WAY

'I like you,' I say, 'it would be cool to see where this goes. I'm not ready for marriage just yet. That's about it.' The conversation has sent my stomach into turmoil. I'm half expecting her to stand up and leave. She runs her fingers up and down the stem of her Champagne glass.

'I'm older than you and whilst I'm not ready for marriage or anything like that, I'm...' she frowns and sips her glass. 'What I mean is-'

'Lauren, I know exactly what you mean. You're not wasting your time,' I say. She nods slowly.

TWENTY ONE – BUY ONE, GET ONE FREE

'Would it be high maintenance of me to I ask if you could put those photos somewhere else?' Lauren asks.

'No, not at all,' I say, embarrassed. 'Should have done it ages ago.' I immediately stand up and grab the photo of Svetla. I walk into my bedroom and snatch the photo by the bedside and throw them under the bed. I do a quick check to make sure there's nothing else liable to cause offence and head back to Lauren.

'Thank you,' she says, sincerity in her eyes. I feel stupid. Humiliated. Why hadn't I done it before now? Too late, bloody amateur.

'No worries. I'd better just check on the main course,' I say, clearing the table and heading back into the kitchen. I dump the plates, still self-flagellating. Stupid, stupid. I breathe out, open the oven and check the chicken. It looks pretty good and smells fantastic. But it still needs another ten minutes…I think. I shove it back in and close the oven door before heading back into the living room for round two. I sit down and notice Lauren has finished her glass of Champagne, so I pull the bottle out of the ice bucket and pour her another. I must have lost just under a glass full in spillage.

'I really like your flat, it's cosy,' she says.

'Yeah it's okay,' I reply. 'So what about you and your ex's?'

'Ah, here we go,' she replies, smiling, 'come on then. What do you want to know?'

'You and James?' I say. She closes her eyes slowly then looks at me.

'James and I used to see each other. Only for a short while. He's very happy with Sarah but yes, we did go out. Problem?'

'No, I just…don't get it.'

'What don't you get?' she says, leaning forward, showing me more cleavage that I try not to notice.

'I just think he's a bit of a-'

'Prick?' she finishes.

'Well, yeah. Look I don't want to offend you, because you work with him and you're obviously friends but, seriously.' She chuckles.

'Don't hold back Ollie, tell me what you really think.'

'Sorry.'

'No I get it. James is a bit cocky and up-his-own-arse but deep down, he's actually a really sweet guy.' I consider what she says.

'Okay,' I say, 'main course.' I stand and walk back to the kitchen to collect and serve the chicken. When I pull it out of the oven, it does look a little well done. Shit. I shovel it onto a plate with some veg but somehow it all looks just a little bit crap. Nothing for it but to serve it and hope I don't kill the both of us. I carry the plates in.

'Oo,' says Lauren. I place the plate down in front of her. If she's disappointed she covers it well. We start eating. Sure enough the chicken is overcooked and has a rubbery texture to it. Damnit.

'Sorry, it's a little well done,' I say.

'It's perfect,' says Lauren in a reassuring voice. I smile, gratefully. A thought hits me.

'Oh, I did an interview with the Prime Minister the other day.'

'Really?'

'Yeah, the statement on North Korea. That was me. Except I totally fucked it up.'

'Oh? How come?'

'Urgh, he started talking then he screwed it up and said 'shit, can we go again?' on camera.'

'Right.'

'Unfortunately it was a pool statement which means we play it out to the other broadcasters and when we played it out, rather than starting it in the right place we played out the whole thing, including him saying 'shit.''' Lauren's eyes widen, she's hooked.

'Oh no.'

'Yeah,' I say. Her mouth is open, hanging on my every word. 'Total fuck up and everyone took it live so it went out like that, raw,' I say.

'Oh God, what happened?'

'I got a massive bollocking from my boss with the whole newsroom watching. Wasn't good.'

'Shit, Ollie. Is it okay now though?'

'It will be. These things happen sometimes. Just because it was an important statement and these things always get Downing Street pissed off. Don't blame them but it was a genuine mistake. It'll be fine. It's not like I did it on purpose, the clip just started playing from the wrong point.'

'Wow. You have such an interesting job. I know it went wrong then but I wish I could do what you do.'

'I'll have to bring you in, show you the newsroom.'

'That would be great. What do you want in return?' she replies. I suddenly feel her foot on my crotch. I look up at her, she winks and carries on chewing (three or four times before swallowing) her chicken.

'I...nothing.'

'Sure?' she asks, 'you're sure there's nothing I can do for you?'

'Well. Umm,' I say, pretending to think. Her naughty face is back. She looks so hot, a sudden urge fires up inside me. 'Yeah, I think there probably is something you could do.'

She stands up, pulling the hem of her dress down and walks over to me. She bends down and kisses me. My hand moves around her waist and runs down to her bum. Damn that feels good. Her hand moves down to my crotch and starts rubbing. Before I know what's going on, I feel her pull at my belt and unzip my trousers. Her hand moves over my boxers and yanks them down. She is so damn sexy I can barely comprehend what's happening. She nestles herself between my legs, I look up to the ceiling. I move a hand over a breast. Large and perfectly formed.

Suddenly the front door slams.

'Jesus,' I say. Lauren is off me in a flash, I yank my trousers up quickly. I hear someone walk past the living room with heavy footsteps and down the corridor to Parker's room.

'Who is it?' Lauren whispers.

'Must be Parker, fuck's sake. Sorry,' I reply. I stand and do up my trousers. My erection is still visible so I try to walk with my bum sticking out a little. I poke my head out into the corridor.

'Parker?' I call. Parker's door is open and the light is on. I walk slowly towards it and look in. I'm surprised to see Ashley sitting on Parker's bed. Her makeup has run down her face and she stares out to nothing.

'Hey. What's wrong?' I ask.

'Nothing,' she replies, her eyes in another world.

'Doesn't look like nothing.' She doesn't respond. I glance back towards the living room and sigh. 'Listen Ash, I've got Lauren over-'

'I'm sorry. I'll stay in here, you won't know I exist.'

'Come on, we had an agreement,' I say, aware of my insensitivity. She nods slowly, a tear rolling down her cheek.

'You're right. Sorry. I just...,' she says, standing.

'Hey, come on. What happened?'

'I had a thing with Norman and I quit. So now I have no job, no place to live and no boyfriend. Why am I such a...?' She whispers something I don't hear and wipes her eye. 'Sorry Ollie. Excuse me.' She tries to get past.

'Hold on, hold on,' I say, blocking her way. Lauren appears behind me.

'Everything okay?' Lauren asks. Ashley turns her head, hiding her face with her hair.

'Yeah, sorry. Lauren, this is Ashley. Ashley, Lauren,' I say. Ashley nods, still shielding her face.

'Hey. You okay?' Lauren asks.

'Uh, Ashley's had a bit of a bad night and she's just going to stay in Parker's room.'

'You guys need your space. I'll find somewhere else,' Ashley says.

'No,' I reply, 'are you okay if she stays in here?' I ask Lauren. A frown appears on Lauren's face. More confused than angry.

'Uh. Sure,' Lauren says.

'There you go,' I say. 'You going to be okay here?' I ask. Ashley nods.

'Yep. I'm sorry Ollie. Please, go back to your dinner,' Ashley says.

'Okay,' I say. 'We'll speak tomorrow.' I close the door and we head back to the living room. 'Sorry about that,' I say to Lauren.

'No problem. Who is she?'

'Ashley. She's a friend from school who got into trouble recently and didn't have anywhere to stay so she's sort of staying here. Temporarily.'

'Oh. I thought you just lived with Parker.'

'Yeah. Like I said, it's only temporary.'

'Well you can't just leave her in there. She's upset.'

'I know, but it's our date,' I reply. I know I'm being selfish but a few seconds ago she had her mouth on my-

'Ollie...' Lauren says, her head tilted.

'Okay' I reply. Jeez, I don't know what the right thing to do is. Okay, maybe I do and maybe I just enjoyed...you know what, nevermind, moment's over now anyway. I walk back to the bedroom and knock on the door.

'Yeah,' Ashley says. I push the door a little.

'Hey. We're drinking Champagne, want some?'

'Don't really feel like celebrating to be honest.'

'Come on, you can't sit in here-'

'Yes I can. I can sit in here until Parker throws me out.'

'I've got brownies,' I say. Ashley shakes her head slowly. 'They're good, chocolate chip.' She blinks slowly then looks at me.

'I don't want to interrupt anything.'

'You're not. Please. I've baked enough for the Chinese Army, we can't possibly eat them all.' She thinks about it for a moment before she says,

'Okay. Thanks.'

'There you go,' I say, reaching for her hand and pulling her up. She stares at me then leans her head on my shoulder. I immediately move it off, don't want anyone to get the wrong idea. My hands move round to her cheeks, I hold her head. 'Hey, it's going to be fine, okay?' She nods. 'Come on.' I lead her to the living room. Lauren stands as we walk back in.

'How you feeling?' Lauren asks.

'Pretty shit actually,' Ashley replies, taking a seat on the couch.

'What happened?' Lauren asks.

'Oh this guy I've been dating. I thought, with

someone called Norman I'd be alright. But it turns out even geeks are arseholes,' Ashley replies. I pour her a glass of Champagne and hand it to her. 'Thanks,' she says, taking a sip. She looks at Lauren. 'You're so pretty.' Lauren brushes it off.

'Nah,' Lauren says.

'Yeah, you really are. Look at your skin, it's like perfect. Mine's got little lumps all over it.'

'No it doesn't,' I say without thinking. Lauren glances at me. Awkward.

'So you guys met when Ollie came to interview you?' Ashley asks.

'Yeah. I was really nervous, but Ollie had a way of making me feel comfortable and relaxed.'

'Don't believe it for a second, he was just trying to get into your knickers,' Ashley says. I glare at her. She glances at the both of us, unsure if she's just overstepped the mark. She chuckles nervously. Lauren joins her.

'Oh I get it, great,' I say.

'So you've known each other for a long time then?' Lauren asks.

'Yeah, I know Ollie better than he knows himself,' Ashley replies. Hang on, what the hell is happening now? I'm to be the subject of ridicule, is that how this is going to play out? Not sure I like this.

'What's the most embarrassing thing he's ever done?' Lauren asks.

'What? Wait a minute-' I say.

'Most embarrassing thing?' Ashley says, thinking.

'Ashley, don't you dare.'

'I was going to say your performance-'

'Ash, I mean it,' I say.

'-at the school play,' she says. I breathe out and frown.

'He's getting cross now, I'd better keep quiet or I'll be out on the street.'

'Nonsense you can stay with me in Pimlico,' Lauren says.

'Really?' Ashley says.

'For dirt on Ollie here, it's a small price to pay,' Lauren says, smiling. I know they're winding me up but I don't like it.

'Ha ha,' I say.

The night progresses in much the same vein. Ashley and Lauren tease me and I feel like I'm fending them off from revealing anything personal about me to each other. Of course, Ashley has all the dirt on me. Any story she tells could prove disastrous for my relationship with Lauren. But she seems to know this and keeps on the right side of appropriate. They get on well and I suddenly find myself with two girls I've had sex with getting on with each other. This is weird, right? You know when your work friends meet your school friends, bit like that.

The evening progresses to shots. Ashley gets upset when the conversation draws back to Norman and other men she's been with. She's amazingly honest about it all. Lauren is sensitive with her questions and repays Ashley's honesty with stories of her own. Turns out she went out with Johnny Dougan, lead singer of the Time Travellers. You know, the Time Travellers? Okay, they haven't done anything for a bit but come on. Cheater? That's an awesome track. My girlfriend went out with him. Is that something to be proud of? Is she my girlfriend? Not sure on either of those points.

The clock hits two and it's time for bed. We're all wankered.

'It was very nice to meet you, Lauren. You're not like most of the girls Ollie goes out with.'

'No?' Lauren replies.

'No, he normally picks shy, easy to manipulate types.'

'I do not,' I say. Then I think about it. 'Do I?' Ashley laughs, Lauren joins her. 'So see you in the morning, Ash,' I say.

'Yeah. You two have fun. And try not to keep me awake,' Ashley says, pulling off the cushions on the sofa to get the bed out.

'We'll try,' I say, glancing at Lauren, who's staring at me with goggle-eyes.

'He lasts for ages,' Ashley says. I laugh loudly, shaking my head. Lauren's smile disappears but quickly comes back.

'Night then,' I say, taking Lauren's hand and leading her to the bedroom. I close the door as she walks over to the bed and sits down. I know what's coming.

'So you've slept with her?' she asks. I nod slowly, walk over to her and sit down next to her.

'That a problem?' I ask. Lauren shakes her head, her drunken eyes looking at the floor.

'No. Just...didn't know.' We sit in silence. Lauren starts chewing a nail.

'Are we okay?' I ask.

'Yeah, of course.' she replies, looking at me.

'Look, I don't want you to think...I mean, I've

just got out of a long relationship and I'm still a bit....but, then we met and I dunno, we got on so well-'

'Yeah we did.'

'Yeah. But I don't want to mess you around or promise you something I can't deliver,' I say. She crosses her legs and takes my hand in her lap.

'I knew you were trouble,' she says. 'I just don't listen to myself.' She sighs.

'Hey,' I say. She turns to face me. 'I promise, I will not screw you around. Whatever happens, I won't fuck you over. All I can do is be honest.'

'Are you being honest?' she asks.

'Yes.' At least, I hope I am.

TWENTY TWO – A DRIVE TO THE COUNTRY

I lay awake, Lauren snoring beside me. Okay, it's not loud but you can definitely hear it. Sunlight tries and fails to push through my curtains. Although the conversation got heavy, it didn't stop us having sex for a large chunk of the night. When I say that, don't misunderstand me. I'm not that good. I just mean we were physically intimate. That's a better description. I guess we're both in different stages of vulnerability. Have to be so careful with her. Note to self, Lauren is lovely and pretty and I must not be a shit in any way. I still don't understand how she can be so into me after such a short space of time. My job must be more appealing than even I thought. No, it's more than that, I'm sure of it. What would Svetla make of all this? I'd like to think she'd be jealous that I'd managed to bag such a stunner. Maybe she'd even be happy for me? At least I'm moving on, not thinking about her all the time. Would she approve? Approve of my behaviour? Of me? I said I wouldn't keep talking about Svetla and what do I do the moment my mind starts to wander...?

Was I a crap friend to Ashley? When she came back last night, she needed to talk. Properly talk, with someone she knew and trusted. Was I there for her? Maybe I was a bit annoyed she happened to have boyfriend/shag drama on the one night I asked her not to be here. What the hell is going on? How can I, Ollie, have a three way problem with women? Me, when I've had so few girlfriends to speak of. It never rains, it pours, I guess.

I turn over to face Lauren. She lies on her back, eyes still closed. I watch her breasts move up and down under the sheet. She is so lovely to look at. I stroke her hair slowly and kiss her forehead. An eye opens, quickly followed by a smile and a stretch.

'Morning,' I say. She pulls the sheet up over her mouth.

'Morning,' she replies in a muffled voice. I frown, unsure what she's doing. 'Bad breath,' she says. I smile, pull the cover away and kiss her lips. Closing her eyes, she allows herself to be taken by the moment. I join her, relishing the feeling.

'Did you sleep okay?' I ask.

'Yeah.'

'Yeah?'

'Yeah,' she says, smiling.

'What do you fancy doing today? Are you around?' I ask. She looks at me, not saying anything. 'What? What's that look for?'

'It's just after what we said last night, not sure I'm the girl you really want.'

'Hey, come on. That's not what we said. I want to give this a proper go, don't you? Don't want to walk away without really trying?' She rolls the covers away and gets out of bed, naked. She starts picking up pieces of clothing from the floor and pulling them on one by one.

'Yeah, that sounds nice but when you've tried as much as I have, you end up deciding not to sit around waiting while the guy figures out whether or not he wants to be with you.'

'That's a bit unfair. I said I didn't want to be anything other than honest,' I say. She pulls on her dress and shakes it down.

'I get that Ollie. Really. It's just...I don't know,' she says, irritated.

'Where's all this come from? Last night-'

'Last night we were drunk and I didn't know what I was doing. Today I can see what's going on.'

'Yeah? What is going on?' I ask, glancing at her dress.

'I'm going home.'

'Come on,' I say, touching her arm. She stops suddenly, not turning to face me. 'Please don't misunderstand what I was saying. I really do like you and I want to give this a go.' She turns to face me and stares straight into my eyes.

'I don't know,' she whispers, looking up and shaking her head

'Just give it a try. That's all. Don't let fear destroy us before we've even begun.'

'You sound like a self-help book,' she says. A sting of hurt ripples through me. She stands and goes to the window. She pulls the curtains open and closes her eyes, letting the sun bathe her face.

'Sorry.' She looks over to me.

'Don't be,' I reply, standing and walking over to join her. I place a hand on her shoulder. She tilts her head, touching it with her cheek. The sun shines over both of us.

'Damnit, how can you look like that when you just got out of bed?' I say. She turns to face me.

'Like what?'

'Like this. This good. Look at you. Most girls at this point in the morning look like they've slept in a cardboard box. You look ready for a movie premiere,' I say. She smiles and ruffles a hand through my hair.

'Ohh. What is it about you, Ollie Hayward?' she asks, putting her arms around me.

'I'm devastatingly gorgeous? My supreme personality? Good basic hygiene?'

'Ah yes, good basic hygiene, that's it,' she laughs. I laugh with her and stroke her back as we embrace again. 'So, what did you have in mind for today then?'

'I wouldn't say a plan has formed yet. I'd like to spend it with you,' I say.

'Are you working tomorrow?' she asks.

'Tomorrow? Uh, Sunday, nope day off again. I rule,' I reply. She frowns, an idea forming.

'Well, we could go to my cottage in Stroud in the Cotswolds.'

'Wait a minute, you have a pad in the Cotswolds?'

'Yeah, used to be my parent's house but it's mine now.'

'Holy shit, what the hell are we still standing here for?'

I pack a bag quickly as Lauren undresses and showers. I check in on Ashley in the living room. She's still asleep. She'll be okay, we can talk when I get back...from my night away! How cool is this, the girl I'm seeing owns another property. Not that I've seen her first place yet but what the hell. She owns two houses! That is definitely a pro. Once we're both dressed and ready (Lauren takes an hour to get ready, I'm not kidding, an hour!) we head out to her car. She owns a lovely white Porsche.

'This yours?'

'You're putting your stuff into it, aren't you?' she replies.

'Yeah, I guess. Nice car,' I say.

'Thanks.'

We get in and she starts it up. Revving far more than is necessary, we head out of my driveway, through Clapham and down the A3, towards the M25. She drives aggressively, which surprises me. We get way too close to cars in front before she pulls out to overtake them. I figure, as it's her car and she's driving I probably shouldn't criticise but I'm tense as we narrowly avoid causing another mass pile up. I try not to scratch the dashboard with my fingernails and suppress the urge to scream like a cheerleader. I glance down at the radio and turn it on to take the temperature down a notch. Radio One, as good as any. Bit of Rhianna, nice.

'You think she's fit?' Lauren asks me.

'Who, Rhianna?'

'Yeah.'

'Yeah, I guess. Not as fit as you,' I say. Lauren rolls her eyes, immediately seeing through my pacification. We drive on, the motorway climbing and winding westwards.

'So, you said your parents used to own this house?' I say.

'Yeah,' she says, tensing.

'So, do they live somewhere else now or...?' I say. She glances at me and shakes her head.

'Nah, they're dead now.'

'Oh, sorry,' I say. She shrugs.

'At least I got the house, right?' She says it as a half-hearted joke but doesn't feel quite right. Suddenly we sit with only Radio One between us. 'Sorry. Not sure why I said it like that. Sounds like I don't give a shit. I do. Just...not easy to talk about.'

'Sure. I understand.'

'Anyway...have you ever been up this way before?'

'Cotswolds? Nope, never.'

'Good. I think you'll like it,' she says. I glance at her as subtly as I can. I notice her swallow and clear her throat. I look back to the road.

We arrive in Stroud around lunchtime. There are so many coaches. That is all I will say. Many, many coaches. Lots of people with bum bags. We drive along London Road then out to Slad Road and into proper countryside.

'You slad,' Lauren says, smiling at the road sign.

'That's outrageous. You're the slad.'

'No, you're a slad. A big, giant slad.' We chuckle at the joke. I look out, watching rolling fields and farmland race past (I use race because we are flying). She obviously knows these roads but...that's a blind corner. Slow down, Christ, what's she looking for, a chequered flag? I claw back a whimper, tighten my arse and hold on to the door with both hands.

'Sorry, not used to coming here with someone else in the car,' she replies. Turns out, my whimper was out loud.

After a couple of minutes, we slow down and she indicates right. We turn and head down a gravel drive. We arrive at a Cotswold stone house, and I mean house. When someone says cottage to me, I have this quaint idea of something small with low head clearance and maybe a thatched roof. This is more like a forever home. We pull around and park in front of a wooden garage door. We get out of the car and I stare at the house in front of us, sunbeams coating it in a glorious yellow light.

'This is your cottage?' I ask.

'Yeah, well...yeah.'

'More like a stately home,' I say. She chuckles.

'Come on, it's not that big,' she replies. I gawp at the stone pathway leading to the front door, the white wooden shutters covering the windows and the abundance of lavender and bees.

'I mean, Jesus,' I say, my mouth unable to close. She smiles.

'Grab your bag and we'll go in. Assuming I can find my keys,' she says, riffling through her handbag. I pull my bag out of the Porsche and throw it over my shoulder. I look out at the absurdly stunning view before me. Sheep dot a landscape of patchwork hills and in the distance there's a small forest. She probably owns that as well. You can see for miles. I try to process as much of it as I can before-

'Ah here we go. Ready?' she asks.

'Yeah,' I say, following her along the path to the front door. She inserts a large key into the lock and opens the door.

Inside, a hallway leads to a simple dining room with a wooden table and four chairs. To the right is a large kitchen with separate bar area. To the left is what looks like a spacious living room. Except the shutters are closed so I can't make out the detail.

'I'll open the shutters round the back, you...just stand there and look good,' Lauren says.

'What, like this?' I reply, striking a hands-on-hips superhero pose. She laughs. 'Or...this,' I say, placing my fingers on my chin in an accentuated thinking pose.

'Very good, yes, stay like that,' she says and disappears around the corner. I hear a door unlock and open. I notice some photos on the wall. Two middle-aged people smiling into the camera. Parents perhaps? I hear the shutters creak open and light suddenly fills the living room. It's a stunning room with wood beams running the length of the ceiling. There are two large sofas and a table in the centre. I note the lack of TV. But the piece de resistance is the concertina doors which open out onto quite possibly the most stunning garden and view I have ever seen. Lavender and roses wherever you look. Then a lawn that drops away to reveal the great British countryside. I stand in awe.

'Fuck me,' I whisper to myself. I hear Lauren open other shutters around the front of the house. My eyes return to that view. I shake my head. Even if I were to be promoted and scaled the heady heights to management at TBN, I doubt I could ever afford something like this in my job. The thought makes me feel depressed. I turn and look back at the living room. Lauren is leaning against a wooden beam looking at me, her arms folded across her chest.

'You like?' she asks.

'This is amazing. You're so lucky,' I say.

'Yeah, I am,' she replies, quietly. 'So, tea? Coffee?'

'Tea sounds lovely.'

TWENTY THREE – A NIGHT UNDER THE STARS

We sit down with a cup of tea and a packet of biscuits.

'You know, I think you're only the second boy I've brought here,' Lauren says.

'Really? I'm honoured.'

'You should be.'

'Who was the other guy?'

'Johnny,' she replies, looking down. I nod slowly.

'Do you still have a thing for him? Don't get me wrong, I would understand if you did. He's pretty cool,' I say. She shakes her head.

'Nah, me and Johnny have definitely been there and done that. We just don't work well when we're together. He's a good friend. Nothing more.'

'So, how often do you come here?'

'Not as much as I should. This place is calm. Peaceful. Something I definitely need more of in my life but, I don't know, somehow other stuff takes over.'

'Is the lack of TV deliberate?' I ask. She smiles and nods.

'Why, something on tonight you're going to miss?'

'No, not at all-'

'I know what you mean. I just thought, this place needs to have no distractions. Just somewhere I can be myself. So no TV, no mobile reception, no internet. I'm not even sure you can pick up FM here.'

'I like that.'

'Yeah? I get a lot of reading done when I'm here.'

'I want to apologise in advance.'

'For what?'

'I'm afraid you're not going to be doing a lot of reading whilst I'm here,' I say. She smiles and raises an eyebrow.

'Right. So...what will we be doing?'

'Hmm,' I say with an exaggerated expression. 'I'm sure we can think of something.'

'Okay, but before we start any of that, probably need to head to the supermarket and stock up. There's a Tesco in Stroud.'

'Oo, a Tesco.'

'Up yours. Finish your tea, and when we get back I'll show you exactly who's boss.'

We get the shopping in and Lauren starts cooking. I'd like to tell you I offered or had thoughts or input into anything but I'd be lying.

She knew what she wanted to cook and got on with it.

She tells me to set the table. Doesn't seem fair but what the hell. I walk around the house, inspecting the odd photo or painting. I reach the patio doors and open them. The last of the summer light just touches the edge of the garden which slopes away leaving nothing but rolling English countryside. It's a sight to behold. High above me I see the vapour trails of a plane. There are seemingly hundreds of different varieties of flowers and plants. She obviously has a gardener or someone who tends to them as everything looks immaculate. I walk along a stone pathway down to the end of the garden and look out across the hills. In the distance I can see sheep, horses and the occasional farmhouse. Stunning. I turn and look back towards the cottage. I watch Lauren washing her hands at the sink. She's unaware of me gazing at her as she sings to herself. Or is she talking? I can't tell. She still looks hot even in that Fifties flowery apron. I smile. Am I...falling for her? Is that what this is? She turns the tap off and shakes her hands, disappearing to dry them. I watch the empty space then look up at the mauve sky above me. I can just make out the first star. It flickers silently in the twilight. From somewhere I hear birds chirping their final song before going to bed or whatever birds do at night. I breathe in deeply, savouring the fresh, clean air. Today is a good day.

'Where are you?' I hear Lauren say. I turn and walk back towards the house.

Before long, dinner is ready. I watch as she brings out endless bowls of food, although secretly

I'm enjoying watching her bum in those tight jeans. Even the baggy wool jumper looks sexy. She starts serving what can only be described as a banquet...for two people. Roast pork, potatoes, vegetables, gravy, homemade Yorkshire puddings and so on. It smells amazing. It tastes even better. I look up from the plate, Lauren's searching my face.

'I hope it's okay,' she says.

'It's more than okay. Bloody perfect,' I reply. She smiles and we get stuck in. If I were to tell you I couldn't finish it, you'd probably think me rude but I'm not over-egging it when I say banquet. Needless to say she doesn't take offence at what's left on my plate. I pour another glass of red.

'So what was it like going out with Johnny Dougan?'

'Really? That's what you want to talk about?'

'I'm just curious. Was he a dick?'

'No. Well yes...a little. But he was also quite delicate. Vulnerable,' she says, glancing at me. 'But mostly, yes he was a dick.'

'Must be strange going out with someone famous.'

'No, I was with him before he became famous. And it wasn't strange, it was horrible. He got into drugs which he had never touched before and he changed. Became an exaggerated version of himself. I'm probably not making sense. He was just swept up in it all and I tried to hang on. Probably for too long.'

'How did it end?' I ask. She sighs, looking down at the table. 'Sorry. Maybe this isn't the proper conversation-'

'It's fine. He caught me in bed with another guy,' she replies.

'Shit,' I say.

'Yeah well, probably a fucked up way of getting away from him. I don't know.' I nod slowly, scanning her face for any emotion she might be feeling. She breathes in then looks back at me. 'What about you?'

'What about me?'

'This girl you were hung up on.'

'Svetla.'

'Right. What's the story?'

'First girl I properly loved. I've been with a few girls, not many but a few. And she was just...I dunno, different. Normal. I could be myself with her. I didn't have to think before I spoke, that sort of stuff.'

'Can I ask you a question?'

'Sure.'

'Will you be honest with me?'

'Depends on the question,' I reply. She smiles but nothing more.

'In your heart of hearts, are you still in love with her?' she asks. My stomach feels like I've just base-jumped off an impossibly tall waterfall. My heart is thumping and my throat is suddenly dry. I look down at the table then back to Lauren. Can she read me? Does she know the answer before I even give it?

'No,' I reply, eventually.

'You sure?' she asks. I nod slowly.

'Yeah. We're done. We had our moment and that moment is gone. Time for something new. Don't you think?'

'For me, definitely. For you...I don't know,' she stands and clears the plates. I watch her go, guilt now strumming me. I watch her in the kitchen, appear then disappear behind the door frame. Am I being a royal shit to this girl? Using her for sex with no intention of going any further? Am I becoming the thing I saw in other men that I always used to despise? She walks back in.

'Come,' she says. I stand, follow her to the patio doors and step outside. She looks up. 'See how much more you can see in the country.' I look up. She's right. The night sky is filled with the awe-inspiring sight of the Milky Way. Thousands upon thousands of stars flicker in a truly spectacular spectacle.

'Wow,' I whisper, 'that is amazing.'

'Yeah,' she replies. We stand in wonder at Nature's display, my hand brushing against hers. A shooting star flies silently through the sky. We gasp and smile together. I glance down at her face, as she peers up into the night sky. 'Something so simple, yet so utterly beautiful,' she says.

'Like you,' I say. She nudges me.

'I'm not simple.' I stare at her beautiful face, lean in slowly and kiss her. I move my hand around her head and run my hands through her hair. She smells of a subtle vanilla. I breathe her in and release her.

'Why am I always attracted to guys I can't have?' Lauren whispers.

'You can have me,' I say.

'Yeah?'

'Any time you want. You lucky thing,' I say. She smiles and flicks her eyebrows. My heart suddenly melts. I feel so lucky. This moment. This girl, all suddenly so...perfect.

'Let's go in and get those trousers off.'

I wake the next day slowly and calmly. The sun streams through the window and birds sing outside. It's so quiet. No planes, no cars, just silence. It's slightly disconcerting, as someone who comes from the city, you get used to all the noise. The shouting, the sirens, the planes on final approach to Heathrow. Here, nothing. Just birds. As I lie, listening, I feel Lauren stir next to me. I glance over towards the bathroom and see a broken picture frame on the floor, glass shards scattered. What happened there? It's then I notice the room looks like a bomb has hit it. A chair lies on the floor, drawers have been pulled out of the chest. Shit, we've had a break in during the night. Quickly I turn back to Lauren.

'Hey,' I whisper. She doesn't move. 'Lauren, wake up.' Slowly she sighs. 'Lauren.'

'What?'

'I think someone burgled us,' I say. Her eyes flick open and she sits up, looking around the room. Then her shoulders relax.

'Is that supposed to be funny,' she says, lying back down and closing her eyes.

'No. Look at this place,' I say. Her eyes open again and she looks at me with a 'are you crazy' look.

'Can you seriously not remember?' she says. I stare at her, frowning.

'We did this?' She chuckles and ruffles my hair. And slowly, one by one, memories start to return. We began in the living room on the sofa. Then we ended up on the floor. We made our way quickly to the wall and then the stairs. I have a vague recollection of things smashing but really, all this? Then the banister, I'm not going to tell you what happened there. I put my hand across my mouth as the memory hits me. Then the bathroom. I think there was a shower involved. I shoved her against the chest of drawers. Shoved. Me. It was all quite rough but I think she liked it.

I swing my feet around the side of the bed and stand up. I feel an instant bolt of pain in my side. I look down to see a massive purple bruise running my from under my armpit to my waist.

'Jesus,' I say.

'Oh my God, Ollie,' Lauren says, staring at the bruise. 'Be careful, I wouldn't move around until we've had a little tidy up, there might be some glass on the floor.'

'Yeah and maybe...I dunno, some ice?' I say. She smiles, her eyes wide and alive.

'We are so bad,' she says.

'You're insane,' I say.

'I think I might be. It's your fault. If you hadn't got me so excited, none of this would-'

'Oh right, of course. My fault, yeah. Great,' I say, smiling at her.

'Come on. Let's clean this up and go for a walk.'

TWENTY FOUR – DRUG SELECTION WITH A BEATING

We get back to my flat in Clapham around seven. Lauren doesn't come in, we sit in her car and kiss for what feels like an insanely long time. Eventually she lets me go and I wave goodbye. I watch the Porsche disappear, listening to the engine slowly fade into the distance. I walk up the steps and arrive at the top. Tristan's front door opens and he steps out. His excited facial expression says to me 'I've just seen Jesus but he told me to keep it a secret.'

'Hey,' he says.

'Alright,' I reply.

'Nice car.'

'Yeah.'

'That your girlfriend?'

'Um, sort of,' I say.

'She drives a very nice car.'

'Yes, she does.' A pause between us. I glance at him and frown. 'Was there something else?'

'No, no. I just wanted you to know I appreciate nice cars.'

'Okay. Thanks.'

'I've got a few Moggies left if you want some.'

'Moggies?'

'Moggies. You know..?' I shake my head. 'Moggies. Downers, roofies, rugby balls. Moggies.' He looks at me like everything has now been suitably cleared up.

'Mate, I don't know what you're talking about.'

'Jeez man, what do I have to spell it out for you? Rohypnol. Date rape?' he says, shaking his head at my lack of drug terminology knowledge. I nod.

'I've heard of that,' I say.

'Good. That's good Ollie. It's fifty quid for six.'

'Thanks but I'm good.'

'Then what the fuck are you doing, wasting my time?' Tristan says, frowning. He walks back into his apartment and slams the door with such force, the number three falls off. I try to process what just happened and realise that doing so would probably cause a stroke. I open my door and go inside.

'Where've you been?' Ashley asks when I walk in.

'Out to Lauren's house in the Cotswolds,' I reply.

'Could have left a note. I've been trying to call you for two days.'

'What's the problem? No one's dead, are they? Or...the Queen? Is the Queen dead, have work been trying...?'

'No, the Queen's not dead. I just didn't know

where you'd gone, that's all.'

'I think, as I own this flat I can come and go as I please,' I reply.

'Yep, you can. Sorry, I just needed to talk to someone but...it's fine.'

'Well I'm here now, so...talk,' I reply, dumping my bag down.

'I can't afford rent. With losing my job and everything I just...I wouldn't have anything left to live on.'

'Don't worry about it. I said you don't have to pay me anything,' I reply. 'Have you spoken to Norman?'

'Yeah. He wants some of my salary back. Can you believe that?'

'What?'

'He said we get paid for the two weeks we've just done and two weeks in advance and now he wants that money back.'

'What a cock.'

'Yeah. Except he really means it and I just don't have it. What am I going to do, Ollie?'

'You're going to ignore him. He doesn't know where you live, does he?'

'Well, yeah he sort of does,' she replies. Off my look, she says, 'When I started there you had to fill in name, address, date of birth...'

'Well I'd say he can fuck off. What exactly happened anyway?'

'With what?'

'Norman.'

'Nothing I..,' she starts to say then stops. 'Okay, we had a disagreement about where the beer barrels were stored.'

'What?'

'He wanted them in the staff room and I told him it was illegal to store pressurised barrels in the same place as the staff hang out.'

'Is it?'

'I've no idea but the staff room is small enough as it is, you put barrels in there, there would have been nowhere to sit down,' she says. She's thrown away a job because of this?

'Christ, Ashley.'

'I know, I know. I'm shit. Got no money, no job, no friends. Nothing really.' She looks down. I walk over to her and put my arm around her.

'You've got plenty.'

'Yeah? Why do I keep fucking it up then?'

'Because you're pathologically self-destructive.'

'Sounds about right,' she says. 'How was your trip anyway?'

'It was nice. She has a massive house near Stroud and-' I say. Ashley stares at me. 'It was nice.'

'Good. Glad one of us is happy.'

'Yeah.'

Suddenly there's a heavy knock at the door. It makes us both jump.

'Jesus,' I say, 'if that's Tristan, after slamming the door like that, I'm going to be mightily pissed off.' I stand and walk to the front door, opening it. A man stands in front of me that I've never seen before. He's sporting short blonde hair, muscles and an anchor tattoo! Perhaps he's a Popeye wannabe? I mean, what is this, nineteen fifty-three?

'Yes?' I say. I feel sure he isn't here to sell

double glazing.

'I'm looking for Ashley, I was told she lives here,' says the guy. He has a deep voice. Like the guy who does movie trailers.

'Uh...who are you?' I say.

'I'm Gary. Her boyfriend,' he says. This orangutan is Gary? The guy that beat her up. I pull the door closer to me.

'There's no Ashley living here,' I say. I hear Ashley behind me.

'For Christ's sake Gary, what, are you stalking me now? That's an excellent way to get me back,' she says, pulling the door from my grip to reveal herself.

'Babe, I just want to talk, that's all.'

'We're done talking. Now piss off and leave me alone,' she says. Why do I get the feeling this is going to end badly? Gary looks at me.

'This the new boyfriend then?'

'No, Gary...piss...off,' she says.

'Are you?' he asks, eyes burning. No, but we have engaged in the sexual act a number of times and places if that helps answer your question, good sir.

'No. I have a girlfriend. A different girl. Not Ashley,' I say. Yeah okay, not exactly the most convincing I've ever been but what the hell, he came out of nowhere.

'Yeah? You sure about that?'

'For fuck's sake, piss off!' Ashley says.

'I think she wants you to leave,' I say with zero authority or stature. He takes a step towards me and looks into my eyes, our foreheads almost touching.

'Yeah? Make me.'

'No, you know, I'm just saying,' I start to say. As I try to move out of his stare, I accidentally brush his forehead. This, apparently, was the trigger he'd been waiting for. He forces me to one side. And what I mean by that is, he rams his elbow into my face in the same place as the Nazi did the other week. Pain shoots through my cheek and I stumble, desperate to try to stay on my feet. I steady myself as Gary steps inside my flat and grabs Ashley. I touch my cheek, this is never going to heal.

'Gary! GARY, what the fuck are you doing? I'm warning you, get out, right now.'

'I just want to talk, babe. Come on, you owe me that.'

'This is not talking, this is assault. Let go of me or I swear to God you'll be sorry.' I go to rugby tackle Gary but the guy is built like a concrete bunker, so now I'm just a guy holding Gary's legs. Hmm, this didn't work as well as I'd hoped. He kicks out at me and catches my chin. More pain hurtles through my face. I let go, regretting ever opening the door.

Then suddenly Ashley elbows him in the stomach, flips him over and takes his legs out from under him. He crashes to the ground, surprised by her moves. She grabs his arm and rolls him onto his front. Little Ashley against brick shithouse guy? I watch with amazement. She pushes his arm up his back, threatening to dislocate it. He yells in pain. She leans into his ear and says,

'If you ever come back here or even so much as think about me again I will break your arm in so many places you'll need a full-time carer just to have a wank. I put up with your shit for too long. You hear me?'

'Fuck,' I hear Gary mumble out. 'Yes, yes!'

'I'm going to let you go now. You try something stupid, I will break your right knee then your left, understand?'

'Yes,' he says, more softly now, beaten.

'Okay,' she says, loosening her grip on him, she pulls him up. He feels his arm, looks at Ashley then me.

'Station's that way,' says Ashley, pointing towards Clapham High Street.

'I just wanted to say I'm sorry,' he says.

'You've said it. Goodbye Gary,' she says. He walks away, still rubbing his arm. I go over to her and we watch him leave together.

'So...where did you learn to do that?' I ask.

'I've been taking free self defence classes down the leisure centre. Turns out it's something I can actually do. You okay?'

'Apart from a nice new shiner, great.'

'It doesn't look that bad,' Ashley says, examining my face.

'Yeah, that's what everyone said about the last one.' Ashley walks back inside, leaving me to comprehend what just happened in my hallway. Christ. Life gets stranger by the day.

TWENTY FIVE – THE TRIP

Eight-thirty AM. I walk into the office.
Everyone is in the early editorial meeting. I sit
down and log onto the computer. It's strangely
quiet. No real news. As soon as my computer boots
up, I quickly sign into Facebook and request that
Lauren Bates be my friend. I look at my News
Feed. Very dull, nobody has anything of value to
say except, what the hell? Oh...my...God. I lean
forward, staring at the screen. Svetla has uploaded
some new photos of her at some swanky hotel
somewhere near Bristol. She's not alone. There
are fifteen pictures and four of them have the same
guy in them. I know, sounds paranoid, right? It's
not like he's even doing anything. There's no
kissing or hugging, but there's something
intangible. They're having fun, laughing at the
camera with a glass of wine in their hands. I move
the mouse and hover over his face. Nothing. I click
to the next picture and hover again, this time his
name comes up. Svetla has tagged him. 'Rupert
Gilbert.' Who the fuck is Rupert Gilbert? I click his

name. His public profile comes up. Unfortunately, there's almost nothing on it, he keeps his profile private. There are a few photos though. I click on the first picture and I'm taken aback by what I see. It's a photo of a bunch of people posing at the camera. Svetla, Rupert Gilbert and...Parker. I can't believe it. Parker knows Rupert fucking shitarse Gilbert. I check the date, the photo was posted last week. What the fuck does this mean?

People start filing back into the newsroom now, the meeting has ended. I scan further. I click on Parker's profile and photos, searching for Rupert Gilbert. My heart is in my mouth, feels like I've swallowed an anvil and can barely breathe, let alone move.

'So first thing you do when you get in is look at Facebook, is it Mr. Hayward?' Paul says, standing behind me. I close it down immediately.

'Sorry,' I say.

'Can you call Angela at Millbank and tell her we want her at St. Stephens Gate at ten please?'

'Sure,' I reply.

'You okay?' Paul asks.

'Yeah, couldn't be better.'

The day wears on and on and my mind is almost on fire with all the thinking I'm doing. I can barely hold a conversation, so consumed in working out what all this means. I need to call Parker. Or...maybe I should wait to see him. Do it in person? How could he? Calm Ollie, it might be perfectly reasonable. Yeah right, like my best mate has been working to supplant me.

Supplant...that's a word that doesn't get used all that much nowadays. Why am I thinking this?

Rupert and Svetla. Together. Svetla Gilbert...best man, Parker. What an arsehole. If he...God, I don't know what to think. As soon as I'm out of here, Parker is toast.

'...yeah okay, let me ask him,' Paul says, covering the phone. 'Ollie, how'd you fancy taking some money to Danny Arnold in Jo'burg?'

'What?' I reply, looking over the desk to Paul.

'Charles Wavery has just taken over the Congo in his little coup, right? You watch the news, yes?'

'Uh, right, yes,' I say, having no idea what he's talking about.

'Right and the team in Jo'burg need to go in tomorrow. But they need twenty thousand dollars in cash when they go, for bribes or whatever. So you need to book a taxi...have you got your passport?'

'Yeah, in my bag. Why don't you just wire the money?'

'Not safe. People get attacked outside those places in Jo'burg. Plus, it's cheaper just to fly you.'

'Right,' I reply.

'Okay, so book a taxi to Heathrow, pick up the cash and get on the next flight to Johannesburg. Once you've delivered the money you'll have to come straight back but it'll be a nice little adventure.'

'Uh, okay,' I reply, confused.

'Jason, when's the next flight to Jo'burg?' Paul shouts to the travel guy, Jason. A guy that looks like he should be doing shampoo adverts. Jason looks up from his monitor.

'Hang on,' he calls and peers back at his computer. 'Nineteen twenty-five, Terminal three,' he says. Paul turns to me.

'You okay with this?' he asks.

'Sure, you can count on me,' I say. Johannesburg...South Africa...fuck yeah!

As I sit in the cab on the way to Heathrow I ponder on the circumstances that lead me to this moment. Here I am, Ollie Hayward, a nobody on the way to Heathrow, paid for by someone else to take a shitload of cash to colleagues in South Africa. Outstanding. I'm still pissed off with Parker but what can I do about that now? He'll have to wait.

The cab pulls into Terminal three and I jump out. I have nothing on me other than the clothes I'm wearing and my passport. I walk into the terminal and look for the check in desks. I join the queue and wait patiently. Excited but also nervous. Jason gave me a few pointers and key pieces of information on the way. In no particular order, they are:

- My flight code is JSZTRD.
- When I pick up the money, I have to count it and count it again.
- When I go through customs, I MUST NOT get caught with it in my pocket. I MUST NOT say anything to anyone (this part sounded a bit naughty but what the hell, I take the drugs mule attitude to this sort of work.)
- I MUST NOT tell anyone how much cash I'm carrying.
- When they give me one of those green cards to fill in on the plane, I MUST tick 'Tourist.'

I finally get to the front of the queue. The pretty brunette at the counter smiles as she calls me forward.

'Hello sir, where are you travelling this evening?'

'Uh Johannesburg,' I say, trying not to fidget.

'May I see your passport, please?' I quickly hand it over. She taps something into the computer and scans my passport. The computer beeps, an eyebrow heads north. She looks at me. I smile and swallow at the same time, my face displaying a slightly druggy look. She picks up the phone and waits. Oh shit. She knows. She knows what I'm doing is illegal and I haven't even got the cash yet. Doesn't matter, she can see right through me. She's calling security. Maybe I should just walk away. Oh God, Jason didn't tell me what to do in this situation. She whispers into the phone, I can't hear what she's saying. I glance round at the passengers waiting, they stare right back. They know. They all know. I want to scream 'I'm not a drug's mule! I'm a journalist!' but I can't. Have to wait for judgement to pass. She puts the phone down and looks at me.

'I'm sorry sir, there is a little problem here. We seem to be overbooked on this flight,' she says.

'Oh, right,' I reply. Unexpected. I suppose, good, given a second ago I was thinking arrest and incarceration.

'I'm afraid we will have to upgrade you to First Class.' Afraid? She's afraid she's going to have to upgrade me! That's a hoot.

'Oh, that's fine,' I say. Fine? It's the fucking best thing that's happened all year. A boarding pass prints out and she hands it to me.

'Here you go sir. I'm sorry for the inconvenience,' she says with a face that appears genuinely sorry.

'No, it's a good thing, really. Thank you,' I reply, taking the boarding pass. I can't believe it. First Class. I'm going to fly to South Africa First bloody Class!

I head over to the travel money counter. I flip out the reference code Jason gave me. A tall man in a waistcoat but no jacket greets me. He has too many teeth for his mouth and his smile is mildly uncomfortable.

'Hello sir, how can I help you?'

'Ollie Hayward from TBN, I believe you have some US dollars for me,' I say. I hand over my passport and Press Pass.

'Yes indeed sir, hold on two seconds,' he replies. He leaves the desk but quickly returns with a clear plastic bag. He pulls out a chunk of money. My eyes widen. Each note is one hundred dollars with the entire wodge being the thickness of a brick!

'Twenty thousand US Dollars. Would you like me to count it for you?'

'Yes please,' I say, not taking my eyes off the money. He counts it out. It takes five minutes. That's right, five minutes. Because I make him do it three times, after which, I sense he wants me to leave. I sign for the money and tuck it into the inside pocket of my coat.

I head towards security. Moment of truth, this is where I either get on a plane in First Class or go to jail for money trafficking. I show my boarding pass to the man on the entrance, he examines it and stares at me. I attempt a non-guilty smile, he frowns. Shit. He looks back at the boarding pass then waves me through. Phew, first bit out of the way. I join a security queue and shuffle along patiently. I feel the wodge in my pocket then quickly remind myself not to draw attention. I glance at the security men in front of me. The first guy is asking a whale of a man to remove his belt. Hope nothing falls down, that would be horrible. Fatty walks through the metal detector, it beeps. Another security guy wands him then waves him through. I get to the conveyor belt and remove my jacket, careful to fold it so nothing is visible. All change and metal goes in the little box and I step up to the metal detector. I don't look at the x-ray machine as my coat moves slowly inside. I step through, nothing happens. The security man indicates for me to carry on. I head to the end of the x-ray conveyor. The belt has stopped. The guy on the monitor is peering intently at it. Oh shit. He's seen it. This is it. Nice one Ollie. Should have had the cash on my person. So stupid. The conveyor moves, I see my coat pop out and roll towards me. I glance at the security man on the monitor again. His face has resumed its bored expression. I grab my coat and carefully put it back on. I subtly feel for the money, it's still there. I walk into duty-free hearing nothing but the cheers of imaginary people inside my head.

TWENTY SIX – A FLIGHT INTO THE WILD

When I board the plane (before anyone else), I show my boarding pass to the stewardess.

'Welcome onboard Mr. Hayward, this way please,' she says, smiling as First Class stewardess' do. Because they don't have to deal with the riff-raff. Only people of a certain class, First Class, one might say chuff, chuff.

She leads me to the left which is my new favourite direction when boarding a plane. She takes me to my seat which also doubles as...a bed. A freaking bed! I know, I know I need to calm down but look at this.

'Here you go, sir,' she says.

'Great, thanks,' I say, barely able to contain myself.

'Would you like a glass of Champagne, sir?' Hmm. Would I like a glass of Champagne? Interesting question.

'That would be lovely,' I reply, exactly like

someone who does this every week. The stewardess disappears to the bar. And I mean proper bar. Not the place at the back and middle of the aircraft you're not allowed to see because they close the curtains. I mean bar like you get in London. With bartender and everything. Brilliant. I can't help it, I've got to call someone. I dial Lauren's number. It rings, once, twice-

'Hello?'

'It's Ollie.'

'Hi, I was just leaving work,' she says. I glance at my watch. Ten past seven.

'Bit late, isn't it?'

'Had some bits to catch up on. A weekend away is great but there's always payback when you get back. How are you?'

'You'll never guess where I am?'

'Uh, having tea with the Queen?'

'No. I'm sitting on the tarmac at Heathrow, about to start drinking a glass of Champagne on my way to, wait for it...Johannesburg.'

'What?'

'They want me to take some cash to a reporter there. So,' I lower my voice to a whisper, 'I'm sitting here with twenty thousand dollars, in cash, in my pocket, and they put me in First Class! How cool is that?'

'That is very cool. You lucky sod.'

'I know. I can't believe it.'

'How long are you out there?'

'Not long, I have to come straight back but even so...'

'Still very cool. Have one for me, okay?'

'I will, oh she's coming back, better go. See

you soon.'

'Okay, bye,' she whispers back. Don't know why she was whispering but still. The stewardess returns with a tall glass of Champagne and sets it down next to me.

'There you go, sir. Would you like a massage during the flight?' If there had been a camera filming me at this point, I would have turned to face it and pulled a big smiley face. Hmm, would I like a massage during the flight, let me think, uhh-

'Sure,' I say. The stewardess smiles. I obviously gave her the right answer.

'Very good sir, I'll come and find you once we're airborne. If there's anything at all you need, please do not hesitate to call me. I'm at your disposal.'

'Thank you,' I reply.

We take off and I swear I cannot stop smiling. What's wrong with me? I know it's not that amazing but somehow these things are always more special when someone else is paying. I feel light-headed from the Champagne. One thing I'm not doing is thinking about Rupert 'crapshag' Gilbert. The seat belt sign clicks off and the stewardess comes to find me, just as she said she would.

'Is now a good time for your massage, sir?'

'Sure,' I say.

'Come this way please,' she says. I stand, remove my coat (with the twenty thousand inside) and follow her to the bar area, leaving the money on my seat. What? It's First Class, no one's going to steal anything here. Twenty thousand is small change to these guys. A couple of other passengers sit at the bar chatting to each other. The stewardess asks me to sit in a special seat and lean my face forward into this towel covered ring. I do exactly as I'm told.

'So what brings you to Johannesburg,' she asks, beginning to kneed and push my skin through my shirt. I need to tell her a believable story here. I'm a businessman going for a set of meetings. No, I'm professional skier, South Africa is great this time of year. I don't know what to say.

'I'm a journalist working for TBN, I'm supposed to take twenty thousand US Dollars in cash to the correspondent out there and give it to him then take the next plane back.' Shit. I don't see her reaction but her voice doesn't sound surprised.

'Oh, that sounds very important, sir,' she says. Hmm, maybe it isn't that impressive. I guess if you hang round these sorts of people all the time, movie stars, important business men, I guess my story is a little lame. I'm aware suddenly that I'm looking at the floor, away from my seat with the money sitting in my jacket. And I just told this girl where it is. Yeah I know, pretty stupid.

Luckily she finishes the massage and I head back to my seat to discover...the money is still there. Phew! Close one. Ha, you thought something was going to happen with the money, didn't you? Well it didn't, so there.

I arrive in Johannesburg, rested and more ready for the day than after any flight I've ever been on. I move cautiously through customs. For some reason I'm not so nervous going through passport control here, couldn't tell you why. I make it to baggage pickup and await my luggage. I stand for maybe two whole minutes before remembering I don't have any bags. Feeling mildly stupid and cursing myself for wasting time, I head to the 'Nothing to Declare' corridor. Here we go. There are four guys in blue uniforms wearing baseball caps. Two of them have already got passengers, but the other two are on the lookout. Shit. Just stay cool. What you're doing is totally legal. Twenty thousand dollars. Twenty thousand dollars. Just here. In my pocket. I walk, eyes front, as we all do. I would tell you the customs guy asked me to stop. I would say I nervously turned to face him, only for him to hand me the wallet that had dropped out of my back pocket. And both you and I would breathe a sigh of relief. However, that would be embellishing the story. It just didn't happen and I'm not going to lie to make you like me more.

I walk out of a set of double doors and into a crowd of people, most of whom hold signs. I search for my name. Nothing. I get to the end of the line then I spot someone almost hiding behind a large woman with a silly looking hat. 'Ollie Hayward – TBN.' I walk over to him.

'Hi, I'm Ollie Hayward,' I say.

'I am Jeffrey. I am here to take you to Mr. Arnold, sir. Do you have any bags?' he replies. Jeffrey is a broad, black man with what looks like a small scar on his cheek. He's in his mid-forties and wears a smart suit.

'No, I'm good thanks mate,' I say.

'Please,' he says, indicating to follow him which I do. We walk out of arrivals and I'm immediately hit by the warm air and smell of aviation fuel. Everything looks different. There are different cars, different looking people with different clothes. Jeffrey takes me to the airport car park and over to a white Mercedes E-Class with blacked out windows. We get in and drive away.

'Did you have a pleasant flight, sir?' Jeffrey asks.

'Yeah, great thanks,' I reply, 'hope you weren't waiting too long?'

'Not long, sir,' he replies. We don't speak much more, I stare out of the window at the various types of car on the road and the people driving them. I note the dry landscape and huge township to my left as we travel to our destination. I find it all fascinating. I've heard so much about this place, it's exhilarating. I half expect to see a lion or an elephant walking along the side of the motorway, instead I just see people. There are loads of makeshift vans and overloaded trucks which can't possibly be roadworthy or legal.

Eventually we turn off the motorway and into a private estate. I stare as we drive past one massive house after another, all with ten foot high electrified fencing with signs that say things like 'ADT – Armed Response.' People really don't want you to come in around here unless you're invited. We pull up outside a gate, Jeffrey takes out a remote and presses the button. Slowly the gates open. We head along a winding driveway, surrounded by immaculate gardens, to an impressive two storey house. Large blue trees are dotted all over the estate and the house is covered in wisteria and what looks like the South African version of ivy. It's a beautiful place. The car stops and we get out.

'Ollie?' a tall, handsome man wearing an open white shirt greets me. Danny Arnold. Seen him so many times on the TV. He looks different in real life, older perhaps.

'Danny, hi. How's it going?' I say, shaking his hand.

'Good, how was your flight. Everything okay?'

'Yep, everything was great,' I say, trying to reassure him. The money is here. I still have the money. I didn't fuck it up.

'Come in, come in,' he says. 'No bags?'

'No, just me,' I reply.

I follow him inside. It's an open-plan house, the doors and windows letting in all the available air. I glimpse a swimming pool in the garden. We walk through the hallway and into the kitchen to see a woman with her back turned to me.

'Darling, this is Ollie,' Danny says. The woman turns round, a vague expression on her face, as if she had been a million miles away. She smiles and offers her hand which I shake.

'Hi Ollie, I'm Martina glad you made it. Was the flight okay? It's so long, isn't it?'

'Yes, but I got upgraded, so it was actually pretty cool.'

'Really, they upgraded you?' Danny replies, eyebrows rising.

'Yeah, not sure why. Something about being overbooked.'

'That Jason, he knows how to manipulate the system. Would you like something to drink? Coke, orange juice? Something stronger?' Martina asks.

'Uh, Coke's fine thanks,' I say.

'You boys go outside, I'll bring it out,' says Martina. We do as instructed.

The garden is bigger than I first thought. The pool goes back at least ten metres. But the most impressive thing are the big blue trees. They look like oaks except all of them have bright blue flowers.

'What are those trees?' I ask. 'They're everywhere.' Danny glances in the direction I'm pointing.

'The trees? Jacarandas. They look great but those flowers get in the pool and it's a real pain in the arse,' he replies. We walk over to a white metal table and chairs and sit down.

'So Ollie, you have the money?' Danny asks.

'Yep, here you go,' I say, pulling out the wodge and placing it in front of him. Feels like I should have bought a briefcase to go with that much money.

'Great,' he replies, 'I hope you don't think me rude but I'd better count it.'

'Go right ahead,' I say. So I sit and watch, while Danny counts the money. Martina brings out Cokes for everyone and sits next to Danny.

'Is he counting it in front of you, so rude,' she says, smiling.

'It's not rude, if I'm even a hundred dollars down, that comes out of my wages darling,' Danny says. They exchange a look.

'Don't worry. I understand,' I say, interjecting. Martina turns to me.

'So Ollie, what do you do at TBN?' she asks.

'I'm a producer. Doing interviews, looking after

court cases, that sort of thing,' I reply. Martina nods.

'And do you have a girlfriend?' she asks. Danny looks up from counting.

'Jesus Christ Martina, you can't ask him that.'

'I can ask him anything I want,' she says. Awkward. I try to calm things down again.

'I don't mind,' I say to Danny. 'I did, but we split up.'

'Ahhh,' Martina says.

'No it's okay. I've found someone else. At least, I think I have.'

'Not sure about her?' Martina asks. Danny looks up from counting and sighs.

'No I am. I am. Just, it's new and...she's quite different to Svetla.'

'You still have feelings for your ex?' Martina asks.

'Darling, maybe Ollie doesn't want to talk about this stuff,' Danny says with forced politeness.

'No it's fine, really. We were together for a couple of years and maybe I just need to let go but...'

'A heartbreaker?' Martina asks. I nod slowly.

'Yeah. But then, maybe I broke hers? So I guess we're even,' I reply. I opt not to start talking about Rupert Gilbert, whoever he is. Not going to think about him, he'll only spoil my trip to South Africa but when I get home-

'And what about this new girl?'

'Lauren? She's great. She's better than great. Yeah. She's really pretty.'

'Nice tits?' Danny asks. I smile.

'Daniel Arnold,' Martina says, frowning. Danny chuckles. I laugh.

'Yeah,' I say.

'Just have to get used to her not being your ex-girlfriend, right Ollie?' she says. I look at Martina. Something about her looks tired and yet this line of questioning seems to have engaged her.

'Right, I guess,' I say.

'Sometimes you can spend your entire life searching for someone who's right in front of you. Except you don't realise they're even there because they don't match what you think you were looking for. That's how it was with Danny and me. I was his producer, setting up his interviews, doing his interviews, writing his scripts-'

'You rarely wrote my scripts,' Danny says.

'Okay darling,' she then mouths me to me, 'I did.' I smile. 'What I'm saying is, you've got to look at what's in front of you, not what's behind you. Because you could be missing out on the best thing that ever happened to you and you wouldn't even know it because you were too busy looking the other way.' I nod slowly. 'Although fifteen years later, let me tell you it does lose a certain degree of its romance.'

'Thanks for that,' Danny says.

'Well, he's always off somewhere or other. I'm stuck here being housewife. It's funny, how you imagine things will end up and how they actually do.' Danny clears his throat, they exchange a look.

'Let's not do this now, huh?' he says.

'Whatever you want. Darling,' she says. The tension is uncomfortable.

'Shame I can't stay longer. Would have loved

to see more of South Africa,' I say.

'It is a shame. I could have taken you out to a friend's farm. He's got all the Big Five there and some black rhino as well,' Martina says.

'Big Five?'

'Elephant, lion, buffalo, rhino, leopard,' she replies.

'Maybe he should call London,' Danny says, turning to me, 'check in, you know?' I nod.

'Yeah, maybe I should,' I say, unsure exactly what I'm supposed to do, given this is my first ever foreign trip.

'You can use the phone inside, I'll show you,' says Martina. I follow Martina into the living room and over to the phone. There are paintings of lions and elephants. There are also strange African statuettes dotted around the room. 'Why don't you call this girl?'

'Nah, couldn't use your phone-'

'Don't be silly, TBN pick up the bill anyway. Go on, call her, I bet she'd love to hear from you, time difference is the same as London too,' she says. I nod. Why not, what harm could it do?

'Okay, thanks.'

'If you need anything, just shout,' she says, walking out. I dial the foreign desk number and check in with Robert, the foreign editor. He speaks with a posh accent, you'd never guess he was born in Peckham. He seems surprised I'm calling.

'I thought you were coming straight back,' he says.

'I am, just...Danny said-'

'I've got an earthquake in New Zealand, three British soldiers dead in Afghanistan and a G20 meeting. I'm hoping you can make the flight on your own,' Robert says. Jesus. Alright, no need to be an arsehole about it.

'Okay, yeah...sorry. See you later.'

'Yeah,' he replies, hanging up. What a cock. I shake my head and dial Lauren's number.

'Hello?'

'Lauren, it's Ollie.'

'Oh hi, Ollie I'm just in a meeting, can I call you back?' she whispers.

'Uh, yeah. Well no, I'm sort of at the reporter's house.'

'What about your mobile?'

'Not sure I can receive the calls, you can try.'

'Okay, you get there okay?'

'Yeah. Hey, if I don't speak to you, I'm...thinking about you,' I say.

'Me too, speak soon. Bye,' she says. Probably the two most unsuccessful back-to-back phone calls I've ever made. Then a name pings back into my memory. Rupert Gilbert.

TWENTY SEVEN – HAVING WORDS

Saturday. My flight touches down at Heathrow at six in the morning. I spend the entire flight pondering two things. Martina's advice and the state of her relationship with Danny after being together so long and what I'm going to do about Rupert 'fucktard' Gilbert.

If I really do want to heed what Martina said I should just leave Mr. Gilbert and Svetla to it and let them be happy. I shouldn't make Parker feel bad about being friends with a shitkicking bumclot like him or for being in touch with my ex behind my back. I should just let it all wash over me. I have a wonderful new girlfriend. There's no need to continue pining over Svetla. And yet...I want to know. I want to know why Parker is friends with this guy? How does he know him, how does Svetla? I want answers and I'll explode if I don't find out.

I accidently (on purpose) bang the door shut when I get in. It's 09:25 A.M. Both the living room and Parker's doors are closed. All is quiet. I walk down the hallway and into my room, listening for

233

any signs of life. I sit down on the bed and run a hand through my hair, breathing out slowly. Then I head into the kitchen to make coffee. I wait as the kettle boils, my mind playing over what I'm going to say when Parker shows himself. I glance out of the window, mostly blue skies with a few clouds dotted around, should be a nice day. Do I need to do this? Couldn't I just rise above it all, like Martina said? Maybe I could try, maybe I could just see how-

I hear Parker's door open. I wait, almost counting the steps until he appears at the door.

'You ever heard of entering quietly?' he says. He's wearing boxers and a T-shirt and let me tell you ladies and gentlemen, it is not a pretty sight. He looks like a fat Jesus, except without the beard or street-cred. I say nothing, trying to gather the words. He apparently doesn't find this strange, or he's still half asleep. He walks over and pulls the milk out of the fridge.

'You making coffee?' he asks, yawning.

'No, I'm inflating a bouncy castle,' I reply. He opens the cupboard and pulls out another mug.

'Why is there always a sarcastic reply to that question? A simple yes would have sufficed. Two sugars, please,' he says.

'I've been living with you for two years, I know how many sugars you have,' I reply. My tone is mildly threatening and judging by the way his eyes dart left and right, he seems to be processing that.

'Everything go okay in South Africa?' he asks.

'Yeah, everything went great,' I reply, with a needless amount of sarcasm.

'Am I missing something?'

'Loyalty,' I say under my breath.

'Huh?'

'Okay, I'm going to ask you something and I'd appreciate the truth.'

'Sounds heavy, can I have my coffee first?' he asks. What the hell do I say to that? No?

'Fine,' I say. The kettle boils, I pour the water into the mugs. We stand saying nothing to each other.

'Well...this is awkward,' he says.

'Are you friends with someone called Rupert Gilbert?' I ask. He stares at me, blinks, then after what feels like an age, he sighs.

'Yeah,' he replies, looking down.

'Who is he?'

'Fuck I knew this would happen. I told her-'

'Try telling me, huh?' I say, trying to reign in my anger.

'Okay, look I met him at this party ages ago. He knew Svetla-'

'How?'

'I don't know. Maybe he worked with her or...I don't know.'

'And?'

'And she introduced me to him and we sort of got on. He owns a Harley dude. But...obviously that's not important. Svetla left to talk to other people and I was sort of stuck with him but he was cool, you know.'

'Okay, but why are you still hanging out with them?' I ask.

'I dunno man. I just...he's cool. I should have told you but I knew you'd go nuts so...I won't see either of them ever again if that's what you want,' he says. I breathe in. It's fine. So what if she's going out with someone Parker happens to know and like. She's single, she can go out with anyone she wants I suppose.

'Well, it has been six months, she was always going to meet someone else eventually, I guess,' I say.

'Yeah, just a bit of an arse they met when you guys were still together.'

'What? Jesus Christ, Parker-'

'I know. I should have said something but you and Svetla were having a really bad time of it back then. Just before you split up, remember? You were arguing and shouting at each other and I didn't want to make it worse. I sort of told myself, I don't know, maybe she wasn't shagging him. Maybe I'd misunderstood.'

'So, this is who she's with now?'

'I'm not sure-'

'Don't bullshit me,' I say. He looks to the ceiling and puts his hands on top of his head.

'Yes,' he replies. I stare at him, unable to speak. Rage courses through me. The fact he even knows this, tells me all sorts of things. My best friend has been keeping the biggest secret from me. That my girlfriend and some guy were shagging around behind my back. My best friend thought he didn't need to tell me. My best friend, who's also 'friends' with said shagger. I try to think of something to say that I won't regret but find myself wondering why exactly this guy is my best friend.

'Where is she?' I ask.

'What do you mean?'

'Where's she staying?'

'Mate, I don't think-'

'I don't give a shit what you think, where the fuck are they living? You must know, you're friends on Facebook, so cough it up,' I say.

'It doesn't have addresses on Facebook,' he replies, quietly. I glare at him, eyes on fire. 'Shepherd's Bush. He owns a house on Brackenbury Road.'

'Number?'

'Mate, don't do this. Just leave her alone-'

'What's the fucking number?!' I shout, shaking with anger. He's shocked at my tone. So am I, but I'm so furious I can barely control myself.

'I don't know! It's a big blue house at the end of the street, it's obvious. Mate I-'

I turn and storm out of the flat before he can say anything further. I stomp along Northcote road towards Clapham Junction. Thoughts smack me as I walk. How long were they shagging whilst she was with me? When did she decide to leave me for him?

I turn the corner and up St John's Hill to the main entrance of Clapham Junction station. I slam my Oyster card on the reader and head through the barrier, marching towards the Overground platform. The train takes what feels like an age to arrive. I jump on and even though there are plenty of seats, I stand. I try not to let my thoughts form into sentences or questions. I stare out of the window as the train moves off towards Shepherds Bush. Houses and trees trundle past. We ride over the Thames, in the distance I see Battersea Power Station. Four massive cooling towers are all that remain of the ugly shell of a building.

By the time we pull into Shepherd's Bush station I'm standing next to the doors. They open and I'm away. I get out my iPhone and type in Brackenbury Road into the map. It's a twenty minute walk. Fine. Whatever it takes. I head west, following my iPhone.

In a record fifteen minutes, I round the corner of Brackenbury Road and start looking for a blue house. Parker said it was at the end. I walk down the street and come across...a big blue Georgian terraced house. I look up. Stone steps lead up to a blue door. It's three storeys and it has a basement with a window. Every house along this road looks the same. There's a window box with pink flowers under the first floor window. I walk up the steps and bang on the door. I hear someone coming, and ready myself. The door opens and a man steps out in front of me. He wears wire-thin glasses, a dressing gown and slippers. He also has a half smoked cigarette in his mouth and a bowl of cereal in his hand. He looks like a drug addict with zero prospects. This is the guy she left me for?

'Can I help you?' he asks, politely.

'Does someone called Svetla live here?' I ask. He eyes me suspiciously.

'Yeah. Who are you?' he asks, frowning. From behind him, I hear her voice.

'Who is it?' she asks, suddenly appearing at the door. Her surprise is clear when she sees me. 'Ollie? What are you doing here?'

'I thought we'd have a chat,' I say, calmer than even I thought possible. Rupert glances at Svetla seemingly unsure whether he has to fight me or not.

'You shouldn't be here,' she says, moving past Rupert. She wears tracky bottoms and a hoodie with a worn Thundercat logo. The hoodie she used to wear when we had days off together.

'I just want to know how long it was going on for,' I say.

'Shh,' she whispers, turning back.

'Listen mate, I know it's hard-,' Rupert starts to say.

'I'm not talking to you, I'm talking to Svetla,' I say, my heart about ready to burst.

'Rupert, just let me handle this, okay. Go inside. Please,' she says. He looks at me and shrugs, taking another spoonful of cereal. I watch him go, buoyed by this smallest of victories.

'Let me get some shoes and we'll go around the corner, okay?' she says. I roll my eyes but say nothing. I'm not the sort of arsehole that makes people walk around with no shoes on, even if the person is my cheating whore of an ex.

She reappears at the door and steps out, closing it behind her.

'Let's go,' she says. I follow her as we walk away from the stupid blue house. Who paints their house blue anyway?

'So?' I say, after fifty yards.

'Did Parker tell you?'

'Doesn't matter who told me, just tell me you weren't screwing around with dealer boy there whilst you were still with me.'

'He's not a dealer. We just got up.'

'Were you?' I ask. We stop walking, she turns to face me.

'Look Ollie-'

'No. I want the truth.'

'Yes. Okay, yes.' Her words cut straight into me. I involuntarily step back, I think I might be sick. 'We were miserable. Don't you remember? We went days where you barely even acknowledged me.' I can't believe what I'm hearing, I sort of believed...hoped that this was some sort of misunderstanding. I know there was overwhelming evidence but even so. She looks at me, her worried expression almost passing for convincing. 'I'm not excusing what I did,' she says. 'I should have just left but I couldn't. I couldn't leave you. You mean more to me than anyone. And leaving you was the hardest thing I've ever done. I'm still not completely over it, even now.' I pick up on that last part. She's still not over me. Good. I hope you never are. 'Should I have done it sooner? Yes. Should I have been fairer to you? Yes, I should. But there are two people here. Two people that made mistakes. I'm willing to accept my part but you've got to accept yours.'

'Yeah right. I didn't fuck someone else though,' I say. She looks down and sighs.

'You want revenge? You want to hurt me? Say the things you want to say and go. Maybe we both need some finality here.'

'Big word. Rupert teach you that?' I say. She glares at me, then her eyes relax and she smiles.

'Say what you want. I never stopped loving you. And you know what's really sad about all this, what's so pathetic on my part. I still do. I still bloody love you. Even after all the shit you put me through. What kind of a person does that?' A tear rolls down her cheek, she brushes it away. I won't let her get to me. She has questions to answer. But look at her. She's beaten. What am I supposed to do now, carry on? Have her run off? Think of me as an even bigger arsehole. She's right, I drove her away. I've got as far as admitting that to myself. Maybe I did deserve this.

'I hate that you can still do this to me. It's pathetic,' she says. My breathing is calmer now, although my heart is thumping like it's trying escape from my chest. I look at her. The girl I once loved. The girl I can't let go. This one person who showed me everything I know about love and the meaning of being close to someone. Reduced to this. What a waste.

'And Parker?' I ask.

'He kept telling me to tell you. I just couldn't...find the moment. He said you'd find out, that I wasn't being fair. He even threatened to tell you himself. I persuaded him not to. Just to let things be as they were. We were practically split up anyway. What was the point of making things worse?'

I lean against a wall and look up at the sky. What a karzi.

'So this Rupert guy. Do you love him?'

'I don't hate him. And I didn't have a place to stay so...thought it made sense but...we're quite different. He's got a kid. Not sure I'm ready for all that. She's such a little brat as well.' I smile. We say nothing for a moment. A thought enters my mind, a stupid, immature question I mustn't ask.

'What about the sex?' I ask. She looks up, confusion on her face.

'Are you kidding?' she asks.

'No.'

'All this, and you want to know if he's better in bed?'

'Yeah, I think I have a right to know. Maybe that was the real reason you left.'

'I just told you it wasn't.'

'Yeah well, you would say that. I mean, what you going to say, 'sorry Ollie, Rupert's a fucking porn star in the sack?' She frowns at me then shakes her head.

'Well?' I say. Another tear runs down her face.

'No, Ollie. I loved you. You were my first and my most special. You think someone like Rupert can come anywhere close.' She sighs. 'I'm tired Ollie. Tired of this, tired of you. I think it would be best for the both of us if you just left me alone.' I take a step back, suddenly everything is very real. I feel panicked by her words.

'Right, so this is it?'

'No,' she says. 'It was 'it' six months ago. Neither of us has had the courage to admit it. I'm done. With all of it.' She turns and starts heading back towards the house.

'Hang on, where you going?' I ask. She turns back to me.

'Fuck off Ollie. I mean it. Leave me the fuck alone,' she shouts back to me. I hear her voice tremble on the last word. In the entire time we were together, Svetla had never sworn like that. I watch her go, helpless. I want desperately to stop her but she's made herself clearer than ever before. Leave her alone.

TWENTY EIGHT – GETTING OVER

The journey back from Shepherd's Bush seems to take forever. A thousand memories fly through me, each presenting itself in absolute clarity before being replaced by another equally painful, happy snapshot with Svetla. All those moments. All those special times dissolved to shit. Memories that now leave a sour taste. Somehow even the arguments seem preferable to this. I feel drained, empty and desperately sad. It's all I can do to stop myself from breaking down in the middle of the street. Svetla, out of my life forever.

I get to the station and swipe my Oyster card. I stand on the platform staring down at the track, in a trance. I just can't believe it. Somewhere, I guess I thought, maybe we'd...I don't know what I thought.

When I open the door to the flat, I hear voices talking. I enter quietly and close the door behind me. Ashley and Parker are talking in the living room, I stand and listen in the hallway.

'...he doesn't hate you. Just needs to calm

down, that's all,' Ashley says.

'So stupid, I just didn't want to cause him any more pain, been through enough already and they had pretty much split up anyway-,' Parker replies.

'I know.'

The conversation stops. I open the front door again and close it loudly. Parker opens the living room door.

'Alright?' he asks.

'Not really,' I say. My anger for Parker has all but gone. I don't hold anything against him. He's not the sort of person who would deliberately screw me over.

'Did you see her?' he asks.

'Yeah,' I reply. Ashley appears next to Parker.

'Hey,' she says.

'Hi,' I say.

'I'm making coffee, you guys want?' she asks. Parker looks at me. I shrug.

'Take that as a yes,' he says to Ashley, 'I'll have a cup as well, if that's alright?' She nods, and touches my shoulder as she moves past us. Parker heads back into the living room and sits down. I follow him. We sit opposite each other, neither saying anything for a moment. I hear the kettle boil in the kitchen. 'So what did she say?' he asks.

'She told me never to contact her again,' I reply.

'Did you shout at her?'

'No. I was angry but I didn't shout. She said she was tired of dealing with...this. Don't blame her. I have been slightly psychotic about it.'

'Yeah. Still, be better if your friends were more supportive,' Parker says. I glance at him, he looks genuinely sorry. I go to say something but Ashley walks in with two cups of coffee and some Digestive biscuits on a plate.

'Try the biscuits first,' she says, 'I have no idea how long they've been in there.'

'Thanks,' I say.

'Parker told me what happened,' Ashley says.

'She told him she doesn't want to see him again,' Parker says. Ashley looks at me.

'Ah,' she says, sitting down next to me. She starts to rub my knee.

'What she actually said was fuck off,' I say. Parker raises his eyebrows.

'Svelta said fuck off? Wow,' he says.

'Yeah. Never heard her speak like that,' I reply, replaying her face in my mind as she said those words.

'You gonna be okay?' Ashley asks. I nod, automatically. The truth is I have no idea if I'll be okay. If she means, will my heart keep beating, will my lungs keep taking in air, then yes, I'll be okay.

'Sorry guys, I know I'm being pathetic,' I say.

'No you're not,' Parker says. I look at Ashley who gives me a sympathetic smile.

'He's right. You're just sad. Understandably. We've all had relationships not work out, and it's horrible when that happens. The fact is, it ended a long time ago and you've been holding on to it. On to her. It's time to let her go. You've got Lauren-' I almost sneer as she says Lauren's name. Don't get me wrong, Lauren's great. She just has one problem. She's not Svetla. 'Lauren's really nice and she's got big tits which has to be a positive when we're looking at these things,' Ashley says. I chuckle, so does Parker. 'Don't dismiss Lauren just because you've had your head up your arse over Svetla.'

'You know what we should do?' Parker says. 'We should go out. All of us. You, me, Ash, Lauren, Nicola. It'll cheer us up. Ashley's only just split up with Norman-'

'Yeah, thanks for reminding me,' Ashley says.

'So, let's go out. Clubbing.'

'I really don't feel like clubbing,' I say.

'Of course you don't...until you get there,' Parker says.

Jamboree. I stare at the sign above the door. I don't want to do this but Parker just wouldn't shut up. What I wanted to do was sit in my room and feel sorry for myself whilst thumbing through old photos and watching videos of me and Svetla.

The air has a chill to it, summer coming to an end? It barely even started. Anyway, present are myself, Ashley, Nicola, (who's wearing knee-high boots) and Parker who's wearing a shirt and has something in his hair that makes it look permanently wet. What a sad case. Do women go for that? Nicola seems suitably impressed. Thank God girls care more about things like personality than looks. I called Lauren but she didn't answer, so I left a message telling her what we were doing, where and when. I'd like to see her again but I don't want her to pick up any self-pitying vibes, so it would be fine if she didn't come. We pay our ten pounds entry fee (ten pounds, Jesus I'm getting old) and go in.

We are immediately greeted by thumping R&B music. It's already rammed and I feel an immediate urge to leave. Ashley presses her finger into my back pushing me to carry on. The bar runs along one side, a blue neon strip lighting the floor directly underneath it. People dance wherever they can find a space. The place is full of girls who wear very little and guys who spend a lot of time in the gym. We find a dark corner and stand looking at each other.

'Drinks?' Parker asks.

'I'll get them,' I say.

'You stay where you are,' Parker replies. 'What do you want?'

'Beer, anything,' I reply. Parker goes round, taking orders then disappears off to the bar with Nicola.

'Is Lauren coming then?' Ashley asks.

'I don't know. She didn't answer. Probably not,' I reply.

'Then you'll just have to settle for me,' Ashley replies.

'I don't 'settle' for you. You're a good friend.'

'No I'm not, but thanks for the sentiment.'

'Heard anything from Norman?'

'You don't have to small talk with me, Ollie.'

'I'm not, just asking.'

'No. Norman is gone.'

'And job hunt?' I ask.

'Nothing yet but I'm looking. Don't worry, you'll get your rent.'

'I don't care about that.'

'Yeah you do.'

'Maybe you should do something with the piano stuff. You were really good.'

'Thanks,' she replies, offering nothing more. 'Look at that girl there.' I look to where she's pointing.

'Who?'

'Who?' she repeats, sarcastically. 'You know exactly who I'm talking about.' I'm afraid Ashley is right. There's a girl dancing in the middle of four guys who has almost nothing on. I'm not kidding. She's wearing what looks like a swimsuit type thing with a skirt so short it's almost unworthy of the title 'skirt.'

'Yeah okay,' I reply.

'You think she's fit?'

'No,' I reply, automatically. Ashley turns to me, her eyebrow raised.

'Alright yes, but in an obvious way.'

'Look at those guys staring at her.' We watch her moving and gyrating to the music. All attention within a five-metre radius focused on her. 'Maybe I should start doing stuff like that, at least I'd get a shag.'

'Well, if that's all you want,' I say, smiling. She chuckles.

'You're off limits now, you have a girlfriend.'

'Yeah. Bummer.'

'For you. Definitely,' she replies. I smile. Parker and Nicola return with drinks.

'Stella for you,' Parker says offering me the glass. 'The white wine is for Ash,' he says to Nicola who hands Ashley the wine.

'Thanks,' Ashley says.

'So, Parker tells me you've been stalking your

ex,' Nicola says. I stare at Parker who looks like his eyes are about to pop out of his head. He quickly shakes his head.

'What? No, that's not what I said,' Parker says.

'I'm not stalking her. I just...' I stop in mid-flow. What was I doing? Trying to get her back? Making her feel guilty for not taking me back? '...had trouble accepting it was over.'

'But you've got a new girlfriend now?'

'Baby, I don't think you should-' Parker says.

'It's okay,' I say to Parker. 'Yes.'

'But, you don't like her as much as your ex?'

'It's new and I'm...adjusting.'

'As I previously indicated, she does have a very nice pair though,' says Ashley.

'Why do you keep bringing up her tits?' Parker asks.

'Yeah, why do you, Ash?' I say.

'What? A woman can't comment on another woman's tits?'

'Sure. In fact I actively encourage it. But you seem to have a mild obsession with Lauren's,' I say.

'Is she fit then, this girl?' Nicola asks, the alcohol clearly loosening her tongue. Ashley nods.

'Yeah, a bit too fit actually,' Ashley replies.

'Girl crush?' Nicola says. Ashley smiles and sips her drink.

'Girl crush?' I ask.

'Yeah. Ashley has a girl crush on Lauren,' Nicola says.

'Do you?' I ask. Ashley shrugs.

'Maybe,' Ashley says, eventually.

'Cool,' says Parker. I smile.

THREE WAY

Before long, Ashley and Nicola have us all dancing. Or whatever you call what I'm doing now. Still, no one seems to mind and I admit I am enjoying myself. Svetla and I never used to dance, mainly because of me. I'm quite self conscious and I don't really go in for big public displays. In this instance, alcohol is helping. I feel my phone vibrate in my pocket. I stop dancing and whip it out. It's a text from Lauren which says 'Hi, just got your message. Don't think I can make it there now, prob too late but you could come over after if you fancy? L x.' I consider her offer. I will, of course, be a lot drunker by the time I finish here. Do I want to spend the night at Lauren's? Do I want free sex and a warm body to cosy up to? What sort of questions are these? I click reply 'Sounds good, not sure what time. Will you still be up at 1?' I click reply and carry on dancing.

'Who's that, Lauren?' Ashley asks. I wipe a bead of sweat from my forehead and nod.

'Yeah,' I say.

'Is she coming down?'

'No. But I might go over to hers once we're done here,' I say.

'Mate, we're pulling an all-nighter. Can't bail halfway through,' Parker says.

'Are we? No one told me.'

'I'm telling you now,' he says. My phone vibrates again and I check the message which says, 'Maybe rain check. I'll call you tomorrow.' I feel slightly disappointed. Okay, I understand why she didn't want to come down at this late stage but meeting up would have been nice.

'Well?' Parker asks.

'Rain check. Guess she wants to go to bed,' I reply.

'So we're still on for all night?' he asks.

'What the hell,' I reply.

TWENTY NINE – A SURPRISING TURN OF EVENTS

Sunday. Feel horrible. Where the hell am I, anyway? Doesn't look like my room. I open my eyes wider. The floor is on the ceiling. What...oh hang on. I pull myself up. A rush of blood to my head sends me back onto the bed. I now stare at the correct ceiling. It's still not a ceiling I recognise though. I rub my eyes, scratching sleep out of them. I feel like I've been hit by a train. I sit up, slower this time, and look around. I'm in a dimly lit girl's room. Everything is pink. There are fluffy toys everywhere and a poster of Barbie on the wall. I hear distant voices behind the door. I also seem to have an erection. It's fine, just need to find a toilet and that will be gone in a jiffy. I stand, get out of bed, wearing only my boxers and walk slowly over to the door. I carefully pull it open and listen. The voices sound like Parker and someone I don't recognise. Am I in some sort of alternate universe where our flat has been girlified? Is this, in fact, my bedroom? I don't have any answers and in my desperation for the toilet, I look down the corridor searching for likely candidates. Where the rest of my clothes are, is anyone's guess. I go for it, sneaking to the first door on the right. I open it. Bathroom, close but no toilet. I pull the door closed and move to the next door. Suddenly I hear the female voice change location. She's moving closer. Shit. I open the next door and sneak in. It's dark. I look for a switch. Rather, I feel for a switch. Eventually I locate it and click it on. Turns out I'm in a small girl's bedroom. Annoyingly, the small girl also occupies said bedroom and now her eyes are open, looking at me. We stare at each other, unsure what to say. I turn away as best I can, a pathetic attempt at hiding the lump in my pants. Oh this is so bad.

'Uh...I was, uh looking for the toilet,' I say. The girl's expression has now changed to one of unmitigated terror. She pulls the covers up to her eyes and then points towards the door. I interpret this to mean she wants me to leave. I nod slowly. You know what I do then? Really dumb. I put my index finger in front of my mouth and do a 'shhh.'

'MUM!!!!!!!!' the girl screams. I open the door and run out into the corridor where, in my haste, I knock over someone who was just outside. We both fall to the floor.

'Shit! Sorry,' I say. The person I've floored is a woman, early forties wearing an apron. Girl's mum perhaps? She looks like an older Nicola. Then Parker appears in the corridor with Nicola in tow. Parker's hand slaps over his mouth as he tries to stop himself from bursting with laughter. My hands try to cover my erection but only draw more attention to it.

'Oh, jeez,' says the woman sitting up. I stand up quickly.

'God,' says Nicola, 'Ollie, where are your clothes?'

'I don't know. I'm sorry...' I start to say. It then dawns on me this must be Nicola's mum's house. Parker's in fits. Nicola elbows him but he can't stop himself. The laughter is unleashed, filling the hallway. I run back to the room I came from and slam the door. I pull the duvet off the bed and cover myself up. I hear Nicola talking to her mum.

'Are you okay, mum?'

'I think so. Who is that man?'

'Parker's friend. Hey, it's not funny, stop it now!' Parker's laughter still fills the corridor. I hear someone walking towards my door and a soft knock.

'You okay in there, Ollie?' Nicola says.

'Honestly, I've been better,' I reply.

'Can I come in? Are you, decent?' she asks. I want to die. We all know what she's referring to. I shake my head.

'Yeah,' I say. The door opens and Nicola walks in, carrying my clothes.

'Here, found them. Probably should have got undressed in here,' she says.

'I'm so sorry Nicola. I don't really remember anything.'

'It's fine. We all got quite drunk and ended up coming back here,' she says.

'Right,' I say, trying to remember a semblance of anything from last night. 'What about Ashley?'

'She's in the living room. Do you need the

toilet?' she asks, glancing down at my groin. I look down and see the faintest outline of my erection.

'Yes. Please,' I say. I want to die. She smiles.

'This way, try not to scare the children,' she says. I nod and follow her. She indicates the correct door this time and I walk inside.

'Thanks.'

'Take your time,' she says.

Once I've been, thrown water on my face, crept back to my room, clothed myself and tidied the room as best I can, I head into the living room. Ashley sits on a chair reading a magazine. Nicola sits on Parker's lap. The little girl I scared the crap out of is lying on her front on the floor, colouring a drawing with crayons. Probably practising for when the psychiatrist asks her if the picture is a butterfly or a cloud.

'Ah, here he is, paedophile Ollie,' Parker says. Nicola nudges him in the chest. The little girl looks up from her colouring. She stares at me. I force a smile. Floor swallow me now.

'Hi,' I say. I glance at Ashley who is smiling sympathetically.

'Why are you all up so early?' I ask.

'It's eleven-thirty, dude,' Parker says. 'We were waiting for you to get up so we can go home, I wanted to throw water on you but...I was voted down.'

'Right,' I say.

'This is my younger sister, Joanne, my other sister, whose room you slept in is over at a friend's,' Nicola says. 'Joanne, this is Ollie.'

'They've already met,' Ashley says. Everyone cracks up. I nod. Even Joanne laughs, although

THREE WAY

I'm not sure she knows why.

'That's just great,' I say.

Thursday. Lauren and I have agreed to have dinner at hers tonight. Quite excited, haven't seen her place yet. Bet it's amazing. I start wondering what the bed looks like and whether we'll end up using it for non-sleep purposes. However, all that is at least ten hours away. I'm running late and every train that comes into Clapham Junction is rammed. I hate queuing to get on a train when I've already paid an obscene amount just for the privilege of standing under some stranger's armpit. London bloody transport.

I transfer onto the Northern Line at Waterloo and again, have to stand. My iPod is about the only thing that keeps me sane on these sorts of days. I stand against the Perspex and glance down at the woman sitting next to where I stand. She's thumbing through her diary but quickly comes to rest on a page. I look at the entries.

14th September - cut hedge row.

15th September – take John to rugby. Boring. Then another entry grabs my attention.

16th September - nothing written.

17th September – Ken's birthday – blow job. I blink then immediately smile. I glance at the woman, she's no looker for sure but Ken is about to get very lucky. The train pulls into Goodge Street and I step off, my mood much improved by the possibilities for Ken's birthday.

As soon as I get in Paul asks me to try and

find an address for a radical Islamic preacher who has just managed to get bail. He's thought to be living somewhere in South London.

'Can you see if you can track him down? There's a crew for you when you're ready,' Paul says.

'Sure,' I reply. I log in and get to work. Using the various funky programs and ultra-modern tools we have, I manage to find out shit all. In the end, I ask Paul if I can just go out with the camera crew and chance it. Sometimes you get lucky. Me and a cameraman called Rooney start searching South London for a radical preacher located in a safe house somewhere. Not an impossible task but I think lowering expectations in such a quest is advisable. We drive around endless residential streets looking for any sign of police protective detail or two constipated guys sitting in a car outside a house with a flask of coffee and a box of doughnuts. Unfortunately we spot nothing even close.

Two hours later, we've reached the end of the road and the end of my shift. I decide to call it a day. I call Paul to tell him we've had no luck. He's disappointed but says he isn't surprised. Thanking me, he lets me go home. I jump on the tube and change onto the Victoria line. Pimlico only takes ten minutes and before I know it I'm walking down Lauren's street. She lives in a posh neighbourhood.

Her place is a white Georgian terrace. Large bay windows jut out next to the front door. I walk up the steps and knock. I hear movement, the door opens and there she is. She's gone all out, wearing a beautiful long red dress, shoulders exposed. Her hair is straight and she wears just the right amount of makeup, subtle and restrained.

'Hi,' I say, breathing in as I take in the sight. She smiles.

'Hi, nice to see you,' she replies.

'You look beautiful.'

'Thanks, come in,' she says, turning away from me and heading up the stairs. I close the door and follow her up. I hear the mellow tones of Birdy in the background. Her flat is nicely decked out. Neutral colours, high ceilings and a good finish. The kitchen is modern and looks expensive. The lounge has plenty of light coming through those big windows and there are two tall bookshelves on either side of a grand fireplace. Vases of flowers are dotted about the place and she's lit some candles.

'Champagne?' she asks, turning to face me with a bottle of Don Perignon in her hand.

'Sure,' I say. Blimey, I could get used to going out with a rich girl.

'Can you do the honours? I'll just check on the food,' she says.

'Yep,' I reply, taking the bottle from her. I unwrap the cork and pop it open, pouring the Champagne into two long-stemmed glasses. I nearly screw it up by pouring too fast, a little spills over the top. I really do need more practice doing this. I guess, if Lauren and I are going to be a permanent item it's something I'll get better at with time. I check to see if she's still in the kitchen and wait for the bubbles to go down. She walks back in and takes the glass I offer her.

'Cheers,' I say.

'Cheers,' she replies. We clink glasses and take

a sip. It tastes like liquid money.

'So what are we celebrating? Apart from you being with me, of course,' I say, a vague attempt at humour. She smiles then assumes a serious face quickly.

'Well, uh...shall we sit down?' she says, gesturing to the sofa.

'Yeah.'

We relocate to the sofa and place our glasses on the table in front of us. Not sure why but I feel like something is wrong. I look at her, she isn't saying anything and looks uncomfortable. Would she offer me Champagne then dump me? Pretty cold.

'Ollie, we need to talk about something,' she says. Holy crap, she is dumping me. Who the hell does that? Who opens a bottle of Don Perignon and then tells her boyfriend/shag to get lost? That is so twisted I might have to-

'Right,' I say, interrupting my thought process. I'm nervous now, anxious at what she will say.

'I've got a new job,' she says. I blink, that's not what I was expecting. She isn't dumping me, that's definitely a positive. I breathe out, realising I'd barely been breathing at all.

'Oh right, that's great. Congratul-'

'It's in New York.' Ah.

'Oh.' Silence. I glance at her, she stares at me for a reaction. I blink, trying to process all the implications of this bombshell. She touches my hand.

'I know this isn't what you want to hear and to be honest I don't really want to go but it's quite a big promotion and it will only be for a couple of years-'

'A couple of years?' I repeat, still trying to take it in.

'I know you're not going to be happy about it.'

'Why would I be happy? I mean, I'm glad you've got a new job and all that but, I dunno. I thought we were going somewhere.'

'We were. But, we haven't exactly been going out for that long,' she says. I note her use of the past tense there.

'Right.'

'Look, I'm disappointed too. But I can't pass this up. United is huge over there, I would be just below board level. It's a massive opportunity.'

'Okay. So, we're breaking up then?'

'Hang on. I don't go until October, still plenty of time to see each other,' she says. I nod, miserable. 'Also I was thinking, and don't freak out when I say this...you could, maybe...come with me?'

'What? To New York?'

'Yeah. You could get a job at one of the American TV networks, we could find a big apartment to live in. Even if you had trouble finding a job, you could still stay with me. I earn a fair bit and you could come out, see how it goes? I know it's fast and I haven't thought through all the implications but...sorry, what do you think?' Live in New York? With a girl I barely know. I thought this was just another date, now it's turned into this, whatever you call this. 'It doesn't have to be the end, Ollie.' She stares at me, scanning for any reaction. I feel numb and strangely more upset than I would have expected. I thought we had something here. I know I've been a bit all over the place with Svetla but I thought Lauren would be the one to pull me out of that. I thought we'd end up together. Even if I never phrased it like that in my head, that's sort of where I figured we were heading. And now she hits me with this. 'Talk to me,' she says.

'I don't know. What do you want me to say?' I reply.

'Just be honest, tell me what you think.'

'This is...I don't know. I like you. A lot. Maybe more than I was even admitting to myself but I can't go to New York. My friends are here. My life is here.'

'It's a five hour plane journey. You can come back whenever you want, on me,' she replies. I sigh and stand up, walking over to the window. The sun is setting, its orange light glows everywhere. Magic hour, beautiful.

'I don't know if I want to rely on you for money,' I say.

'I understand. Okay, don't go anywhere, I just need to check on the food,' she replies. I nod slowly and watch her leave. I turn back to the window and stare out. What the hell? I've been quite relaxed about Lauren until now. I don't want her to leave. Why can't she just stay here? Could I live in New York? My immediate reaction is absolutely not. Can't up sticks and leave everything I've worked for. I'm fairly young, I guess I could do it for a couple of years. As she says, New York is only five hours away. But what about my flat, all that saving up to finally buy my own place and I'd...what, sell it? Rent it out? I don't know what to do. I down the rest of the Champagne and pour myself another glass. Lauren appears at the door and walks over to stand behind me. She puts her arms around my chest, holding me tight.

'I'm sorry. I know this sucks. But do you understand at least why I'm doing it?'

'I do,' I reply. I want to say more but I can't slot the words into the right order.

'Like I said, it's not until October, we've got a couple of months,' she says. I nod slowly. She releases me and walks around me, rubbing my back as she goes. We face each other. I can barely look her in the eye. I feel let down, disappointed. Fucked. She smiles at me. Her beautiful smile. I'm suddenly overcome with emotion. What the hell is the matter with me? This was supposed to be just an intermediary thing, until The One came along. Don't tell me all this time, Lauren was The One and I missed it completely. That would be just like me. She was right under my nose and I was too busy looking at Svetla to notice. Exactly as Martina said in South Africa. 'Hey. This is a celebration even if it is bittersweet. So, let's celebrate.'

She takes my glass from me and places it on the table. She leans in and kisses me, I close my eyes, savouring her taste, her smell. I try to imprint this moment into my mind. Remember this. Remember her. I feel her hands move over my groin. She rubs and kneads. I feel myself become hard. Our kisses become more urgent, passionate. The sensation whips around my head. The conflict inside me is intense but soon, the urges take over and we're having sex on the sofa. Our bodies so close. As close as you can be with someone.

Lauren Bates, who was there all along. Until right now.

THIRTY - CONFESSION

'What's the matter with you?' Ashley asks when I walk into the flat the next day. She sits with her legs tucked under her bum, watching daytime TV.

'Nothing,' I reply. Although what I really mean is everything.

'Yeah? You look like you're going to kill someone.'

'This is my face, Ash. When I relax all my facial muscles this is what it looks like, okay?'

'Okay.'

'What are you doing?' I ask.

'Taking a break.'

'A break from what?' I ask. She shrugs and says something I don't hear. 'What?'

'From playing the piano,' she says. I turn.

'Yeah? You been playing something?'

'I've been thinking about what you said, and maybe I could try and record some of the stuff I play.'

'You should. You're good,' I say, heading into the kitchen. I switch on the kettle and find the tea bags. Ashley appears at the door.

'You see Lauren?' she asks. I pause and glance down, nodding. 'Something happen?' I turn to face her and sigh.

'She's got a new job,' I say. Ashley waits, then raises her eyebrows when I don't say anything else.

'Right? So..?'

'In New York,' I say.

'Ah. Shit. That sucks.'

'Yeah,' I say, sighing again.

'What does that mean then?' she asks.

'I dunno, she wants me to go live with her,' I say.

'Really? You gonna go?' she asks. I look at her then over to the window.

'I don't know.'

'Hey, come on,' she says, stepping towards me. She puts her arms around me. Feels good. 'Just have to work out if she's worth it. Is that what you want to do? Big thing, moving to another country.'

'I just don't think I can. And it's not like we've been going out for very long. It's a bit too soon for this sort of stuff.'

'Do you love her?' Ashley asks. I consider the question. Do I love her? I can't possibly love someone after such a short amount of time. I was begging Svetla to have me back only a few days ago, how can I possibly be in love with Lauren?

'I don't think so.'

'You need to let this sit. Can't make any decisions yet. When does she go?'

'Not until October.'

'Right, well that's like two months away. You've got a bit of time. Maybe things will change, anything could happen. She could get fired,' she says, smiling. She's trying to make me feel better and I appreciate it, but it doesn't change the sinking feeling in my stomach. I finish making the tea.

'So...you want to hear my song? I'm not saying it will cheer you up or anything but...' she asks. I smile.

'Sure,' I reply. Why not, can't make me feel any worse. Maybe this will take my mind off it all.

I grab my cup of tea and we walk into Parker's room. I sit on his bed and she takes a seat at the piano. She switches it on and plays a couple of notes to check it's working.

'Okay, so just remember this is really rough and I haven't quite got the lyrics right yet.'

'Sure,' I say.

'Okay,' she says. I hear the nerves in her voice. She starts to play, a slow melancholy song. I watch her move with the melody, her eyes close and she starts to sing.

Where I am
The place you dwell
A place for my heart
The place we died

The song becomes more stirring, her voice more emotional.

We lived, we soared
We died, we fell
Where I am
Take my soul
The lies from your mouth
The lies
Those lies
Were all you had

That's where I am

I'm spellbound, my heart moving with every key she plays. It's one of the most beautiful pieces of music I've ever heard and I'm not over-egging it. I breathe back the emotions that build inside me. My mind flashes to Lauren. Lovely, beautiful Lauren. Don't go, Lauren.

Ashley slows right down to note after note, then stops. I swallow, she opens her eyes and turns to me. I close my mouth and shake my head, trying to find something appropriate to say.

'Jesus, Ash.'

'You hate it, don't you? I can see you hate it.'

'I don't hate it. It's one of the most beautiful pieces of music I've ever heard,' I say, still in mild shock.

'Shut up,' she says, smiling.

'I'm serious. That was absolutely amazing,' I say, grabbing her arm. She looks at my hand then at me.

'Really?' she says with a raised eyebrow.

'Yeah. You seriously don't know how good that was?'

'I'm just...playing around.'

'Fuck me Ashley. If that's you just playing around, I can't imagine what it'll be like when you really put your all into it.'

'Are you being serious, because you're starting to get my hopes up?'

'I wouldn't joke about something like this. You need to get this recorded and burned onto a CD. I'll help you.'

'Okay.'

'Have you got any other songs?'

'Of course, loads,' she replies. She really has no idea how much talent she has. And to think she was a barmaid last week. My friend is going to be a superstar. At least one of us has it figured out.

I sit at my laptop trying to burn Ashley's songs onto a CD. The bloody program is being an arse and won't do what I need it to. This should be so easy, so why is it turning into such a mare? My mobile rings, I glance at the display. Lauren. I answer it.

'Hi,' I say.

'Hi,' she says. She sounds upset.

'You okay?'

'Yeah, you know, just...having trouble with this job thing. You?'

'Yeah, me too.'

'I have to go. I can't not go,' she says.

'I know. I get it. It's just, sad.'

'Yeah,' she says. Silence on the other end of the phone. I swallow. God, this is so bloody tragic. Maybe I should take charge, end it now. I can't, I don't want to. 'What are you doing now?' she asks.

'Nothing, just burning a CD. Or trying to.'

'Can I come over?'

'Sure, that'd be nice. Ashley's here.'

'That's okay. I'll be over in an hour or so.'

'Cool, see you then,' I say, hanging up. I stand and walk into the living room. Ashley sits on the sofa, a cup of tea in her hand.

'Did you get it burned?' Ashley asks, sipping her tea.

'No, still messing about with it. Lauren's coming over.'

'Oh. Do you want me to go out?'

'No, it's cool. We'll just go to my room,' I say, sitting down on the sofa next to her.

'You're really upset about her, aren't you?' she says. I look up and shake my head. 'Oh Ollie,' she puts her cup down and wraps her arm around me, giving me a hug. Why am I being such a fucking girl? What the hell is the matter with me? I'm not crying by the way because that would be really crap. But I'll admit I'm a little emotional.

'If I hadn't spent so long worrying about Svetla and actually paid attention to Lauren, I mean properly paid attention, maybe-'

'She'd still be going to New York,' says Ashley.

'Yeah. Right.'

'But you're right, sometimes the person you love is right there in front of you,' she says.

'Exactly,' I say. Ashley breathes out fast then glances at me, a strange look in her eye. She starts chewing a fingernail. We sit in silence for a moment then she says,

'I need to tell you something.'

'Oh?'

'Yeah and you may not like it,' she says. I turn to face her. She's staring at me with a very strange look. Oh God, what now?

'What?' I reply. When I get no response I say, 'what is it?' She sighs and looks away, her eyes staring at the floor.

'You remember Claire Arthur's eighteenth birthday party?' I frown and think for a moment. Man, that feels like a lifetime ago.

'Vaguely. I was very drunk. As were you.'

'Yeah. You remember Jane Sommers?' Where is she going with this?

'What is this, a history lesson of my ex girlfriends?' I ask.

'You remember me saying it wasn't going to work with Claire?' she says. I chuckle at the memory.

'Yeah, you really didn't like her.'

'No. Or Jane or any of them frankly,' Ashley replies, her voice calm. I don't like this. I'm suddenly scared about what Ashley is going to say.

'Yeah, but Jane was a girlie girl. You're not really like that.'

'I got you to split up with both of them.'

'No. We just decided or rather they decided-'

'Ollie, every girlfriend you had at school never lasted longer than a few weeks. Didn't you ever ask yourself why that was?'

'Maybe I wasn't too bothered about them, and every time I broke up with someone-'

'We'd start fooling around,' she finishes.

'But...we were always just friends...weren't we?' I say. Ashley shakes her head, a simple smile on her face.

'Men are so stupid sometimes,' she says. We stare at each other. I suddenly know where this is headed. Surely...she can't be telling me-

'So...what are you saying?' I ask. She tilts her head.

'What do you think I'm saying?' she says. I shake my head, trying to come up with an answer. This is huge. This is more than huge.

'I...I didn't think you were interested. I mean,

you always said you didn't want to get attached.'

'Come on, Ollie. First rule of 'friends that shag,' someone always wants more.'

'So? That was ages ago.' I'm playing dumb, I know I am, but I can't get my head round this. Ashley raises her eyebrows.

'Do I really have to spell it out for you?' Oh. My. God.

'Shit, Ashley...all this time?' I say. She closes her slowly eyes then flicks them open to me.

'I don't expect anything to change. You're with Lauren and I bet you end up going to New York. And even if you don't, I don't want anything from you. I'm...I'm just sick of carrying this around,' she says. I honestly don't know what to say. Ashley and me? A proper couple? Christ. I mean, I always thought it was just about the sex. We'd attempted a relationship before, it had never worked out. This makes things more complicated.

'We tried going out, remember? It never worked,' I say, quietly.

'No we didn't really try, Ollie. There were simply times when neither of us was with anyone else.' I breathe out fast and shake my head.

'So...all this time...' I say. She nods slowly.

'I love you, Ollie. Always have, probably always will.' I stare at her, unable to find suitable words for the bombshell exploding around me. 'Okay, well...thanks for telling me, I guess,' I say.

'No worries,' she replies. A silence descends into our conversation. I don't know what to say. Fuck. Then she says, 'In fact, I think I will go out. Leave you two to talk properly.' She stands and clicks the TV off.

'Hang on, you can't just throw that bomb in and leave.'

'Why? Not like you're going to split up with Lauren and be with me. Not even sure I want that, it's been unrequited for so long, I'm sort of used to it,' she says, rolling her eyes. 'God, listen to me. Pathetic. Excuse me.' I grab her arm.

'Wait, Ash. Let's talk properly. This is pretty big, right?'

'Yeah. But it'll hold,' she says, looking down at my hand, 'can you let go of my arm, please?' I do as she says. I follow her out into the hallway where she takes her coat off the hook. 'I feel bad Ash, don't go.'

'Don't feel bad, you didn't know. I'll see you later, okay?' she says. I watch her open the front door and leave. What the hell is going on?

THIRTY ONE – A WANDERING MIND

I wait for Lauren to arrive. Alone. Images race through my head. Memories of me and Ashley. All those times when I just thought...we were friends that fooled around. What a karzi. This stuff just doesn't happen. Does it? I mean, in reality. No one, especially someone like me, ends up having to fret over three girls. What am I, some sort of male sex robot alien person? Yeah, not sure where that came from either.

I stand up and walk to the bathroom. I look at myself in the mirror. Are you really the guy that has a problem with three separate and distinctly different women? Ashley...I mean, we're friends who, occasionally...I like her. She's funny, easy to be around but she's a bit of a scatterbrain and can be harsh with her criticisms sometimes.

Lauren, beautiful, said it a thousand times but saying it again. I have a genuine connection with her. She seems into me, maybe more than I'm into her. At least, she was. But now she's leaving I feel...an urgent need to, what, go with her? Be with her? I don't want to be with her in New York, I want to be with her here.

And Svetla. The woman who broke my heart and somehow, to this day continues to dominate my thoughts and feelings. Yes, Lauren is a great distraction and makes me feel better about myself but Christ, me and Svetla were supposed to be together. Except I fucked it up. And she fucked Rupert fucking Gilbert. I'm swearing more, I know I am, but this stuff is serious.

A knock at the door disturbs my thoughts. I walk over and open it. Lauren stands in front of me. She's wearing spray-on jeans and a tight-fitting white top under a dark coat. Her boobs look amazing.

'Hi,' she says.

'Hi, come in,' I reply. I close the door behind her. We head to the living room.

'No Ashley?' Lauren says, taking off her coat.

'Uh, no. She had to...she left. Have a seat,' I reply. She does as she's told. 'Do you want some tea or coffee?'

'Nah, thanks,' she says. I sit down next to her. It's suddenly awkward, the elephant in the room looming large between us.

'So...' I start to say and stop, having nothing to add. Our eyes lock. She leans forward and kisses me. My head is light and the back of my throat dry. Our lips break contact and we stare at each other again. She sighs and smiles.

'Fuck,' she says, leaning back theatrically.

'Yeah. Why can't they just promote you here?'

'I don't know. Because that's too easy,' she replies. I lean back and put my arm around her. She snuggles next to me. 'I know you're probably going to think I'm stupid but I...' she pauses then says, 'I missed you a little bit.'

'I missed you too,' I reply, feeling the truth of the statement. I did miss her. Less than a day and I missed her. She strokes my chest slowly.

'We're not going to talk about New York or the job or anything. We're just going to enjoy being with each other today, okay?'

'Okay,' I reply, but somewhere I know we're both just pretending now. We sit in silence for a moment then she says,

'It's not working, is it?' She pulls away and looks at me. She lightly hits me across the chest and smiles. 'Damnit, this is all your fault.'

'Me? How is it my fault?' I reply.

'I don't know but I'm sure I could make it your fault,' she says, chuckling.

'Brilliant. Well most things are, to be honest.'

'Ollie, Ollie, Ollie,' she says.

'Oi, oi, oi,' I reply. The clock is ticking and it doesn't matter what either of us do. From now until she leaves, the clock is the only thing that will define how we act and what we do.

'Have I met the man I'm supposed to be with, only for it to be doomed to fail yet again?' she asks. I'm unsure if she means it as a rhetorical question.

'What if, and I'm just throwing it out there, what if you didn't take the job?' I ask.

'I've thought about it. And yes I could turn it down. But...just feels like a step backwards. If I don't take it, someone else will and my career will pretty much grind to a halt.'

'It's not only about ruling the world,' I say.

'Yeah okay. But what happens if I don't take the job and we split up, I've lost twice.'

'Good to see you have so much faith in us.'

'No, but come on.'

'I don't know. There are no certainties in anything, are there?' I reply.

'Are you really asking me to give it up?' she says. I consider her words. Am I?

'No. Not really. I just, don't want you to go, that's all,' I say. We kiss again, I run my hands through her hair.

'Maybe we should just have sex. Take our minds off it,' she says.

'Maybe we should.'

We do. It's great. It's fun. What it's not, however, is a problem solver. And we do have a big problem. As we lie there, in post-coital tenderness, the elephant stirs.

The door bangs shuts. Someone's home, Ashley? Parker?

'Hello?' I hear Parker's voice echo in the hallway.

'Hi,' I call back. I hear him approach.

'You having a wank?' he asks. Lauren smiles at me.

'No, Lauren's here.'

'Oh, hi Lauren,' he says.

'Hi Parker,' Lauren calls. She's naked and she's talking to Parker through a very thin door. Sexy. Or am I just weird for thinking that?

'Hi guys,' Nicola calls from somewhere beyond Parker.

'Jesus,' I whisper, rolling my eyes. 'Hi,' I call back. Lauren smiles at me.

'Maybe we better get dressed?' she says.

'Yeah,' I reply.

When we eventually surface, Nicola and Parker have moved into the kitchen. We walk in sheepishly.

'Hi,' says Parker.

'Hi,' I reply, 'uh, Parker this is Lauren. Lauren, Parker.' His eyes have gone weird, like he's staring at a ghost or something. I frown, unsure why he's pulling that face. Then I guess, he hasn't met Lauren before. Nicola nudges him in the ribs.

'Hmm? Sorry yes...this is Nicola,' Parker says.

'Nice to meet you,' Nicola says. 'Ashley was right, you are gorgeous.'

'Yeah,' says Parker, in some sort of trance. Nicola glances at Parker again.

'Oh no, really,' Lauren says, shaking her head. 'It's lovely to meet you both.'

'So...you guys joining us for dinner?' Parker asks. I glance at Lauren, unsure whether she is or isn't. Lauren shrugs then says,

'Sure, why not.'

'Okay,' I say.

'You guys make yourself comfortable in the living room I'll whip something up,' Parker says.

'Really? Sure you don't need any help?' Lauren says.

'Nope, please. You ladies are guests here. Allow me to work my magic,' he replies. I glance at

Lauren who smiles and then looks at Nicola who shrugs and chuckles. Parker turns round. 'What?'

'You're a dick,' I say.

'Better be nice if you want dinner.'

'Okay, I would like some of your dinner, Mr. Parker, sir,' I say.

'Please vacate the kitchen,' he says. Nicola and Lauren walk out. I follow but not before Parker mouths a silent 'wow' to me, accompanied by other male 'go on my son' hand gestures. Jesus, he's immature.

'I'll put some music on,' I say, walking into the living room and over to the iPod dock. Lauren and Nicola sit down on the sofa.

'So what do you do Lauren?' Nicola asks.

'I'm a trading manager, working in the City,' Lauren answers. I set the iPod to start playing a little Madeleine Peyroux, nice.

'Oh okay,' Nicola replies.

'You?'

'I'm a teacher, so...not as interesting but-'

'I'd say infinitely more interesting,' Lauren says. I find a bottle of red wine in my very limited collection. I know nothing about wine and I'm mildly embarrassed that Lauren seems to be used to drinking expensive Champagne on a daily basis. I hold it up.

'Sorry, is this okay?' I ask, looking at Lauren.

'Of course,' she says. I show it to Nicola who nods. Probably just being polite.

'Hey douchebag?' Parker calls from the kitchen.

'Yeah?' I reply.

'Is Ashley joining us?'

'Uh...don't know. Don't think so,' I reply. I look around for a corkscrew, I thought it was just here. That's so annoying.

'How long have you and Ollie been together?' Nicola asks Lauren.

'Not long, a few weeks but feels we've known each other a lot longer,' Lauren replies, glancing at me. I smile and continue searching for the corkscrew. It's no use, it's not here. I walk into the kitchen. I hear Parker on the phone. He turns to face me, phone against his ear.

'Oh...okay. No I get it, I understand. Just...yeah, okay. Bye then.'

'Who's that?' I ask.

'Ashley,' he says. I pause then move to the utensil drawer.

'Did you guys just have a soul baring session?' he asks.

'Well she bared her soul to me, if that's what you mean,' I reply.

'Seriously, how did you not know?' Parker asks.

'What do you mean?'

'Everyone knew she was in love with you, always has been. You really didn't know?'

'No. I just thought...we were friends,' I say, checking to make sure I'm not overheard. 'I didn't know she liked me...properly.'

'Jesus, man.'

'I know, I'm crap. Is she okay?'

'Surprisingly, no. You know what Ashley's like, all defensive and whatnot but underneath she's all soft and gooey. Bit like a Cadbury's Crème Egg,' he says.

'Right. Shit, I didn't know. How was I supposed to know?'

'Open your eyes, start paying attention to shit,' he says. I open a drawer, find the corkscrew and begin opening the bottle of wine.

'Lauren's going away anyway, so maybe it will all work out,' I say.

'What do you mean? Where?'

'New York. In October.'

'Shit. For how long?'

'A couple of years by the sound of it.'

'Man, that sucks. Could you...?'

'Go with her? Yeah. But then I'd be fucked,' I reply. I open the cupboard and pull out some glasses. Parker nods.

'Shit. That really sucks. She's a keeper as well.'

'Don't remind me.'

'Then just make sure you really imprint however many sex sessions you've got left. You know, for when she's not here,' he says.

'Parker...' I honestly don't have the words to respond.

'What?' he says. I shake my head, pick up the glasses and wine and walk back to the living room. The girls are talking about Lauren's jeans and where she got them. I pour them both a glass of wine which they acknowledge but carry on their girlie talk. I sit and listen and pretend to be interested in what they're saying. I watch Lauren as she talks and reacts to Nicola. She's so gorgeous, maybe I do need to give serious thought to moving to New York. Would it be so bad? A new start. Yes, I wouldn't know anyone and I would have to get a new job and new friends and a new place to live and everyone might hate me. Can I really just let her just leave?

And Ashley. Where is she? Just upped and left. Upset and embarrassed. Maybe I should be out there looking for her? Or maybe she just wants to be by herself, away from me. I love Ashley, I really do. But I don't see her like that. She's attractive, of course, but she's a friend. A friend that has, on occasion, been more. Am I an arsehole for not seeing the truth of the situation? I guess there's always someone more into these things than the other but with Ash, because she's so thick skinned, I just thought she didn't care. If Lauren left, could I hook up with Ashley? Or would she just be a consolation prize whose heart I'd end up breaking to solve my apparent inability to be alone? There is no obvious right answer here and I know that if I don't make a decision I'll probably end up losing everyone. But then maybe that's what needs to happen. No more than I deserve. I keep going on about how I need to make a decision and yet I'm not really deciding. What is it I want?

'...don't you think, Ollie?' says Nicola.

'Huh?' I reply.

'Lauren's jeans. Do you think they're sexy?' Nicola says.

'Yeah, very,' I reply. Lauren smiles. I return the grin. My mind, on the other hand, is somewhere else.

THIRTY TWO – SPIRALLING DOWNWARDS

I try calling Ashley on the way into work the next day. Her phone is switched off so I leave a message.

'Hi, it's Ollie. Just phoning to make sure you're okay. I don't know whether you didn't come home last night because of me or something else or...anyway, just give me a ring.' I hang up and consider where she might be, quickly coming to the conclusion I haven't the faintest idea. I transfer to the Northern Line and actually find a seat. I know, amazing, right? I grab a copy of today's Metro newspaper and settle in. The doors ring, a women jumps into the carriage just before the doors close. She wears a large baggy white dress and has wet patches under her armpits. Gross. I glance at her then back to my paper.

'Excuse me,' she says. I glance up, she can't possibly be talking to me. Turns out, she is.

'Um, yeah?' I ask, wondering if she's going to

kill me.

'Can I have the seat please?' she asks. I spot a bump in her stomach. Shit. I huff and stand up, annoyed. I never get a seat at this time of day and the one time...just let it go Ollie. And breathe. It's fine. She needs it more than me.

My phone rings just as I'm showing my ID to the security guard at main reception. Ashley? I pull out my phone. Blocked Call.

'Hello?' I say.

'Ollie, it's Julie. Paul's asking if you can do a coffee run?' she asks. What am I, the newsdesk bloody gopher?

'Sure,' I say, unable to hide my annoyance.

'You don't have to,' she says, detecting my mood.

'No, it's fine. What do you want?'

'Can I have a skinny latte and Paul wants a double shot cappuccino.'

'Right.'

'Thanks, Ollie.' Yeah whatever. I head over to the lifts and up to the canteen.

A chirpy bottle blonde teenager with an eastern European accent takes my order. I wait, glancing at the muffins and assortment of croissants available to me. No, need to be good. That panettone bread looks like it needs to be eaten.

'Here you are sir,' the blonde girl says.

'Cheers,' I reply, taking the coffees. My phone rings again. I place the coffee on an empty table and answer the phone.

'Hello?'

'Hi, it's Lauren,' she says, her voice strange.

'Hey, how's it going?'

'Uh, not good.'

'Oh?'

'They want me to go to New York tomorrow.'

'What?'

'Just for a couple of weeks, then I'll be back. I'm not moving for good yet, don't worry.'

'Right.'

'I know, it sucks. But I sort of have to-'

'I know you do,' I say. Silence descends as we both try to find the words. 'What time is your flight?'

'Twelve-fifteen.'

'Okay,' I reply. I consider offering to see her off at the airport but is that a bit-

'Don't fancy seeing me off, do you?' she asks. I do have a day off tomorrow but do I really want to-

'Uh, sure-' I find myself saying.

'You don't have to, just thought it might be...nice.'

'Yeah, I'm on a day off anyway.'

'Jesus. You get a lot of days off, part-timer,' she says, chuckling. She means it as a joke but the comment annoys me. 'Maybe you could come round after work today?'

'Uh sure. I didn't bring a bag or anything.'

'Well it's only for one night.'

'Okay, I finish around six, so be there by six-thirty, seven?'

'Great.'

'See you later.'

'Bye,' she says. I hang up and breathe out, realising I'd been holding my breath for what felt like the entire conversation. I'm losing her, I know I am. She is slipping through my fingers and there seems to be fuck all I can do about it.

I walk back into the newsroom with the coffee and hand the cups to Julie and Paul.

'Great stuff mate, how much do I owe you?' Paul asks.

'Nah, it's fine,' I reply.

'It all adds up,' he says.

'You can buy me one next time,' I say.

'Okay, thanks. Nothing for you so far, so just log in and I'll let you know if something comes up,' he says.

'Sure,' I reply.

'You okay, Ollie?' Julie asks, ripping a sachet of sugar and tipping it into her coffee. I look at her and consider my response.

'Not really,' I say.

'What's up?' she says.

'My life's a mess.'

'Why?'

'I just...can't seem to slot the pieces in order,' I reply.

'Is this about Lauren, Svetla or your schoolfriend?'

'Lauren,' I say.

'So?'

'Guys, can you have this conversation offline?' Paul says. 'Sorry Ollie, but Julie has work to do.'

'Sure,' I say. I glance at Julie who gives me a concerned face.

'If you're around at lunch, maybe...?' Julie says.

'Yeah, okay,' I say, walking to my desk and sitting down. I feel like shit. I have no control over

anything important in my life. Ashley's gone
AWOL, Lauren's flying to America, Svetla is living
with fuckface. I'm wallowing, I know but I can't
help it. Need something to go right. Some good
news. I turn on the news and watch people
shooting one another in Afghanistan. This is not
going to cheer me up. I log in and load up the news
program, looking through the wires and news
stories. I grab a couple of papers and settle in for
some reading, trying not to think about Lauren or
Ashley.

I spend the day achieving nothing. Unless you
call finding out how much a return flight to New
York costs. It's a lot. I know Lauren said she would
pay but I wanted to know anyway. My lunchtime
conversation with Julie is fairly pointless and
short-lived as Paul calls her back off her break for
some breaking story in Norfolk about a gunman
shooting a police officer. Strange when those sorts
of stories kick off, the newsroom goes nuts but as
it's outside London I have very little input into the
story. I leave at six, the newsroom still as chaotic,
even four hours later.

I walk to the tube station and head down to
the platform. The train comes in rammed, blowing
hot air and sheets of discarded newspaper around
the platform. I breathe in as I board. The doors
close and we move off. I transfer to the Victoria line
and find a seat. In rush hour! I know, second time
in one day! Except, and you won't believe this,
another pregnant woman stands right in front of

me. I pretend not to see her but I can't do it. I look up at her. She gives me puppy dog eyes. Sighing, I stand and let her have the seat. Maybe, if you're pregnant, you just shouldn't be allowed on public transport. Or is that like a racist thing to say? Just annoying, that's all I know. Did the city run out of contraception or something? I arrive at Pimlico station just after six-thirty and head towards Lauren's flat. As I walk, Parker calls me.

'What do you want?' I ask.

'I need some advice.'

'From me? You need advice from me?'

'Yes. Now shut up and listen.'

'Okay.'

'Now I'm being serious when I say this, right?'

'Right.'

'Okay, and I'm not saying it's her or anything but-'

'Yeah, yeah, yeah,' I say quickly, wanting him to hurry up.

'Okay. Well, you know about Nicola and her gas...issues,' he says. I smile.

'You've mentioned it,' I reply.

'And...you know, that's normal because lots of people have those sorts of issues, right?'

'Yes. That it?'

'No. See, because last night, I get up and go to the toilet, like I usually do at three in morning, right?'

'Right. It's bloody annoying-'

'Okay but, I finish and I flush the toilet and I head back to the bedroom and...I mean we did drink quite a lot last night and I don't really remember that much about what happened

but...okay...' Christ, how long is this going to take?
'On the floor, was...'

'What?' I say.

'A poo.'

'Uh, what?'

'Yeah.'

'Wait a minute...you're saying she...shat on
the floor?'

'I don't know, man. I mean, it wasn't me and
we don't have any pets so the conclusion I've come
to is...yeah.'

'Okay, just so we're clear and there's no
confusion...you're girlfriend...took a shit...on my
spare bedroom floor?'

'I'm not a hundred percent it was her.'

'But for the sake of argument, let's say it was.'

'Right.'

'You're asking me what...you should do about
it?'

'Yeah.'

'I would start by clearing it up-'

'For Christ's sake Ollie, I did that. I mean what
should I do about her? Should I tell her? Should I
just pretend it didn't happen?' he asks. This is one
dilemma I never imaged I'd be giving advice about.

'Jesus, I don't know. Is she liable to do it
again?'

'No, I mean...I don't know.'

'Then maybe you'd better have a chat with
her?'

'Yeah,' he says, almost disappointed with my
answer.

'I don't really want her shitting all over the
flat,' I say.

'She's not shitting all over the flat, she was probably a bit drunk and, I don't know, couldn't hold it or something.'

'Parker. You're a good friend. And as a good friend I'm going to be completely honest with you.'

'Okay.'

'I don't want your girlfriend shitting on my floor! I mean, Jesus Christ.' I don't think it's unreasonable to ask people to go to the toilet in the actual toilet, do you? What is this, the Bronze Age? 'Look, do I think you guys need to sit down and talk about this? Yes. Does she need to know that I know? Possibly not.'

'Okay. I'll have a talk with her.'

'Good luck,' I say.

'Yeah. Thanks.'

'Anytime.'

'Okay, see you later.'

'I'm staying at Lauren's tonight, she's going to New York tomorrow, so I'm going to the airport with her. Only for two weeks.'

'You're going to the airport for two weeks?' he asks.

'No, she's going to New York for two weeks, shit-for-brains.'

'Okay. I'll see you tomorrow then.'

'One more thing, have you seen Ashley?' I ask.

'No. Why?' he replies.

'Nothing just...doesn't matter. I'll see you tomorrow.'

'Okay, bye.'

'Bye,' I say, hanging up. As I round the corner to Lauren's road, I feel as if life has taken on a certain eccentric tone and I hope and pray I can return to some semblance of normality as soon as possible. The image of Nicola taking a dump on my floor keeps popping into my mind. I smile to myself but I hope she hasn't stained the carpet...you know what, let's just stop thinking about this.

I knock on Lauren's door and she opens it quickly. She's on the phone and indicates for me to follow her inside which I do.

'...exactly, but just make sure James knows everything about the Anderson account because I don't want to come back and find there are still issues with it...yeah...no Mark, I've told you how it should go, so make it happen...' I follow her into the bedroom. Her clothes are out in piles on the bed and her suitcase is open with nothing in it. The image of the piles sends my mind straight back to the piles Svetla had when she was leaving. I look up at Lauren. I watch her lips moving as she paces around the room with purpose, barking orders at Mark on the other end of the phone. Another girl, soon to be gone. 'Yep, okay, call me if there's anything else, I mean it. The second anything changes you call me, right? Okay, bye.' She turns to face me and shakes her head. 'Total nightmare.'

'What is?'

'Oh, James Kennedy is fucking about with a client and...' she breathes in deeply, 'you know what, doesn't matter.'

'He's a cock.'

'Yes well...how are you anyway? You want something to drink?'

'Orange juice or whatever?' I say. We head into the kitchen and she takes out a carton of

Tropicana from the fridge.

'How was work?' she asks, finding a glass and pouring the juice.

'Boring,' I reply. She hands me the glass and puts the juice back in the fridge. 'You not having any?'

'No.'

'All ready to go?'

'No. But it'll have to do. Hate when everything is such short notice,' she says. I take a glug of my juice. 'So...you gonna miss me?' she asks. I nod and swallow the juice.

'Sure,' I reply, trying to play it cool.

'Yeah you really sound it,' she says. I sigh.

'I don't...forget it.'

'What?'

'I don't want you to go. I know that's selfish and I shouldn't think like that but that's how I feel,' I say.

'Look I don't want to go either. But I have to.'

'I know,' I say. She walks over and kisses me then we hug. I close my eyes, savouring the moment. 'This sucks.'

'Yeah. But too much of this and I'll be bawling my eyes out before we've even got to the airport. Come on, you can help me choose what to wear.'

THIRTY THREE – GOODBYES

Lauren and I barely speak on the drive to the airport. There's so much more I want to say. I want her to know how much she means to me, that I don't want her to go at all. I can't stop her though, unless I cause a scene at the airport? Could I do that? Could I pretend to have a bomb strapped to me or some other weapon of mass destruction? I watch the scene play out in my head and whichever way I look at it, it doesn't end well. I therefore decide against a terrorist attack.

This is a nice taxi. The driver wears a hat, I mean…right? I glance down at my hand holding hers, then up to her face. She's staring out of the window, in another world. I mirror her, looking out of my window. Could I actually have met the girl that gets me over Svelta? Could she be this close and yet soon be so far away. I rub her fingers slowly. She responds by rubbing back, glancing at me and giving me a sad smile. Her eyes return to the window.

I spot a plane taking off ahead, not far to go

now. I breathe in. This is going to be horrible. I know it's only for two weeks but it's just foreshadowing what's ahead. Like a dress rehearsal before the main event.

We drive to the set down area of Terminal five at Heathrow and pull over. The driver gets out and starts unloading her bags. She sniffs and opens the door. I follow her lead, getting out my side (without sniffing or showing any visible sign of upset.) The noise and wind are intense as is the smell of aviation fuel which hangs in the air. The driver, having unloaded the bags slams the boot shut. She hands him a ten pound tip. Bloody hell, ten pounds! For doing the job he gets paid to do. Man, if he gets ten pounds just for driving her to the airport, I wonder how much...you know what, I'm not going to finish that thought.

We walk into the terminal. It's a bright and spacious area with glass everywhere and plenty of room for checking in. We walk up to the First Class section and she hands over her passport.

'Are you travelling as well, sir?' the brunette check-in girl asks.

'No. Just seeing her off,' I say, wondering if I sound mildly pathetic. The check-in girl smiles and carries on processing the ticket. She hands Lauren her boarding pass and tells her the lounge is on the second level then wishes Lauren a pleasant flight, which is nice.

We head to Carluccio's and sit down. A skinny-looking girl comes over and takes our order. Lauren asks for an espresso, I go for a latte.

'So, here we are,' Lauren says.

'Here we are,' I reply. We stare into each

other's eyes, she looks away first.

'I'm not going to cry. I told myself I'm not going to cry and I'm not. I never cry. I'm not one of those sorts of girls,' she says. I nod slowly. 'Don't look at me like that,' she adds. I frown.

'Like what?' I ask. She sighs.

'I feel...awful.'

'Don't. You have to do this. It's important.'

'Is it? More important than being with you?' she asks. I consider her words and shrug. I don't know. It's not for me to tell her what's more important in her life, is it? Should I be playing it better, making her feel bad for going? I can't. It's a decision she has to make on her own. She runs her finger around her espresso cup and then glances over at a tall guy with a small wife walking past. Looks weird, but I bet they're in love and happy.

'Does Parker know I'm going?' she asks. I nod.

'Yeah,' I reply.

'What does he think about it?'

'Not really his business.'

'I know. Just wondered what he thought.'

'He thinks you have to do what's right for you. I do too.'

'That's such a loaded comment.'

'No. It's true,' I reply. More awkwardness.

'Well, I think I'm going to go through. I don't want to drag this out, I'll be enough of a wreck as it is.'

'Yeah. Sure,' I reply, getting out my wallet. I put down ten pounds for the coffees.

'I'll pay,' she says.

'I got it,' I reply. We stand and walk slowly

towards security. We stop when we get as far as we can go. There are guys dishing out plastic bags and asking people if they have any liquids in their luggage. Lauren turns to me.

'Right well. See you in two weeks, thanks for coming to see me off,' she says.

'No worries,' I reply. I see the beginnings of a tear start its journey down her cheek. I hug her, pulling her in close to me. I feel myself start to go as well and breathe it back. I try to remember her smell as I nuzzle her neck, imprinting it in my memory. Slowly, we release each other. Her makeup has run a little, she must see my reaction because she says,

'I know, how stupid am I not wearing waterproof mascara?' We both chuckle and sniff back our tears. Yes, I'm a little emotional as well. What? Guys cry too, you know. 'I'll sort it out in the bathroom,' she says. I nod.

'Give me a ring when you get there,' I reply. She nods slowly with big puppy eyes.

'God, okay. Sorry. Right, come on Bates, get it together. See you later,' she says, leaning in and giving me a final peck on the cheek. She grabs her bag and walks away. I watch her go, the aching in my heart getting progressively worse. She shows her boarding pass to the official, he waves her through. I wait for her to look back. She does, so briefly that if I'd been blinking at that moment I would have missed it. I wave, but by the time my hand is raised, she's gone. I stand there, watching the space where she used to be. It's not forever. Just two weeks. I breathe in slowly. Goodbye Lauren. I turn and head towards the Heathrow

Express wondering where exactly my life is headed now.

As I ride the train back towards London my mind wanders. That last image of Lauren looking back at me. Two weeks feels like a year. Then I think of Ashley. She probably feels like shit. I need to call her as soon as I get back. Make sure she's okay. I get a picture message from Lauren, it's a photo of her return ticket. I smile.

The train pulls into Paddington Station just after twelve. I dial Ashley's number and walk towards the exit. It rings, once , twice...

'Hello?' Ashley says.

'Ash, it's Ollie,' I reply.

'Hey,' her tone changes.

'You okay?'

'Sure. Great.'

'Where are you? Are you coming back?'

'I dunno, Ollie. Maybe things are a bit too complicated,' she says. I breathe out, thinking of what to say next.

'Doesn't have to be. I'm cool with it if you are.'

'That's the thing. I don't know if I am.'

'Well, if you don't want to come back to the flat, at least meet me somewhere so we can talk.'

'What's the point?'

'Ash, how long have we known each other?'

'I dunno, long time. Maybe too long.'

'We should have a talk,' I say. She says nothing for a moment then,

'Okay, where?'

'Where are you, I can come to you?' I say.

'I'm at Norman's.'

'Norman's?'

'Don't, okay. Just-' she says.

'I didn't say anything. You want to talk at the pub?'

'God, no. Just meet me at Julio's in, what, an hour?'

'Sure.'

'Bye,' she says and hangs up. I jump on the tube and head back towards home.

When I get to Clapham I head over to Julio's, an Italian café halfway up Northcote Road. I'm twenty minutes early so I take a seat by the window. Julio comes over, a fat Italian man in dire need of a shave and a Stairmaster.

'Hey mister Ollie, how you doing?'

'Good thanks Julio, how are you?'

'Ah, you know. So, so. You want coffee?'

'Uh yeah, a latte please.'

'No problem, good to see you.'

'You too,' I say. He waddles off and I resume staring out of the window. I think about Lauren and wonder if she's thinking of me. Probably sitting watching some Hollywood in-flight movie. Could she have forgotten me already? Easily done I guess. Stop it Ollie, stop feeling sorry for yourself.

'Here you go mister Ollie.'

'Thanks Julio.'

'No pretty blonde lady today?' My heart leaps to my throat. He means Svetla. I swallow.

'No...we uh, split up.'

'Oh, sorry to hear that.'

'Yeah.'

'She was a nice girl.'

'She was.'

'You find someone new, don't worry.'

'I have. But she's gone too.'

'Oh. You no have much luck,' says Julio.

'No,' I reply. The door opens and Ashley walks in. She scans the café for me. She's wearing a jean jacket and black leggings. I give her a little wave. Julio winks at me. Ashley walks over, hands in pockets and sits down opposite me.

'What you like, miss?' Julio asks.

'Just a coffee please. White,' she replies. He nods and walks back to the counter.

'So, how you doing?' I ask. She sighs.

'Brilliant,' she replies. I tilt my head. 'What? What do you want me to say? Life's great? I'm happier than I've ever been? I'm with yet another drop out guy, with no prospects for anything. I'm still living with school friends and my life is going nowhere.'

'Just because you live with school friends, doesn't mean your life isn't going anywhere,' I reply.

'Look I appreciate it, Ollie, but I think I need to move out. Can't handle being a fuck up and in love with someone I can't have,' she says. I go to interject but she carries on. 'I know, I know. It's my fault. Just...need to get my shit together is all.'

'What about your music?'

'What music?'

'Ashley, I'm serious when I said you should go pro with that. It's really, really good.'

'Yeah, then why did the Guildhall turn me down then?'

'I...didn't know they did. I didn't know you'd even applied for it. That was quick.'

'Yeah well. They did.'

'Doesn't mean anything.Find another music school. I said I'd help you-'

'I don't want your help-'

'Here you go,' Julio says, placing the coffee down in front of her. She glances at me then down to her coffee. Julio walks away.

'I'm not sure why I came to stay with you. I just remembered I could always be myself with you. And yes, there was always the other stuff but, I dunno...I trusted you. Still do.'

'Listen to me. I get that this isn't easy for you and I won't make you do anything you don't want to but look, you're welcome to stay as long as you like. If it's too hard then I totally understand and I promise I won't hold any bad feelings if you want to move out but...we could try.' She takes a sip of her coffee. I sit back and do the same.

'How's Lauren?' she asks.

'Gone.'

'Gone where?'

'New York. She's there for a couple of weeks, then she comes back for a couple of months. Then, she moves out there for a couple of years.'

'Oh dear,' she whispers.

'Yeah well...'

'What a pair we are,' she says. I nod slowly. 'What about you going out there?'

'I've thought about it. Maybe I could, just...I don't want to. I like her. A lot. But moving countries, pretty hardcore.'

'Yeah. Well, I know I'm probably the last

person you want to speak to about this but for what it's worth, if you need anything...' I glance at her. 'Not that.' We both laugh. 'I mean, if you need to talk.' I nod again.

'Thanks. What about Norman?' I ask. She rolls her eyes.

'He's just...I don't know what he is.'

'Bit on the side?'

'Probably.'

'Do you like him?' I ask. She goes to answer then stops and thinks.

'Not really.' She leans back in her chair, rubs her eyes slowly and sighs. 'Ollie, what am I doing?'

'Your best. Isn't that what we're all doing?' I reply.

'If this is my best, I've got some serious issues.'

NOW

THIRTY FOUR – A FUTURE NO BETTER

Ashley and I head back to the flat. I manage to persuade her that, for lack of a better idea, she should stay around mine until she finds somewhere else. She reluctantly agrees. We walk slowly, not saying much. The sun is out and it's turned into a glorious day. I spot some short sleeves and bare legs.

When we arrive back at the flat, Tristan is sitting on the floor in front of my door smoking a fag. I glance at Ashley who shrugs.

'Hey,' I say.

'Whaddya say you fucking...' Tristan mumbles.

'Hey! You're blocking the door, man,' I say. His eyes open and he quickly shields them from the blinding sunlight. He looks up at us.

'You want some heroin?' he asks.

'Cheers but, no thank you,' I reply. Slowly he gets up and offers his hand to Ashley.

'I don't know you but if you want some heroin,

I have some?'

'Ah that's sweet but I'm okay, thank you,' Ashley replies.

'Why doesn't anyone want my drugs? Fuck, I can't give 'em away.'

'They bust you again?' I ask.

'Fucking pigs. I gotta wear this fucking thing,' he says, pulling up his trouser leg to reveal a tag around his ankle. 'Fascists.'

'Yeah,' Ashley and I say, almost in union.

'You want to know the bitch of it?' he asks.

'What?' I reply.

'It's a real fucker to get off,' he says. I glance at Ashley.

'Sorry man, can we get through?' I say, stepping around him and putting the key in the lock. I open the door.

'It can only get better, right?' Ashley says, her hand on Tristan's shoulder. Tristan looks at her, his face suddenly softening.

'I guess,' he says. I go inside, Ashley follows. She turns to close the door.

'Good luck,' she says.

'Thanks,' he replies. She smiles and closes the door.

'Very nice of you,' I say.

'We can't all be born winners,' Ashley replies.

'I'm not a winner.'

'Who said anything about you?' she says, turning around.

'O...kay,' I reply, keeping eye contact. Ashley turns from me and suddenly starts to move quickly. She becomes almost a blur in front of me, she's moving so fast. And then everything else starts moving in the same way, minutes become hours become days become months. The flat goes from tidy to messy back to tidy. Parker and Nicola come and go, back and forth. Ashley flies around me, then is gone. Day turns to night which turns back to day. Over and over again. I look at the clock on the wall, time is suddenly moving at an incredible rate. The big hand is nothing more than a haze, the little hand barely visible. And then, as quickly as it started, everything starts to slow. The months slow to days and then to hours, before becoming minutes and seconds. The nights turn to days but it takes longer now, until suddenly I'm staring at an empty living room. I look around. Time has settled.

It's been almost a year since that conversation with Ashley and Tristan. I still live here, in the flat. I walk into the hallway and down towards what used to be Parker's room. Empty. Just a spare bedroom. Sunlight pours through the windows showing dust particles in the beams. The flat is empty. I hear my phone ring in the other room. I walk along the hallway and back into the living room. I pick it up from the table.

'Hello?' I say.

'What, no insult?' replies Parker.

'I'm trying to rise above stuff like that.'

'Yeah, right. What you doing?'

'I'm...' I stop, glancing around. What am I doing?

'Having a wank?' Parker finishes the sentence for me. 'Want me to call back later?'

'Parker, I always want you to call back later but as you're on the phone, what do you want?'

'It's Nicola's birthday on Friday and I thought I'd take her somewhere nice. Like, not The Old Cock and I just wondered if you had any suggestions?'

'What, like a bar?'

'Yeah, but a cool bar.'

'I dunno. I went to this place with Lauren once, in the City. Uh, Jo Jo's I think it's called. Quite trendy and hip. Not the sort of place I'd expect to find someone like you.'

'Ta for that. I'll sort something out, you up for coming?'

'I dunno...'

'Nicola has lots of nice single friends.'

'She also shits on floors.'

'We agreed you wouldn't bring that up,' he says.

'We never agreed anything. *You* said not to bring it up,' I reply.

'And yet here we are...still talking about it,' he replies.

'How's the book?'

'Yeah still making an absolute mint from it, being translated into Macedonian. Crazy, right?'

'So you must have more money than God?'

'Not yet, but soon my son. Soon.'

'Nice. Drinks on you then,' I say. Parker managed to get an agent for his book. Turned out that awful thing I read on his computer wasn't actually his book. What he had written (and kept well hidden from me) was a stunning novel about the First World War and a man trying to get home. It was really good and the agent managed to sell it after a bidding war between three publishers. Now it's on the cusp of being released into book shops, he's got some enormous advance and he's living it up. How, you may ask? The answer, dear friends, is I haven't got a clue but I'm happy for him. Suddenly he's become all serious and hardly watches Top Gear at all. Although that may be to do with Nicola not allowing him to control the TV. Yeah, they moved in together and seem happy enough. Most of the time.

'Uh huh. Have you heard from-' he asks.

'Nope.'

'Bitch.'

'No, she probably just hasn't had time.'

'When was the last time you spoke to her?'

'I dunno, couple of weeks ago.'

'Uh huh.'

'She misses me. A lot.'

'Of course she does. So, she's still in New York?' he asks.

'Yeah. I'm planning to go and see her in a couple of months. Maybe after the schools go back.'

'Sure, yeah,' Parker says. I won't pretend having a long-distance relationship has been easy, because it hasn't. We can go days without talking. I try to keep my spirits up but it's hard. She tells me about her deals and the shit they're making her do over there, most of which I don't understand. I miss her. I know, I'm crap, right? But I do genuinely feel sad when we have to stop Skype or hang up. I think she's still in to me. Hopefully as much as before but it's so difficult to tell when you're three thousand miles away from each other. She did come over for Christmas and again in

March. We had a lot of sex. I'll say no more than that. Absence makes the heart grow fonder, I can't even begin to tell you what it does to the libido. I realise Parker is still on the line.

'Okay, so maybe see you Friday then?' I say.

'Yeah, laters dude.'

Friday comes around faster than expected. Nicola decided my idea of Jo Jo's was an excellent one. Be weird if some of Lauren's City bunch were there. Mark did say they went down there regularly. Sod it, I'm sure it will be fine. I pull on my smartest jacket and shirt, leaving the top button undone. I slap on a little Armani Code and I'm good to go. I catch my reflection in the mirror and quickly move on.

I've arranged to meet Nicola and Parker at Jo Jo's. I guess we could have gone together or shared a taxi but I just want to sit on the tube and listen to my iPod, pondering my lot in life. Just as I'm out of the woods with Svetla, Lauren comes along and wheedles her way into my thoughts only to fuck off across the Atlantic, leaving me alone. Could it be that I, Ollie Hayward, am incapable of being by myself? I don't know. The thought makes me more depressed as the Waterloo and City line yanks me towards my destination.

I arrive just after seven at Jo Jo's and look around. It's already rammed. My eyes do a quick scan of the place, searching for people I might know and not want to talk to (e.g. Mark, James, Paul, Julie, my mum.) With no apparent sign of unpleasantness I walk up to the bar. Everyone is dressed in suits or business clothes. After work drinks. Clubby music thumps from hidden speakers. It's just so...contemporary in here. Like someone went nuts with Ikea decorations and lighting and threw them all over the place. In another year or two this place will be like fifties architecture. Hopelessly out of date.

I stand patiently behind the bar waiting to get served, occasionally looking around to see if Parker and Nicola have arrived. Eventually I catch the barman's attention.

'Hello mate, can I get a pint of Peroni, please?' I ask. He pours the beer and takes my money. With uncanny timing, I feel a slap on my shoulder. I glance around to see Parker standing with Nicola and two other girls, all dressed to the nines.

'Alright shithead?' Parker says, smiling.

'Hi,' I reply, 'happy birthday Nicola.' She smiles, leaning forward to kiss me on both cheeks. She looks vaguely hot in a short, red dress.

'Ollie, this is Rachel...' (the one with the tight white jeans and cold sore above her lip) 'and Keely,' (the redhead wearing a smart leather jacket and almost laughable high heels.) I shake both their hands, smiling.

'Nice to meet you,' Keely says.

'You too. You want a drink?' I ask.

'That is the most productive thing you've said all week,' Parker says.

'I booked a table, let's go and find it. Can you help Ollie with the drinks, Parker?' Nicola asks. Parker salutes.

'Sir, yes sir,' he says, saluting. She's not

impressed and his smile soon dies.

'Mine's a dry white wine, if that's okay,' says Rachel. She sounds a bit like a chipmunk, farcically high pitched.

'Me too, thanks,' says Keely.

'Can I get a vodka and Coke,' says Nicola. I nod. The girls wander off to find their table.

'So?' Parker says.

'So what?'

'Which one?'

'Neither.'

'No?' he says, watching them walk away. He turns back to me. 'Picky fucker, aren't you?'

'That's right and I have a girlfriend, cheers though,' I say. Parker looks around the bar.

'Well I asked for trendy and you deliver...a Superdry store without the clothes.'

'I thought it was more IKEA,' I reply.

'Hmm.'

'So what did you get Nicola for her birthday?' I ask.

'Call of Duty for the Playstation,' Parker replies, straight away. I chuckle.

'Nice. Bet she really appreciated that.'

'Well if she didn't, I'll have it.'

'Hmm,' I say.

'Fuck, are any of these guys working...excuse me mate, think we were next,' Parker says. I shake my head. He's so...Parker.

'Yep, what can I get you?' the barman says to me again.

'Two glasses of white wine, vodka and Coke and...,' I turn to Parker, 'what do you want?' Parker stares at me, his eyes narrowing.

'Pint of Peroni,' he says, giving me a look that
says 'you've known me all this time and you don't
know what I like to drink?' I double take, then look
back to the barman.

'Another pint of Peroni,' I say. The barman
nods and gets busy. 'What's wrong with you?'

'Nothing just...not my sort of place,' Parker
says.

'Well, be happy, for Nicola. Right? It's her
birthday.'

'Yeah okay.'

We grab the drinks. I pay. Guess how much
for five drinks? No, go on have a guess? Twenty?
Twenty-five? Nope...the total was twenty-nine
pounds, thirty-three pence! I mean...what the hell?
We find the girls who have been shown to a booth.
It's cosy but there's not a huge amount of space.
We grab our drinks and toast Nicola. A poor
rendition of happy birthday peters out when Nicola
starts shushing us.

'So when you gonna pop the question, Parker?'
Keely asks.

'Keely...' Nicola says.

'Uh,' Parker says. I smile.

'We're not talking about that. It's my birthday
and that topic is banned,' Nicola says. Parker
glances at me. I shrug and sip my pint.

The evening progresses steadily. If I'm honest,
I think we feel a little out of place amongst the
great and the good of the City. When Keely comes
back from buying a round of drinks, she looks like
she's just witnessed a war crime.

'You okay?' Rachel asks.

'Yeah, yeah. It's quite expensive here, isn't it?'

she says, a poor attempt at keeping her tone light.

'Is it?' Parker says.

'Yes it is. You'll see,' I say, smiling. I need a piss and I can't hold it any longer. I stand and squeeze past Rachel who barely makes an effort to let me past. She's off my Christmas list. I wander back to the bar and look for the familiar, internationally recognised male and female symbols. I spot them and head in that direction, pushing through the throngs of people. Christ, you can barely breathe it's so packed. I stop suddenly because ahead is someone who looks exactly like Lauren. It's difficult to see and bloody people keep walking in front of me. I frown. No, it can't be. I carry on, pushing past another person. No, it's not her...phew, that would have been so weird. As I get closer however, the girl who looks like Lauren starts kissing the guy she's sitting next to. I swallow. It can't be her. No, it isn't her, her hair is shorter.

I continue to watch these two strangers with fascination as they go at it, full pelt. The guy isn't wearing a suit, in fact he looks quite dishevelled. They are all over each other, she kisses him and runs her hands over his back. I see him move a hand over her breast as I catch a momentary glimpse of his tongue in her mouth. Her eyes open and I suddenly get a full view of her face. It...is Lauren. She looks different, her hair and makeup...but it is her. Oh my God. Her skirt is pulled up and although they sit in a relatively secluded spot, it still seems inappropriate. What am I saying, it's more than bloody inappropriate. Her eyes roll back into her head, clearly enjoying every second. I want to interject, stop it, stop them from continuing but I can't move. I'm just so...shocked. She's supposed to be in New York. Ruling the world. Breaking the glass ceiling. She's isn't. She's here...in London, sucking this guy's face off. Whoever he is. He runs his hand through her hair and I feel a retch of sick fly up to my mouth. I catch it and swallow. What...the...fuck? Her eyes open again and she stares at him, smiling. But then, suddenly she turns and looks over to where I'm standing. She catches me staring at her. It takes a few moments for her to process who the strange man standing in the middle of the bar is. She jerks away from the guy, a glass smashing on the floor. People glance around at the noise. I stare at her, she frowns, her eyelids heavy. She's drunk but I see the realisation creep over her face.

'Ollie?' her mouth says, frowning. I can't hear her over the music and people but I recognise my name just from lip-reading. The guy turns to face me and suddenly I recognise him. It's only Johnny fucking Dougan, the lead singer from the Time Travellers she'd said she used to date. I look from Johnny Dougan back to her, still completely unable to process what I'm seeing before me. Our eyes stare at each other for a moment longer before I turn slowly and walk towards the front door. I hear a raucous behind me as she tries to push Johnny away.

'Ollie...' This time I do I hear her behind me. I don't react as I walk, now in slow motion, towards the exit. Each step feels heavier than the last, I glance over to Parker and Nicola, catching Parker's eye. He frowns. I get to the door, Lauren's high heels clip-clopping on the floor behind me. I yank the door open and step outside.

'Ollie, Ollie wait!' Lauren shouts. I stop but don't turn around. I hear her walk up behind me. A deafening silence between us. I glance down at the cracks in the pavement.

'I...I'm so sorry,' she says. 'Please, let's just...let's just talk.' I turn slowly and look at her. I want to swear, to shout, to punch something but shock is the only real emotion I'm feeling. Then clarity finds my mind as everything orders itself.

'Don't. Ever, come near me. Again,' I say, my eyes burning. Her eyes fill up at my words. Her lips start to tremble. I turn and walk towards the tube station.

'I'm sorry. I'M SORRY! Ollie! OLLIE!' she screams. I don't look back, focused on getting as far away from her as possible. All that time. All those moments we shared. I believed it all. How busy she was. The job in New York. My God, I'm so stupid. Of course it would end like this, it's so obvious. I'm momentarily confused as to why I'm upset. I carry on regardless, I need to get to the tube. The City rings out with the sounds of drunken people and distant pub music.

'Hey!' I hear a male voice behind me and shoes hitting the pavement, gaining on me. Parker. I don't stop. 'Hey, hey...' he reaches me, out of breath, and puts his hand on my shoulder. I shove it away. 'Okay...what just happened? Was that Lauren?' I turn, face him and nod. 'What happened? I thought she was in New York.' I shrug, trying to form the words.

'Nope. She's here, kissing Johnny Dougan,' I say, surprisingly calmly.

'What?'

'In the bar, just now. I went to the toilet and I saw her. Right in front of me. Kissing him.'

'Shit, man.' I shake my head.

'All that time...when she said-'

'Don't think about it. What a fucking bitch. I'm gonna talk to her, tell her exactly-'

'Don't. Just, leave it alone,' I say. Parker shakes his head and looks back towards the bar. He breathes out and nods.

'What do you want to do?' he says.

'I'm going home.'

'Then I'm coming with you.'

'No, it's fine. It's Nicola's birthday.'

'So? My best mate has just been royally shat on. You are not going home by yourself tonight. Probably find you hanging from the ceiling,' Parker says, taking out his phone. He dials a number.

'I wouldn't do that,' I say. At least, I don't think I'd ever kill myself.

'Uh huh,' he replies, 'hi baby, it's me. Listen something's happened...Lauren was just in the pub, kissing someone else...' as he says it, my stomach drops again. The power of hearing those words. 'Yeah...I'm gonna stay round his, okay...okay. Yeah...' I barely hear the words, my mind replaying over and over the image of Lauren and Johnny. Fucking Johnny Dougan. She said they were just friends. I hear an ambulance siren in the distance. I find myself hoping it's for Lauren. No, I don't mean that. But...how could she? 'Yeah, okay...bye,' Parker says. I stare at the pavement again, tears welling in my eyes. It's too much to try and hide it. Parker puts his arm around me. 'Come on dude. Let's get you home.'

THIRTY FIVE – FINDING A FRIEND

I gradually become aware of my surroundings. I'm in my bed, the curtains are pulled. I blink and rub the sleep out of my eyes. I feel drunk. What on earth did I have to drink last night? How did I even get back here? And then the memories fly back to me. Lauren. Johnny. Hands. Hair. Lips. I sigh, pull the covers off and find my dressing gown.

I walk into the kitchen to find the Nescafe jar out and two cups sitting on the worktop. I switch the kettle on and get some milk from the fridge. Parker is at the door, already dressed.

'Hey,' he says.

'Hi,' I reply.

'How you feeling?'

'Like shit,' I say. He nods.

'I can do this,' he says. I let him. He puts two sugars in each cup and pours the water into the mugs followed by a dash of milk. He hands me a mug and I follow him into the living room. We sit down. I look up towards the window.

'I still can't believe she did that,' Parker says. I

nod.

'Yeah.'

'I mean really. I was thinking about it last night. Who does that? Who plays some massive elaborate game about going to New York and you coming over and long distance Skype bullshit when all the while she's fucking about with that Johnny arsehole?'

'I don't know,' I say and I mean it. I have no explanations. No answers. After all the shit with Svetla and now this. I'm right back where I started. 'You know what pisses me off most? Apart from the obvious. I let her in. I let her get to me. At the beginning, I really wasn't that into it, you know? I know she's gorgeous and everyone stares at her when she walks into a room but I really was pretty indifferent to it all. I just wanted to get over Svetla and she seemed like a good idea.'

'Yeah,' Parker replies, nodding slowly. I take a sip of coffee. 'So maybe you got from her what you needed?' I frown. 'You needed to get over Svetla and Lauren was the person to do that.'

'Yeah but all I've done is swap Svetla for Lauren. I haven't progressed, haven't evolved. Same shit, different person.'

'Maybe you just need to take some time to yourself? I dunno, go travelling or something?'

'Maybe,' I say. I sigh again.

'Or you could try and talk to Ashley?' he says. I glance at him and frown.

'What for?'

'I dunno, she was always good at this sort of stuff.'

'You know what happened between us?'

'Yeah-'

'She won't want to talk to me.'

'Could try, what harm can it do?'

'I think I need to stay away from women for a while. Bad for my health.'

'Amen to that,' he says. My phone rings from my bedroom. I glance over to Parker. 'Don't answer it.' I stand up. 'Hey, seriously don't answer it.'

'I'm not going to,' I reply, heading to my bedroom. The phone ring gets louder as I walk into my bedroom. Sure enough the display reads 'Lauren Calling...' I wait for it to stop.

'Is it?' Parker calls from the other room.

'Yep,' I say, walking back into the living room.

'She leave a message?'

'Not yet.' We both wait expectantly for the voicemail notification beep. I glance over to Parker, he shrugs. Hmm. Maybe she didn't leave one. Even that's a bit shit. BEEP! It almost makes me jump.

'You want me to listen to it, give you the edited highlights?' Parker says.

'No, cheers.' I listen to the voicemail. It's Lauren's voice but she sounds shaky, nervous, unsure.

'Hi. It's me. Look I know you must be...so angry with me. And I know there's no excuse for what I did...(long pause)...I just, umm...I've been having a bit of a shitty week or so and...not that that's your problem but Johnny was just there and I was weak.' She clears her throat. 'Anyway...I just wanted to say please give me a chance to at least explain myself. If, after that, you don't want anything more to do with me I'll understand but...yeah. Okay. Take care.' The click on the other end signifies her ending the message.

'Well?' Parker asks. I look over to him and sigh.

'She says she's sorry and she was having a hard week.' Parker snorts at that.

'Oh right, so it's a hard week when you find yourself in the wrong city getting it on with the wrong guy. That's so crap, doesn't even deserve a response.'

'Yeah. Unless I'm the wrong guy,' I reply, still in a trance.

'Don't say that, don't even think it. This is her fuck up. She knows it. None of this is your fault and you'd be a pussy if you start going down that road.'

'Yeah. I guess,' I reply.

Parker stays for another hour. We talk, I don't learn anything new, we just chew over how shit it all is. I appreciate his presence but find myself just wanting to be alone. He gets the hint and tells me to call him if I need anything. I nod and hug him, man style. He slaps my back on the way out.

'Hey. Be okay dude. Just gotta wait a while. Let time do its thing,' Parker says. I nod.

'See ya,' I say. I watch him walk away. I go to close the door and spot Tristan leaning against the railings watching Parker. He turns to face me. He looks, different. He's had a shave and his hair is gelled back. There are still multiple holes in his jeans and his leather jacket has seen better days but his whole aura seems changed. He looks like a druggie James Dean. Or am I being too kind with that analogy?

'Hey,' I say, nodding to him.

'Alright,' he replies, taking a drag from his cigarette. About the first time he hasn't started the conversation with 'fuck you.'

'Have a fight with your girl?' he asks. I frown.

'Yeah, how did you-?'

'I heard high pitched wailing last night, figured it was you.' I nod, mildly embarrassed. Was I wailing?

'You going somewhere?' I say, eager to change the subject.

'Yeah. Got a job.'

'You have?' I ask. He nods and takes another drag from his cigarette.

'Doing what?' Maybe he's a stand in for Danny in Grease.

'Window cleaning,' he says. I frown, confused. I feel sure there's a punchline in here somewhere.

'Right. So you just...clean people's windows?'

'Yep. The boss is a really nice guy as well.' O...kay.

'Well that's...great. I'm really happy for you?'

'Yeah. Bit of a turn up, someone like me working for a cripple.'

'What?'

'My boss. He's only got one arm,' Tristan says. I stare at him, trying to work out exactly what this job entails.

'So if he's only got one arm, how does he-?'

'Clean windows? I put the leather in the water, hand it to him, he washes them and hands it back to me. I wring it out and so on.' And there it is, the punchline.

'That's...good for you.'

'Thanks man,' he says, checking his watch,

'shit, better go. Don't let the girl get you down.'

'Right,' I say, closing the door slowly.

I walk back inside, sit down on the sofa and listen to Lauren's voicemail again. She wants to explain herself? Fuck her. She doesn't get to do anything. Not now. Not ever. A flash hits me of us at the cottage in the Cotswolds and I breathe out. I hate that she made me feel something for her. I sit in silence, unable to make a decision. I can't call her back. Not this soon. She can sweat. I genuinely don't know what to do. Then Parker's idea fades into my subconscious. Ashley. She always knew what to do in these situations. Is it weird to call her up, ask her advice about this after what happened, especially as she's moved on in such a massive way? Would she even talk to me? I look down at my mobile and I find Ashley's mobile number in my phone. Fuck it. I dial her number. It rings once, twice...click.

'Ollie Hayward,' her voice says on the other end. She sounds cheerful, happy.

'Hey, how's it going?' I reply, trying to sound normal.

'Good, long time no see.'

'Yeah well, you're all famous now so...'

'Doesn't mean I don't have time to talk to my favourite ex shag,' she says. I smile. 'So, how are you? Everything well?'

'Well, you know, same as always...' my voice falters, I can't keep up the act. I clear my throat.

'Ollie?'

'Yeah, sorry. I just, uh...look I'm sorry to just call you up like this but, uh...is there any way you might have time for a chat? Just, I'm going through a bit of a tough time and I could really do with someone to talk to.'

'Of course. I'm in Camden, can you get here?'

'Camden?'

'Yeah, at the Roundhouse. I'm performing three nights. I get busy from about five but if you can come down earlier?'

'Yeah. That would be great.'

'Cool, give me a bell when you get here.'

'Thanks Ash, I really appreciate it.'

'For you Ollie, anytime.'

'Okay. I'll see you in a bit.'

'Bye.'

'Bye.'

I hang up, swallow and head off to find some shoes.

THIRTY SIX – A GOOD TALK

The Roundhouse in Camden used to be an old Victorian steam engine repair shed. Now it's blossomed into *the* place for new artists to play. Looking like a massive stone drum off the busy Chalk Farm Road, it has a vibe about it unlike other venues. I stare in awe at Ashley's poster draped over the main entrance. She's made it. Not that I ever thought she wouldn't but she's had an incredible year. First album, debuting at number three. Top five single with 'Charity' which even made it onto a 'Now' album. Everyone wants a piece of her. Christ, I'm starting to sound like a press release.

I stand, slightly overwhelmed. I knew she'd become successful but I guess it's only when you see it right in front of your eyes you realise how real it all is. I walk inside and up to the desk. I'm greeted by a guy wearing funky thick-framed glasses.

'Hi there, how can I help you?'

'I'm here to see Ashley, I'm a friend of hers.'

'Okay, who shall I say is here?'

'Ollie Hayward, she's expecting me. I hope,' I reply, a little too enthusiastically. The man gives me a polite smile and dials a number.

'Hi there, I've got Ollie Hayward here to see Ashley. Yep. Okay, thanks,' he says, putting the phone down. 'If you take this and head through that set of doors there.' He hands me a temporary visitor's pass.

'Thanks,' I reply and go over to the doors. I push them open and stop when I see the stage. Powerful spotlights are trained on Ashley who sits at the piano. A half-empty bottle of water rests next to her stool. Behind her, a fully kitted out band look ready to start. She's talking to one of the roadies, who's testing the speakers. At least that's what I think they're doing. I'm not a sound expert or anything, I just tell you what I see.

'No, try it a little higher,' she says, playing a small tune on the piano. 'That's it, much better, thanks Josh.' A guy wearing a black t-shirt and jeans waves and heads behind the stage. I walk towards them slowly, unsure if I really am allowed in here.

'Okay, from the top,' Ashley says to the rest of the band. 'One, two...one, two, three...' The band starts to play. I stop, listening to them play. Then she begins to sing, her stunning voice filling the arena.

A friend and something else.
More than a lover, more than friend
Split, the hurt began
I just wanted my friend
My friend

I needed my friend
I needed my friend
I needed my friend

I walk slowly towards her. Her fingers on the keys move deftly on the piano, a total master. She sways slowly to the music as the band lift the song to a foot-tapping, soulful masterpiece.

His ship sets sail
For another land
But I will always miss
Where we came from

As she sings, she spots me and smiles. I wave instinctively and smile back, then glance around, suddenly subconscious.

My friend
I needed my friend
Where was my friend
I needed my friend

Goose bumps ripple across my arm. I shiver as I take in the meaning of what she's singing about. I admit I've been playing her album almost nonstop on my way into work since it came out but I haven't heard this song before. The band build to a rousing crescendo and Ashley's delicate, almost innocent voice, softly finishes the song.

My friend
My lover
My friend

She holds on to the last note for what feels like ages. A beautiful, soulful song. The place falls silent. A moment before I breathe again.

'That was great,' Ashley says to the band. She holds her hand up, shielding her eyes from the bright lights.

'Ollie Hayward,' she says over the microphone so everyone in the hall now knows my name.

'Hi,' I say, walking up to the front of the stage. Ashley jumps up and takes a sip from her bottle of water. She walks down a set of steps and over to me, flinging her arms around me. She holds me tight, it feels good.

'It's so good to see you,' she says. I close my eyes, breathing out.

'You too,' I reply. We hold the embrace a second longer before she releases me.

'How you doing?' she asks, smiling. I shrug.

'Okay, I guess,' I reply. She nods slowly and takes my hand.

'Come on, let's get out of here,' she says. 'Guys, I'm taking a break. Be back in forty-five minutes and we'll start on Charity, okay?' The band voices their agreement to the plan. I follow Ashley through an emergency exit and outside on to the noisy public road.

'So, how are you?' Ashley asks, threading her arm through mine.

'Yeah good,' I say, nodding. She stops and looks at me.

'Really?' she says, tilting her head slightly, eyebrows raised.

'No,' I reply, looking down. She looks at me a second longer then nudges me.

'Come on,' she says.

We find a small park and sit down on a bench facing a deserted playground. There's not so much noise here, I even hear birds singing from the trees.

'So?' she asks.

'So,' I reply.

'Love life?'

'Lauren,' I reply. She leans back.

'Ah. Long distance thing proving difficult?' she asks. I shrug and try to come up with a form of words to tell her the story. Eventually I say,

'When she went to NewYork it started out fine, we talked nearly every day on Skype, sent emails and whatnot. But she got really busy and we just started talking less and less but we were still going out.'

'So...?'

'So,' I say, breathing out quickly, 'I haven't spoken to her for, I dunno, a couple of weeks and last night I went down to this bar in the City called Jo Jo's with Parker and Nicola and a few of her friends. It was Nicola's birthday. Anyway, I go to the toilet and just outside I see Lauren...kissing her ex.' Ashley's eyes widen.

'Oh. Shit,' she says.

'Yeah.'

'So, she wasn't in New York?'

'No.'

'What'd you do?'

'I sort of couldn't believe it really. Like, we'd spent all that time together and she just had so little respect for me, she just threw it all away,' I say. Ashley looks at me with an I-told-you-so smile. She nods slowly.

'Yeah. Doesn't feel good, does it?' she says. I suddenly remember this is exactly what I unintentionally did to her.

'We never talked about us, Ash.'

'Because I didn't want to. Living with you

those last couple of months was hard enough. This isn't about you and me Ollie. Just ironic, I guess,' she says. I look down. 'Hey?' She touches my chin with her hand and gently lifts my head. My eyes meet hers. 'You obviously care about her a lot or you wouldn't be here and you wouldn't have spent a year talking over Skype, right?'

'I guess so. That's why it doesn't make any sense. Is she really that cold hearted?'

'There can be so many reasons, she could have been fired, lost someone close to her...anything could have happened. Your ex is suddenly there, you're feeling all over the place because of...whatever. You know, stuff just happens sometimes.'

'Well, it bloody shouldn't just happen.'

'I know that Ollie, but she's only human. Did she say why?' I shake my head.

'No. She called and left a message saying she wanted to explain everything and that she'd gone through a shit week,' I say.

'Well...maybe you need all the facts before you rush to judge. I'm not saying you shouldn't be pissed off or angry or anything but, maybe just hear her out. You know?'

'I feel so-'

'Humiliated?' she says. I nod. 'You'll get over it. But if this is worth something, you should listen to her. Things aren't always what they seem. Again, I'm not defending her actions or saying you should take her back but if this means something to you, maybe hearing what she has to say is worth the price of your ego.' I nod again, taking in what she says.

'How are you, anyway?' I ask. She smiles and gives me a big hug. I breathe in.

'Ollie, Ollie, Ollie,' she says. Her embrace feels good and I try to stop myself getting emotional.

'Oi, oi, oi,' I whisper. She lets me go and ruffles my hair.

'I'm good. Career has sort of taken over everything.'

'Anyone...special out there?' I ask. Ashley chuckles and shakes her head.

'Nah, haven't got time for any of that nonsense.'

'Because you're rich and famous?' I ask. She shakes her head.

'I'm having my five minutes of fame. Sooner or later someone else will take my place, just have to enjoy it while I can.'

'You're here because you deserve to be here. You're bloody talented and this is only the start.'

'Yeah well...anyway, you and Lauren?'

'I dunno,' I say, sighing.

'I think you do know. You just don't want to admit it.'

'What?'

'That you're totally in love with this girl and you're trying, in a crappy male way, to protect yourself from being hurt again. And I get it. But this isn't going to stop the pain, it's only going to make it worse. You'll spend all your time thinking about her, and in the end that will turn to regret and the whole thing will end up being completely FUBAR.' I frown. 'Fucked Up Beyond All Recognition.' she says. I sigh and nod slowly. 'You need to talk to her.'

'What if we're just not meant to be together?'

'Maybe you're not, but don't you at least want to make sure?' she says. I glance at her and smile. She returns the smile. I know she's right and I know what I've got to do.

'Thanks Ash,' I say. 'Look at us, couple of regular people sitting in the park.'

'Yeah. I don't get too many of these moments anymore. It's nice,' she replies, closing her eyes and leaning her head back.

'Album's doing well.'

'Don't,' she says, not opening her eyes.

'What?' I say. She sits up and looks at me.

'Small talk crap. I know we haven't seen each other for a while and that's mainly because of me. I had to get my head sorted and I couldn't do that with you around. I'm sorry I left without saying goodbye. But you were right about the music. I'm glad I listened to you, 'cos none of this would be happening without you.' Her words touch me somewhere deep inside.

'Thanks for seeing me, especially now. I know how busy you are,' I say.

'We're friends, Ollie. Best friends, and friends look out for each other,' she says, smiling.

I walk Ashley back to the Roundhouse and we say our goodbyes, promising to speak to each other more than once every nine months. I head home, my mind full of new pieces of advice to consider. I probably should give Lauren a chance to speak, but not right now. I know I'm being childish but I want her to know how much this hurt. Then another voice speaks to me, do I really want to be with this girl? She has a lot of good points but there are some seriously questionable ones as well. I don't know.

The tube is quiet on the way back. I walk along my street on autopilot, I know what I need to do, just need to figure out how.

THIRTY SEVEN – AN UNEXPECTED VISITOR (PART 2)

Monday. Lauren has called four times since I saw Ashley. I'm not ready and strangely, the more she calls, the longer I want to wait. I know I'm probably being pathetic and petty but I just can't talk to her.

I sit at my desk, staring at my computer, my mind awash with thoughts.

'Hey, I bought you a latte,' says Julie. I look up at her. She smiles and places the cup down next to me.

'Thanks.'

'A guy cheated on me once,' she says.

'Yeah?'

'Yeah. Kicked him so hard in the bollocks, he had to go to casualty,' she says. I frown. Is she serious?

'Really?'

'Oh yeah. He needed surgery and everything.'

'Jesus.'

'Yeah.'

'Not sure that will work in this situation. She doesn't have bollocks,' I say. Julie thinks for a moment then says,

'You could give her a tit punch?'

'It's sweet you're concerned, but doing a two year stretch at Pentonville for assault just doesn't seem worth it.'

'Hmm,' she replies, considering my answer. My phone rings. Lauren calling...again.

'Is that her?' Julie asks. I nod, staring at the display. Suddenly Julie snatches the phone and answers it.

'Look leave him alone. If he wants to talk to you, he'll answer the phone. You keep calling like this makes you look like a psycho bitch-' she says. I grab the phone from her.

'Hello?' I say. Lauren's gone. 'She hung up. Julie, what the hell?'

'What?'

'You don't do stuff like that, come on. Not cool.'

'I was doing you a favour,' she says. I shake my head. Julie shrugs and walks away. Do I call Lauren back? That wasn't exactly pleasant but then neither was seeing her tongue down Johnny Dougan's throat. I glance over to Julie, maybe she's the psycho? Just get on and do some work Ollie.

The day moves so achingly slowly that by the end, I swear I've managed to grow a tumour just thinking about all this. I say goodbye to Paul and Julie who gives me a sympathetic smile, like she's totally forgotten about the crazy phone-grabbing incident. Weirdo.

The Northern line has severe delays and, after waiting five minutes to get on a carriage, I'm about ready to kill someone. I stand, squashed to the point where no air can enter my lungs. I glance down at a smart-looking Japanese girl. She is reading from her Kindle, her eyes move so fast, I start to wonder if she's reading it at all or just faking so I'll think 'wow you're a really fast reader.' I don't know. Christ, why am I telling you these things? Just get home Ollie.

I open the door to my flat and slam it shut, momentarily leaning against it. I look up at the ceiling and sigh. Somebody help me. God? You hear me? I need some freaking-

KNOCK, KNOCK, KNOCK! Whoever that is is banging the door so hard, I feel the vibrations ripple through my chest. I stand, turn and open the door. It takes a moment to realise that the prick from Lauren's office is standing in front of me. James bloody Kennedy, without tie. Still looks like a dufus in yet another shiny blue suit.

'Hi,' he says. I can't help it, my face has contorted itself into the perfect 'what the fuck are you doing here?' look. 'James Kennedy, you came to my summer party last year.'

'Yeah?' I say. What do you want?

'Can I come in?' he asks. No you can't come in, you can stand there and say whatever it is you want to say then fuck off back to your tall building with the glass and the money and the views and nice stuff inside. Come on, Ollie...yeah I know.

'Uh, okay. How did you know where I live?' I say.

'I'd rather not say,' he replies. Rather not say? Did he pay someone off? Get the information by illegal means? Bribe a police officer? Now my mind is racing with how he found me. He indicates to the hallway. 'May I?' I hold the door open for him. This is weird, right? I mean, semi-strangers don't just show up at other people's houses except in movies or bad television. He steps inside. I close the door behind him. We walk into the living room. I can feel him judging the shitness of everything in my flat. I don't care. He sits down on the sofa and I plonk myself down on the chair opposite. 'It's about Lauren,' he says. No shit.

'What, sent you round to have a chat, did she?' I reply.

'No. She doesn't know I'm here.' So, what?

'O...kay.'

'I know what happened with Johnny.'

'Look, no offence, but I don't really want to talk about this with you.'

'I get it. But just hear me out and I'll leave you alone. I know you don't really like me, not sure why 'cos I'm great.' When I don't react, he clears his throat quickly and continues. 'Look, Lauren really likes you. A lot. And what happened with Johnny,' I roll my eyes, 'she's been having a really bad week and I think you just happened to see her at the wrong time.'

'I'd say I happened to see her at the right time,' I reply. James leans back, his suit reflects the light at my face, temporarily blinding me. Okay, I'm exaggerating but it is a ridiculous suit.

'You know about her parents?'

'I know they're dead. That's it.'

'You know how they died?'

'No.'

'Her mum died of cervical cancer and only a few weeks later, her dad killed himself.'

'Jesus,' I say.

'Yeah. She lost both parents within a couple of weeks,' he says. So, that gives her carte blanche to just do what she wants? Because her parents died years ago?

'But this was when she was a lot younger, right?'

'Well...five years ago,' James says, looking at me intently. I nod slowly, taking it in. 'Five years ago to the day, actually.' I look at him. 'See, the day you saw Lauren with Johnny doing, whatever they were doing, was the five year anniversary of her mum's death and that week is always a bit...tough for her.' Oh jeez. 'Now look. I'm not saying she's an angel. She isn't, at all. In fact, a lot of the time she can be a royal pain in the arse. And she wears this tough exterior precisely because she doesn't want people knowing her weaknesses. But they're there. And she only ever shares them with people she really trusts.' I turn my head.

'Like you?' I ask. He tilts his head, understanding my mild accusation.

'I know Sarah told you we went out for a time. It didn't work out. But with you she's...different. She seems to genuinely like you. Honestly, I don't really get it,' he says, glancing around at my flat, 'but when she's with you, she's happier. We've all noticed it in the office. So, for God's sake, please sort it out 'cos she's turned into a bit of bitch these past few days.' Off my look, James says, 'You know what I mean. She kissed some other guy and you saw. Not great. But given how drunk she was, the closeness she's always had with Johnny and the shitness of the week, you can sort of understand where her head was at.' Can I? Can I understand? Sure, her parents dying like that is pretty horrific but am I just supposed to forgive her because she had some shitty thing happen to her five years ago. Do I sound like an arsehole? I don't know. 'Or maybe you can't. Either way, I thought you should at least know what was going on,' James says, standing. I stand, following his lead as we walk to the front door. He opens the door and turns to me. 'You like her?' I shrug, not wanting to tell this douchebag anything. 'Then fight for her. She's fighting for you. You know she quit the job in New York last week?' I frown at him. He nods at my surprise. 'Came back here, took a pay cut, because she missed you. I think she was going to surprise you,' he says. I nod slowly. 'Like I said, I don't get it.' And with that, he walks away. I stand in the doorway, listen to him get into his car and start it up. I hear him drive away and close the door.

I walk back into the living room and sit down, my mind processing what's been said. What must that have been like, losing both parents like that? I know she's grown up but for anyone losing a parent it's hard, but to lose both like that must have been utterly devastating. I know what it felt like losing my dad and that was fifteen years ago. It was the most gut-wrenching thing I've ever experienced. But then, is all this an excuse for her behaviour? Can I just let it lie? Is kissing another bloke even really that bad? Maybe I'm overreacting.

It's not like she shagged him...that I know of. Did she come back because she missed me? Funny way of showing it. I don't know.

I make some dinner and watch some crap on BBC One. What was it? I can't even remember. My mind is swimming with choices. None of which I seem to be able to settle on. Should I, shouldn't I? Right thing, wrong thing. My phone rings. Parker.

'Hi,' I say.

'Hi. I just wanted to mention that you're gay.'

'So? So what if I was, would that disturb you?' I say.

'Uh, why you talking like that?'

'What if I was gay, Parker, would that offend you?'

'Mate, you know I love you whatever you do. All I ask is you keep your dick in your pants when you're round me. I don't think that's too much to ask.' I chuckle. 'How you doing anyway?'

'Yeah okay. James Kennedy just came over.'

'Who's James Kennedy?'

'This douchebag who works in Lauren's office. You remember? The rich guy who has the apartment near Canary Wharf?'

'Uh, nope.'

'Well anyway, he came over and basically said Lauren's parents died within a couple of weeks of each other and that night at the club was the five-year anniversary.'

'What, when she kissed Time Traveller bloke?'

'Yeah.'

'Right. So he thinks that's like, her reason?'

'Yeah,' I say. There's a slight pause as Parker thinks.

'I guess losing both parents is pretty heavy,' he says.

'Yeah. Her mum had cancer and when she died, I think her dad couldn't take it and he killed himself.'

'Shit.'

'Yeah. So, maybe it's sort of understandable.'

'What do you really think, though?' Parker asks.

'I don't know, mate. I just, can't get it straight in my mind.'

'Maybe you should just go talk to her? See what she has to say? If she doesn't say the right things, then...you're no worse off than you are now.'

'I guess.'

'Fuck it, got nothing to lose,' he says. I hear someone talking to Parker in the background.

'Nicola asks if you want her to bake you something.'

'Bake me something?'

'Yeah, I dunno mate, she thinks her chocolate brownies might make you feel better.'

'Not the same chocolate brownies she left on my floor that time-' I say. Parker bursts out laughing.

'No, not those ones,' he replies. I hear Nicola asking what I said. 'Nothing darling. He says thanks for the offer but he doesn't need chocolate brownies right now.'

'Thank you though,' I say loudly, as if Nicola could ever hear me.

'He says thank you,' Parker says to Nicola. 'So?'

'Maybe you're right.'

'Christ, haven't you learned this yet? I'm always right,' says Parker.

THIRTY EIGHT – GOOD FORTUNES

Okay, now I just need to work this out. Best way forward. Do I go:

a) To her house?

or

b) To her work?

Her house would be more private, I guess. We could talk without fear of being overheard and not have some big soap opera scene in front of the entire bank. What do you think? Bank? Really, you think bank? It's just so... fearless for me to do something like that. But then, I guess the onus is on her. I need to look good as well. Remind her of how great I am and what she's missing. Which, is frankly not a lot but still...might as well make the most of what I've got. I need to get a good night's sleep and-

KNOCK, KNOCK, KNOCK.

THREE WAY

Well, now who the fuck is that? I check my watch, it's nine-thirty. Surely James Kennedy didn't leave something behind, he was only here for five minutes. My flat is like Oxford Circus all of a sudden. I walk to the door and open it. I frown, at first unsure who it is. Then my mouth opens slightly.

'Svetla?' I say, surprise evident in my voice.

'Hi. I know it's wrong to be here and I shouldn't have come but I wanted to talk to someone and I don't know why, but you were the only person.'

'Okay. Come in,' I say, automatically. Don't say anything, I know what you're thinking but I swear nothing is going to happen. I am so over her, she is so yesterday's news. I can tell you don't believe me. Well, watch this scene play out. I close the door behind her, glancing down to her bum as she walks. She's wearing that Thundercat hoodie top and black leggings. Not exactly dressed to impress but hey, whatever. We walk into the living room. She sits down on her side of the sofa which had become mine but I guess now she's here-

'Actually, have a seat here,' I say. She looks at where I point, then up to me. She moves without complaint. Ha, one nil me! Yeah. I sit down in my (formerly her) space. 'So...'

'I'm sorry to turn up like this. The thing is, it's not going so well with Rupert and I just needed someone to talk to.'

'And, you thought of me?' I say, slowly.

'I know. It's crazy, right? But we could always talk. Whatever else, you were always a good listener.' She wants me to listen to the trouble she's having with the guy she shagged behind my back and left me for? This is...so fucked up. And yet I find myself saying,

'Sure, of course. What's happened?'

'He's not getting a divorce. Says he doesn't want one. And that's sort of it. I mean, how can I stay with someone who is still married to someone else?' You can't Svetla, unless you're Hugh Hefner.

'Hmm,' I say, careful not to betray anything.

'I just...I know we didn't really work out but maybe, after this much time...we could be friends? I just...I guess I sort of miss you.' Oh my God. She's making a play for me. The words say one thing but let me tell you, ladies and gentlemen that the body language is clear. She stares at me, those bright blue eyes searching for a reaction. 'Do you...miss me?'

'I don't know what to say to that, Svetla. You destroyed me-'

'You destroyed me, Ollie,' she says straight back at me. 'You remember how we got to splitting up? You remember the things you said?'

'I remember you were fucking someone else,' I say, calmly. She sighs and nods without responding. I breathe out. 'Look, we both said and did some shitty things.'

'Yes, we did. And for my side, I'm sorry. I was...hurt and vulnerable and weak. Sort of like now, actually,' she says. I note that she's moved imperceptibly closer.

'Svetla...I'm sorry about Rupert. Really. But...you shouldn't be here. You just shouldn't. We had our shot. I fucked it up. Or you did, or whatever. If I'm being honest, it was me that screwed it up in the first place by the way I behaved. And I've accepted that. My fault. My selfishness. But whatever the reason you're here, I think you should go. Or we'll do something stupid that neither of us really wants and screw up anything else that might be going on. I love you. I really do. I think I always will. You played such a massive part in my life and I will always be grateful for that. But the success of a relationship isn't always judged by how long it lasts. Maybe we lasted long enough and now, it's time for something else. If Rupert isn't the guy for you, then whoever you end up meeting next may well be. You're a smart, beautiful girl and it really was an honour to be your boyfriend, even if I didn't know it at the time. But for now, I think it's time to say goodbye and move on. Don't you?'

Tears roll down her face. She sniffs and nods, trying to reclaim her composure. She stands quickly. Then, perhaps unexpectedly, she hugs me. I feel the wetness of her tears on my cheek. I rub her back slowly, smelling her skin. That familiar smell I got so used to. But this time, it's different. This time is no longer Svetla time. And somewhere in me, I feel the freedom of knowing I've let her go. We release each another.

'You're a special guy, Ollie Hayward. Whoever you end up with, she'll be a very lucky girl,' Svetla says. I smile and follow her to the door.

'Take care of yourself,' I say. She nods.

'Yeah. And you,' she replies. And then, she's gone. I stand in the doorway and breathe out. The girl I've spent so long thinking about, is gone. And this time, really gone. But there's something about this new fact that fills me with hope. Moving on. I really have moved on.

When I walk into work, Julie has brought in cakes and treats. There's also a bottle of Champagne sitting on the newsdesk.

'What's all this?' I ask.

'Julie's getting married and I'm getting divorced,' says Paul.

'Oh...uh, congratulations,' I say to Paul. He smiles.

'Fuckin' A. Never thought I'd see the day. She's finally out of my life, psycho bitch. Can't tell you how happy I am,' he says.

'Well...that's great.' I look over to Julie who beams at me.

'Hey Julie, fantastic news,' I say, walking over and giving her a hug.

'Thanks,' she says. 'Too early for Champagne now, but if you're around later?'

'Sounds great. So he finally asked?'

'Nope. I asked him. Got sick of dropping hints, so I thought, why does it always have to be the man doing these things? Then I thought, it doesn't.'

'Wow. Was he surprised?'

'Yeah. Fell off his chair, literally. We went to our favourite restaurant, nothing fancy but very us. I got out the ring and went down on one knee and said I'd been waiting for him to get his act together and it was time to take the bull by the horns.'

'Romantic,' I say.'

'Yeah. He was surprised but he got all emotional. Started crying.' What a pussy.

'So sweet,' I say.

'Yeah, except I told him to stop being such a cry baby and give me an answer. My knee was getting dirty and starting to ache,' she says. I chuckle.

'Right. And he said yes?'

'He said yes.'

'Nice one. See, I told you you weren't destined to be a spinster.'

'You were instrumental in all this, Ollie.'

'Really?'

'Of course not.' Amen to that. The newsroom soon settles back into work mode and I walk around to my desk and log in. Nice that my colleagues are happy. I, on the other hand, have to work out exactly what to do about Lauren. I want my happy ending as well, whatever that might be.

'Ollie, do you have a minute?' Jonathan Crawley, scary Head of Home News is standing over me. Oh shit. What did I do now?

'Uh, sure,' I reply. I stand and follow him into his office.

'Have a seat,' he says. I'm nervous now, trying to think of all the fuck ups I've made recently. I can't remember anything that significant. Yes the sat vehicle broke during that Queen's speech to the troops on Thursday, but that wasn't my fault. Or maybe it was-

'I want to ask you something,' Jonathan says.

'Okay,' I reply, holding my breath.

'There's going to be some changes in the

newsroom coming up. One of those changes is Paul is moving over to the Foreign Desk for a bit and I wondered how you'd feel about moving up to be a News Editor?' What?

'Really?' I say, my heart in my mouth.

'You're an excellent producer, Ollie. But I think it's time to step up to the next stage. So, if you're happy...?'

'Yeah, oh my God.'

'It's just a temporary thing to start with, but you will get a bump in pay and if it works out there might be something more permanent for you.'

'Yeah, great. Thank you so much.'

'Okay. I'll get Kirsty to draw up a contract,' he says, standing and offering his hand. 'Congratulations. Don't let me down.'

'I won't. Thank you, really,' I reply. He nods and waves me away. I walk out of the office, semi-stunned. A news editor. I'm going to be a news editor. I wander slowly back to the newsdesk. Paul stands and walks over to me.

'So? You going to take it?' he asks. I look up. He's smiling a big smile at me. I nod and smile back.

'Yeah,' I say, barely grasping my good fortune.

'Good for you. I hoped you would. When Jonathan asked me who would be best to take over here, there was only one person that came to mind,' he says.

'Really?'

'Yeah, David King but he wants to be a reporter so...'

'Oh.'

'You muppet, of course it was you. Jesus.

You're the best producer we've got.'

'Thank you.'

'Don't thank me yet. Wait until you start doing it. It's a lot of responsibility and long hours but it's great fun.'

'Yeah, thanks,' I say. We shake hands.

'Paul, line one is Adrian Banks,' Julie says. Paul smiles, then turns and sits back down at his desk. He picks up the phone.

'Adrian, this better be good news because other broadcasters are running our shots without a TBN strap,' Paul says.

I stare at my screen and try to process what's just happened. I'm going to do my dream job. I'm going to be a home news editor. I can't believe it. This is just too surreal. Maybe life won't be so bad after all. Right, plan of action. As soon as I'm done here, I'm going to head over to Lauren's house (not bank – there's no way I can have that sort of scene in the middle of her office, sorry to those of you who were rooting for that.) Then I'm going to sort this out once and for all.

THIRTY NINE - AN UNEXPECTED VISITOR (PART 3)

At three o'clock, Julie pops the Champagne and shares it with the newsdesk. We stand chatting, enjoying the shared good fortune of Julie, Paul and myself. For once, everyone is happy. My mind still races with what I'm going to say to Lauren. I don't have too much Champagne, need to be focused. My landline rings. I walk over and answer it.

'Newsdesk,' I say.

'Hello, is Ollie Hayward there?' asks the male voice on the other end.

'Yep, this is Ollie Hayward.'

'It's main reception here, I have a Lauren Bates here to see you.' Holy shit. She came here. I momentarily freeze and everything shuts down. What am I supposed to say? I can't do it here. I mean…shit.

'Uh, okay. I'll come down,' I say, replacing the

phone. Julie notices my face because she says,

'You okay?'

'Lauren's in reception.' Julie's mouth opens.

'Oh my God, she's here? That's hilarious. You've actually got a stalker.'

'No I...I think she just wants to talk.'

'Shall I go get her?' Julie asks. Even Paul watches events unfold with interest.

'No. God,' I say. I breathe out and head towards the door.

'Hey Ollie?' Paul says. I turn. 'Good luck.' I nod, appreciating the sentiment.

'Thanks,' I say.

Okay. Come on. I open the door and walk out of the newsroom towards main reception. I scan the people waiting as I walk towards the desk, none of them look like...then I see her. She's wearing a tight-fitting grey skirt suit and dark high heels. Her hair is down and she's looking around keenly. Then she spots me walking towards her and her body language shifts to nervous. I press the button to start the glass turnstile and walk out.

'Hi,' I say.

'Hi,' she replies, staring at me. An awkward moment of silence between us before she says, 'I just...wanted to explain some things. Sorry to turn up like this but...I couldn't get you on the phone.' Little dig there, I opt to ignore it.

'Okay. This way,' I say. The security guard swipes her in and I follow. We walk silently, the tension real and palpable. I go to say something then think better of it.

'Is that the newsroom?' she asks, staring

through the glass wall to the monitors and desks inside.

'Yeah. Would you...like a tour?' I ask.

'I don't know. I mean, maybe it's not...I don't know.'

'I'll show you,' I say, swiping my ID to let us into the newsroom. I clock Paul and Julie watching us. 'This is where the bulletins sit, so over there is the morning segment, on air until eleven. Then the lunchtime news team take over and over there are the afternoon and late bulletins. We walk over to the newsdesk and the general hub bub of people drinking and chatting. Julie looks like she's going to explode. 'This is the newsdesk, where I work. We're having a little mini celebration because Julie here is getting married. Chaps, this is Lauren.' Julie is off her seat and shaking Lauren's hand before I can do anything.

'Oh. Congratulations,' Lauren says.

'Thanks,' says Julie, smiling. 'Sorry about answering the phone the other day but we all care a lot about our Ollie.' I glance at Lauren who meets my eyes.

'Don't worry, I get protective of my friends as well,' Lauren says. Paul stands up and shakes Lauren's hand.

'It's an honour. Heard so much about you and I must say Ollie's descriptions of your beauty are greatly underplayed.'

'Thank you,' she replies, an appreciative smile forming.

'So yeah, this is where we decide what stories we're going to do, which reporters are going to do them, and all the logistics. Cameras, sat vehicles

etc,' I say. Lauren nods. I clear my throat.
'So...anyway. Let's head to the canteen?' I look at
Paul who nods.

'If I need you, I'll call you on the mobile,' Paul
says, winking. I nod.

'Okay. So, this way,' I say.

'Nice to meet you both,' Lauren says as we
walk away. The newsroom chatter has suddenly
become very quiet. I feel everyone's eyes on us. Or
maybe I should say on her.

We walk to the exit, I hit the switch to open
the door and press the button to call the lift. The
doors open and we step inside. I hit six and we
travel upwards. It's awkward as the floors tick by. I
look at her, she glances at me. I look back to the
floor display. The doors open to reveal the TBN
canteen, the place where good food goes to die, as
most of us say. As I said before, the one good thing
about the canteen is the view.

'This is pretty cool,' Lauren says.

'Yeah,' I reply, unable to comment further. I
buy us some coffees and we sit down next to the
window. Lauren plops two sweeteners into hers
and stirs carefully looking at me.

'So,' she says.

'So.'

'I just wanted to explain or...tell you that what
you saw was a one off. I've...I was a bit of a mess
and Johnny was...well he -'

'I know about your parent's and the
anniversary,' I say. She looks surprised and leans
back in her chair. 'James Kennedy came over to
my flat and told me what happened.' She frowns,
as if not understanding what I've just said.

'What was James doing at your flat?' she asks, still frowning.

'He was worried about you and he wanted to put what you did into some sort of context. Which he did,' I say. She leans forward, a worried expression on her face.

'What exactly did he say?'

'He said five years ago your mum died of cancer and that a couple of weeks after, your dad committed suicide,' I reply. She shakes her head.

'He had no right to tell you that.'

'I think he was trying to help,' I say. She doesn't say anything for a bit, so I carry on. 'Look, when I saw you...I was just so...surprised and hurt...I couldn't understand why you would do that? I mean, I know we haven't seen each other properly for a bit but I still sort of thought we were together-'

'We were...we are. I was drunk. I was more than drunk, I was paralytic. And Johnny was just...ugh...he was just being Johnny. I just felt so...sad about my parents. And he just did what he does and I didn't stop him. I'm sorry Ollie.'

'Yeah,' I say, my eyes dart around as I consider my response. What to do? All this time and effort, trying to build something with her. She's given up her job, given up everything. Except Johnny Dougan. The image hits me again like a freight train, that night in the club. Lauren's drunken eyes as she looked at me, her mouth still on his. Can I be the adult here? Can I put this behind me? Start afresh? I know this isn't the first time she's been unfaithful to someone. Even if we did patch things up now, wouldn't Johnny always be there lurking in the background. I look at her, this beautiful girl, waiting for my response. She looks deep into my eyes with expectant worry. I break her stare and shake my head. 'The thing is Lauren...something broke when I saw you there that night. Something that hadn't been right for a while. I know how busy you've been in New York and I realise you've come back here to try and get us sorted out but...I just don't think I can. I'm sorry.' I watch my words translate into surprise on Lauren's face.

'Oh,' she says. The look on her face immediately tells me this wasn't the answer she was expecting. Her mouth is open as she tries to process what I've just said.

'Listen, you're a great girl. And what we had was, great...for a time. But we haven't spoken for almost three weeks. And before that, who knows how long? Like I said, I know how busy you are but-'

'Which is exactly why I came back. That's what I was doing. I came back here to be with you.' she says.

'I know. I'm sorry,' I reply. 'But I didn't know you were coming back and I found out by seeing you snog another guy.' She frowns, still seemingly unable to take in these words. A tear trickles down her face, she brushes it away.

'I gave it all up, Ollie. For you,' she says. I swallow. Guilt suddenly rises through me, I want to say something to reassure her. That she will be okay, in the end. I open my mouth but nothing comes out. She beats me to it by saying, 'so...that's it?'

'I don't know what else there is to say,' I reply. She nods slowly, looking down.

'Can't believe I've fucked up another relationship...' she says. I'm lost on how to make her feel better. 'Okay well, I'd better go.' She stands, I stand. She sniffs and pushes her chair under the table. I do the same. I follow her to the lift. 'It's okay, I can see myself out.'

'I'm sorry, I have to go with you. Security,' I reply, almost chuckling at the absurdity of my words. She nods, presses the button for the lift and we wait for one to come. To say it's awkward would be a massive understatement. I look at her, that beautiful face staring at the floor, and realise this is the last time I will probably see Lauren Bates. I feel strangely empty about it all. DING! The lift doors open and we step inside. I feel the tension between us and hear her quietly sniff. A part of me wants to make her feel better, say I made a mistake. But the truth, in my heart of hearts, is I know this is the right thing to do. Things haven't been right for a long time and I guess I've just been blinkered by it. By her.

The lift doors open and she walks out into main reception, I follow her. She hands her temporary security pass back to the desk and turns to face me.

'Well, thanks for the tour,' she says.

'Lauren-'

'Don't,' she says, holding up her hand, 'I'll be fine. I've been here enough times to know how it goes.'

'I wish...I wish it could have been different between us,' I say.

'Me too,' she replies. We stand, staring at each other. I see the sadness in her face then her expression hardens. Back to Lauren Bates, tough trading manager. She leans in and kisses me on the cheek. 'Take care of yourself, Ollie.' And with that, she turns and walks out of my building and out of my life.

FORTY – THE FINAL CURTAIN

When I return to the newsdesk, Paul and Julie stare at me, scanning my face for any giveaway. I admit it, I'm not acting, I feel sad. Not because I wanted to be with Lauren, but because it didn't work out.

'So?' Julie asks. I look at her, pulled from my thoughts and shake my head. 'Oh Ollie, come here.' She walks over and puts her arms around me, hugging me tight. Sometimes life just sucks. I know I can't complain, this is, afterall, my decision but I'm still sad. Sad for Lauren as well, I hope she's going to be okay. She's always had a thing about how her relationships end up failing for one reason or another. To be fair, she did have quite a big hand in this.

'I'm fine,' I say. Paul stands behind her, a sympathetic expression on his face.

'I would say you're better off without her,' he says, 'but that would be churlish and insensitive.' I force a smile. Julie stands back and stares at me with a concerned face.

359

'I'm fine guys, really. It was my choice,' I say. Paul frowns.

'Wait a minute...you ended it with her?' he asks. I nod. He glances at Julie and raises an eyebrow. 'Are you impaired in some way?'

'Paul,' Julie says.

'No, I just...I don't understand,' he says.

'You don't have to understand. It's no one else's business but mine,' I say. Paul nods.

The remaining hours of my shift move achingly slowly. I can't snap out of my daydream, if that's what this is. Am I wallowing? Maybe. My mind keeps playing tricks on me, showing me all the best memories of Lauren. The trip to the Cotswolds, James Kennedy's barbeque. Then I remember my promotion and suddenly feel a wave of happiness. This is so weird. Fuck.

Paul lets me go at five, he can see I'm down. I walk out of main reception and into the outside world. I feel completely numb. I stop and look left, then right, temporarily forgetting how I get home. I watch cars and buses race past as I shove my hands into my pockets. I breathe in deeply and release it. Breathe in and release. I need to take action. To decide what I want and go get it. I turn and head for the tube.

I walk into the Roundhouse and straight up to the box office.

'Hi there, I was wondering if you had any spare tickets left for tonight's performance?' I ask. The tattooed guy behind the counter smiles and looks at his computer screen.

'Uh, only ones in the circle standing area.'

'How much?'

'Thirty pounds. How many?'

'Just one, please,' I say, taking out the cash and handing it over. The ticket prints and he gives it to me.

'Enjoy the show,' he says.

'Thanks.'

I walk up the metal stairs built into the side of the massive stone hallway and find the correct entrance. I show my ticket to the guy on the door and walk inside. I see Ashley's piano sitting alone on the stage. People have already found their spots and I feel a buzz about the place. I find a corner where I can have a clear view of Ashley. More people are standing in front of the stage below me. People chatter and laugh. Some hold bottles of beer or glasses of wine. Soon the lights dim and the crowd start to cheer. Ashley and the rest of the band walk out. She gives a little wave to the audience and takes her seat at the piano.

'Hello,' she says into the microphone. Her voice echoes around the hall. Some of the crowd shout back. 'Steady, we've got a lot of songs to play. Try and pace yourselves.' That brings a few laughs, myself included. She shields her eyes from the blinding spotlights trained on her. 'I like your shirt,' she says to one person.

'I love you Ashley!' the guy shouts back. More laughter from the audience.

'Feels like we've got a good crowd in here tonight,' she says. More cheers. She looks up towards me. She seems to see me but her eyes quickly move past and cross to the rest of the audience. 'Okay, let's get this thing started.' The crowd clap and cheer. I'm mildly disappointed, maybe it was too much to ask for her to see me. It is pretty dark up here. Things like that don't really happen anyway, far too much like a movie. But then she says, 'This is for someone I thought had got away.' She starts playing the piano, the band join in. It's a song I instantly recognise. The song she played for me in Parker's bedroom, all those months ago. She glances up towards me and smiles. I smile back, unsure if she can even see me.

Maybe things will be okay after all.

ACKNOWLEDGMENTS

I wish to thank all those who gave their precious time to read and review early drafts. Their notes and thoughts have made Three Way what it is. Rekha John-Cheriyan, Caz Coronel, Adrian Pinsent, Charlotte Essex, Alexandra Vanotti and Tamsin Smith.

And to my wife Alison, without whose support this book would never have been possible.

INTERVIEW WITH THE AUTHOR

Where did the idea for Three Way come from?

Strangely enough my original title for Three Way was 'Sex Friends.' I wanted it to be a sort of sequel to Sex Lessons. I knew the main character would be different from James Kennedy but I liked the characters in Sex Lessons and wanted to carry on some of their journeys.

The genesis of Three Way and the reason it was going to be called Sex Friends was because I thought the story was going to be about two people who basically had sex outside of a relationship. But whenever they began seeing each other as a couple, things would always go wrong. As I got further into writing it I realised this wasn't the story that was coming out. I didn't want to force it to become something it wasn't, so I went with it.

James Kennedy, the main character in Sex Lessons, is a secondary character in Three Way. What gave you that idea?

Yeah, I love the idea you can create a main character in one book and have him or her appear as a secondary character in another. After all readers who have read the first book will, I hope, say 'oh

James Kennedy, I remember him.' But I didn't want the reader to have had to have read Sex Lessons. Three Way is a book that stands on its own. But if you have read Sex Lessons, it's sort of an in joke with the reader.

Run through your writing process. How does it start, how long does it take you to write a book?

Three Way took a little longer to write than Sex Lessons mainly because I wrote Sex Lessons on a career break in Australia. When it came to writing Three Way I had a full time job. So I would write on days off sometimes getting my target of 2000 words a day sometimes less, occasionally more. I normally write in my front room, laptop on my lap. I put on a movie soundtrack to get me in the right place emotionally, then I write for as long as I can. Again, it changes every time I do it. Sometimes it's a couple of hours, sometimes it's a whole afternoon. Whenever I have some time and I'm by myself. I have quite a long commute into work so I listen to soundtracks on my iPod whilst thinking about my story and it's almost inevitable inspiration will come. I use Evernote to log my ideas.

What sort of soundtracks do you listen to? Are there certain soundtracks for certain scenes?

Definitely. If I want to write a sad scene, for example a breaking up scene, I'll listen to slow and melancholy music. Thomas Newman, James Newton Howard and Mychael Danna are some of the best at creating slow, sad themes. If I want to write an action scene, I might put on Hans Zimmer or James Horner for a fast paced, upbeat track. All depends on what I'm writing. The one thing the music can't be is distracting. It has to be background music that makes you feel something without distracting you from what you're writing.

Tell me about Ollie, he seems a genuinely nice guy trying to do the right thing, is that how you envisaged him?

Yes. It was really important I make Ollie sympathetic to the reader. He's a good guy and I think in the opening scene with Svetla you do feel sorry for him. He's a man who wants to find the right girl and settle down but he's also scared of not only making the wrong choice but also being alone. It's like his Achilles Heel.

Ollie is a very different main character to James Kennedy, was that deliberate?

Yes. James Kennedy is a bit of a show off and in certain circumstances he can be a bit of a douche. Although his story is hopefully compelling and you do care about his issues because of how honest he is with the reader, I think there are occasions you lose sympathy for him because of his behavior. The key to making any main character sympathetic and getting your audience to relate to him or her is honesty. If your character behaves the way you or I might behave given the situation in front of him, then that will generate sympathy…in theory anyway.

Once you have finished your first draft what's your process to getting it ready for publication?

I normally pat myself on the back, tell myself what a clever boy I've been then forget about it for at least six weeks. I start thinking about my next book or some other idea I can work on. Then once a period of time has elapsed I reread my draft which is normally a slightly surreal experience. There are bits I honestly don't remember writing. Some parts are great, others are truly terrible. But having had that time away from the manuscript it's a lot easier to see the errors. So I do a pass correcting everything that occurs to me as I read. I then let my wife read it. Then I sulk when she doesn't tell me it's the best thing she's ever read but that with a little work it could be. She does some notes, I either agree or disagree and implement them. Then I ask five or six people whose opinion I trust to read it. They come back with more notes and again I implement the ones I agree with. One final pass and it's pretty much ready. Everything I just said is true, except I normally do fifteen more passes over that

time, I'm a bit of a perfectionist. Hope you enjoyed
the book.

Reading Group Discussion Questions

- What do you think are the central themes of the book?

- What do you think about the humour of Ollie and Parker's friendship?

- Do you find Lauren a sympathetic character? On the surface she seems to have it all, good looks, a good job etc. but is there more to her than meets the eye?

- Did you prefer Svetla, Lauren or Ashley?

- Did you feel sorry for any of the characters in the book, if so why?

- Does Ollie's job as a news producer help or hinder his cause to find 'the one?' Does his job make him more attractive?

- How hard is it for young people to find someone nowadays?

- We don't hear much about Ollie's parents or family during the story. Is that a bad thing?

- What do you think happens after the end? Who do you think Ollie ends up with?

Reading Group Discussion Questions
(continued)

- Was the ending satisfying? If not, why not?

- Did you find the book funny? Which moments stood out to you?

GET THE BOOK THAT STARTED IT ALL

'Just because you couldn't get it up once, doesn't mean we cancel the whole thing,' says Jenny. Now, in her defence, she did whisper that last line. However, the fact she's saying it at all, let alone in a public sandwich bar are grounds for a firing squad as far as I'm concerned.'

Straight-talking city trader James Kennedy has a problem ... he's a flop in the bedroom. When his latest romance hits the buffers, James reaches the end of his tether. To make matters worse, his new bombshell of a boss might just be interested. What he really needs is someone to show him how to be a Don Juan between the sheets. To teach him where he's going wrong. But who? Sex Lessons is a frank but humorous tale about one man's extra-curricular inactivity.

OUT NOW!

WHY WOULDN'T YOU?

Printed in Great Britain
by Amazon

85857400R00223